A Promise *in the Keys*

A COCONUT KEY NOVEL
BOOK SEVEN

HOPE
HOLLOWAY

A Promise in the Keys

Coconut Key Book 7

Cover designed by Sarah Brown (http://www.sarahdesigns.co/)

Edited by Lorie Humpherys

INTRODUCTION TO COCONUT KEY

If you're longing for an escape to paradise, step on to the gorgeous, sun-kissed sands of Coconut Key. With a cast of unforgettable characters and stories that touch every woman's heart, these delightful novels will make you laugh out loud, fall in love, and stand up and cheer...and then you'll want the next one *right this minute.*

A Secret in the Keys – Book 1
A Reunion in the Keys – Book 2
A Season in the Keys – Book 3
A Haven in the Keys – Book 4
A Return to the Keys –Book 5
A Wedding in the Keys – Book 6
A Promise in the Keys - Book 7

For release dates, excerpts, news, and more, sign up to receive Hope Holloway's newsletter! Or visit www.hopeholloway.com and follow Hope on Facebook and BookBub!

CHAPTER ONE

BECK

"Someone is glowing, and she hasn't even had a sip of her Mom-mosa, specially made by her darling daughter with only a whisper of OJ and plenty of bubbly." Savannah's eyes twinkled as she offered Beck the champagne flute.

"Oh? Am I glowing?" Beck casually touched her face, which *had* felt a little flushed when she signed off the video call before she came over to The Haven. "Must be a hot flash. They are *really* making their presence known now. At this rate, I'll need ice baths to get through a summer in the Keys." She gave a quick fan of her cheeks, happy for the excuse. Because even her wily daughter couldn't guess that there might be something else making Beck glow. "Thank you, Sav—"

"Uh uh *uhhh*," Savannah sang, drawing the glass away. "Not until you spill."

"Spill what? The mimosa?"

"The truth about what—or should I say *who*—has put the color in your cheeks, Rebecca Foster."

Or maybe her wily daughter *did* guess. Was that possible?

To cover, Beck pointed to the large outdoor deck where her other two daughters were currently chatting with her mother, the three of them cooing over Savannah's impossibly adorable baby son.

"Who? Peyton and Callie, of course. If I'm glowing, it's because my other two daughters made it down from Miami for Girls' Night at The Haven, and we haven't seen them since your wedding a month ago." Beck eyed the drink. "Now hand it over and stop being pesky."

"But I'm so good at it." Savannah sniffed and surrendered the drink. "We'll get it out of you tonight. That's what Thursday nights are for." Then she tipped her head, her smile fading. "And don't expect those two to stay the whole weekend, Mom. Callie's got a paper due and Peyton's got..."

"Val," Beck finished, looking at her oldest daughter and catching the sound of Peyton's musical laugh.

"Her month in Miami has somehow become 'the summer in Miami,'" Savannah noted with a sad sigh.

A year ago, the disappointment in Savannah's voice would have surprised Beck. The two sisters spent their childhoods at each other's throats, but since living in Coconut Key that had changed, and now they were close.

"She had her final walk-through of the townhouse this afternoon," Savannah told her. "And the closing is in a few weeks, but she hasn't mentioned moving into it. Honestly, Mom, I think she's going to sell it and stay up in Miami. Brand-new construction in Coconut Key, on a canal, with that dock in the back? She could turn it over for a tidy profit without ever living there."

Beck nodded in agreement. Before Val had come back asking for a second chance, Peyton, who'd dreamed of a wedding, husband, and children since she'd been a little girl, had been fully ready for what she called "Plan B." She'd live as a single woman in her new home, take cooking classes, and pursue a culinary career. She'd even whispered about looking into having a baby on her own.

But then, things changed in February when she agreed to "test the waters" in Miami with Val...and found those waters to be warm and inviting.

"She's in love and he lives there," Beck mused. "And she's glowing."

"Like a hundred-watt bulb," Savannah agreed. "But, for the record, geographic undesirability *can* be overcome."

Geographic undesirability...like Florida to Australia? The thought danced around the edges of her mind, but Beck managed to push it away. "This is her life, honey, and we have to let her live it."

"I just miss her so much, Mom. I was all for her finding love, and still am, but I want her to have it right here on this little island so I can enjoy my big sister, now that I really know her. And I want Dylan to love his Aunt Pey-pey."

"It looks to me like he already does," Beck said, lifting her champagne flute to the sight of Peyton nuzzling the baby and making him giggle.

"All right, I'll be quiet about it." Savannah leaned in to add, "But not about you, Momma. Something's happening in your life and it's not just running Coquina House B&B."

Beck managed a non-committal smile and rooted around for a subject change. "Is Jessie on her way?"

"She had a late interview for a new busboy at the restaurant, and Chuck is dropping her off after their babysitter comes, then he's meeting my husband—" She gave in to a saucy grin. "Husband. Who'd have thought I'd never get tired of saying that?"

"Now who's glowing?" Beck teased.

"Constantly. Anyway, Nick, Chuck, and Josh are all meeting at Conchy Charlie's to watch a basketball game, so we have *la mansion* to ourselves." She gestured toward the expansive beachfront home she shared with Nick Frye, former movie star and current devoted father and husband.

"Is Kenny with them?" Beck asked. "I know he and Josh have been hanging out a lot lately."

"He's at the high school for Ava's play. They roped him into building the sets for *Mary Poppins*. And, yes, Kenny and Josh are pals now that..." She made a sad face. "You and Josh are splitsville."

But the sad face wasn't necessary. Beck and Josh, a man she'd known since childhood, had tried to make their warm and solid friendship into something more. They'd "dated"—or at least spent a whole lot of time together and some of it included some very long kisses—for a year after Beck moved to Coconut Key.

But ultimately, they'd called it quits when they acknowledged that a spark was missing. They couldn't kindle a fire without that, but they would be friends forever, and each week that passed, that friendship became easier and more natural.

"Josh'll find someone," Beck said. "He's so ready for love. He told me that when we broke up."

"And what about you?" she asked pointedly. "Are *you* ready for love?"

"Oh, please." She tried to make it sound like the very idea was laughable. "I'm running a brand-new B&B which, as you will hear when we go around the table and share problems, is a little light on reservations. That's keeping me plenty busy." She finally took a sip of her drink, hoping the subject would close.

Savannah rolled her eyes. "Fine, Mom. Be coy. While you do, power down that Mom-mosa so we can hear the real story about Crocodile Dundee."

Beck nearly choked on the champagne and OJ. "*Excuse me?*"

"We were not born yesterday," Savannah called over her shoulder as she headed to the deck. "Which you know because, as our mother, you were there."

Beck stood stone still holding her drink, staring at Savannah's swinging ponytail as she waltzed outside.

Wait. How could she—how could *any* of them know? Beck had never whispered a word about her feelings for... Crocodile Dundee. She bit back a smile, thinking of Oliver Bradshaw, who had arrived in Coconut Key the night before Savannah's wedding with the shocking news that he was Nick Frye's long-lost father.

He'd stayed at Coquina House as a guest, so as the live-in proprietor, it was natural that Beck would chat with Oliver. A lot. Like for *hours*.

A widower with a keen sense of humor, a warm personality, and an Aussie accent that ought to be illegal,

Oliver had absolutely fascinated Beck. And the feelings seemed to go both ways.

She'd mentioned that they'd talked a lot, but did her daughters know those chats were deep into the night on the veranda, or while taking long walks on the beach that week?

How could they?

Did they know that Oliver and Beck shared scones and coffee and life stories over breakfast, and chuckled while they worked side-by-side on ads for her B&B? She'd told them that he'd helped her, which was natural since he was a former owner and creative director of an ad agency.

But they couldn't know that those sessions were charged with electricity when their hands would brush over her keyboard, or that belly laughs ensued when she tried to write clever copy that seemed to come to him naturally. Could they?

And had she unintentionally mentioned that since he'd returned to Sydney, they'd been video chatting almost daily—okay, sometimes twice—despite the fourteen-hour time difference? Maybe she'd casually dropped that into a conversation.

But Beck definitely didn't tell them that when they said goodbye, she was already looking forward to the next call, or that her whole body felt a little like melted butter every time she looked into Oliver's impossibly brown eyes.

Nope. No one knew that.

"It's not a party without you, Beckie." Her mother came to the French doors with a quizzical look. "Is everything okay? You look lost, sweet girl."

She pulled her focus back to the moment. "Just thinking about the, um, new guest we have coming tomorrow, Lovely," she said, grabbing an excuse from the all-consuming B&B business she and her mother had launched. "I'm coming." As she got closer to Lovely, she whispered, "Speaking of lost, how's our Peyton?"

Lovely smiled. "Let's just say my infamous lovedar is screaming so loud, people down on the beach can hear it."

"Your trusty lovedar is never wrong."

"Sometimes, though," Lovely said, "I think it's screaming for one couple, but it's really found another." Her mother lifted her brows. "Weird, isn't it?"

Lovely knew, *too*? Or was she just feeling guilty for not telling anyone, not even her precious mother. That was especially tough because she and her mother had promised they'd never keep another secret from each other.

"Yep, weird." She slipped her arm through her mother's and walked through the French doors to the deck.

"What's taking you so long, Mom?" Peyton asked, searching Beck's face as they got closer. "You okay?"

"I'm wonderful," she said brightly, lifting her glass. "I'll toast to having my three girls and mother all gathered together!"

"Water toast," Callie said, holding up a bottle. "Not twenty-one yet."

Savannah chuckled softly as she eased Dylan into a bouncy seat that would keep him happy for a good long time.

"You know, I used to think you were just a complete nerd," she said. "But now I want you and your good sense to be around my little man constantly, teaching him to follow rules. Because God knows, I didn't."

"You followed a journey that got you here," Beck said, settling into the seat across from Peyton and Callie and next to her mother. "And for that, we are grateful."

Savannah smiled and took the head of the table, looking at Peyton. "And what about your journey, Peyote? Have you decided to give in to your favorite Miami vice?"

Oh, she wasn't wasting any time today.

"Savannah," Beck said softly. "Just let her relax for a few minutes before the interrogation starts."

"It's okay, Mom. I get it." Peyton gave a somewhat shy smile, then looked down at her drink. "And as far as vices go, if Val Sanchez is wrong, I don't want to be right."

They all laughed, except Savannah who tried to hide her disappointment. "What about your new place?"

"The walk-through today was awesome; they have just a few things to finish in the kitchen and upstairs bath, and we close before the end of the month."

"Close...and move in?" Savannah prodded.

Peyton shot her a look. "Chill, sister of mine. We'll see. Things with Val are just perfect right now."

"I'm happy for you," Beck said, automatically inching closer to soothe ruffled feathers as mother hens liked to do. "Yes, we miss you, but this is your life." She slid a Mom-look at Savannah.

"Oh, so I'm the one getting Beck Warning Looks for loving my sister?" Savannah scoffed.

Peyton laughed and put one hand on Beck's arm, and one on Savannah's. "I love you, too, all of you. But I'm in no rush to leave him right now."

"They're in a love bubble," Callie chimed in. "Even I can't break it and she's living with me."

"And you have nothing to apologize for, Pey," Beck assured her. "A love bubble sounds..." Like something she would like to get in with Oliver. "Really nice."

Peyton smiled at her. "I know you want your chickens close to the nest, Mama Bear."

"Way to mix metaphors," Callie teased. "And before you get your panties in a bunch, Sav, I like having Peyton in Miami with me. As a transfer student, I don't have a ton of friends at UM, so this has been wonderful. Plus, we're not that far. Mom's fine with it."

"Of course I am." Beck couldn't selfishly demand her daughters stay close to her. "You've waited for the right man and I think you've found him. You deserve love."

"You deserve it, too, Mom," Peyton said softly. "So forgive us for teasing you so much, okay? We're all excited about Oliver."

"Oliver?" She tried for total nonchalance, but, based on Savannah's eye-roll, she failed.

"He's Nick's father, Mom," Savannah reminded her. "Those two talk a lot now that they've found each other. And, well..." She lifted a shoulder, nailing the nonchalance Beck missed. "I might know...stuff."

"You do?" Beck sat up. "What kind of stuff?"

Savannah leaned back and let out a long sigh, obviously enjoying the moment immensely. "I'm just saying Oliver isn't as cagey about this romance as you are."

"Romance?" The word caught in her throat.

"He's downright...talkative," Savannah added, her pretty lips curling up. "And my goodness, does he like to talk about *you*. The man is quite smitten."

"Smitten?"

Savannah choked a laugh, and Peyton and Callie high-fived, and Lovely just looked smug.

"What?" Beck demanded.

"Three one-word answers in a row, your honor," Callie said in her best lawyerly voice. "The jury is calling this one guilty of having a crush and keeping it from all of us."

Beck opened her mouth to argue but…nothing came out. Because she was so guilty, and so crushing, and so not quite ready to share. Except this gang would never let her sit quietly without giving them what they wanted.

She took a deep breath, grabbed her mimosa, and lifted it. "I guess I'm going to drink to that. A crush."

Just as a cheer went up, Jessie came rushing up the stairs, her curls bouncing, her freckled face bright. "If you're toasting good news, I have some."

"What is it?" they asked in unison.

"Heather secured financing faster than she expected, is moving up the house closing, and coming to Coconut Key this week!" She sailed over to the table and put her hands on Peyton's shoulders. "She's arranged for the kids to transfer back to Coconut Key High and finish the semester there. So Heather is ready, willing, and able to steal your job, Miss Peyton Foster."

Peyton looked up at her. "Really?"

"Only if you're not coming back right away." Jessie leaned over and dropped a kiss on Peyton's head, her affection obvious. Jessie might have been Beck's childhood best friend, but Jessie and Peyton had also created an amazing bond for over a year. "Because I will make room for both of you, if you are."

For a long moment, Peyton didn't answer, then she let her eyes close. "I think I'm staying up there for a while, Jess."

Jessie immediately looked at Beck with sympathy.

"I'm okay," Beck assured her.

"I'm not," Savannah said dryly. "But I'll manage."

Jessie let out a sigh of relief as she slid into the only empty chair. "That's good. Is that what you guys were toasting so emphatically?"

"We were cheering Oliver Bradshaw," Savannah said, lifting her water. "And Mom's crush on him."

"Oh, finally we can talk about it?" Jessie asked on a laugh, making Beck's jaw drop. "Please tell me that Aussie is coming back here to sweep you off your feet."

"He's not—"

"Oh, yes he is," Savannah said. "At least he's seriously thinking about it."

"He is?" Beck's voice rose and, dang, nearly cracked.

"Did he forget to mention that in one of your twice-a-day calls?" Savannah shot a brow north. "Momma, surely you know there are no secrets in Coconut Key. I'm pretty sure that's your motto with Lovely."

Beck looked at her mother who tipped her head so that her long gray braid slid over her shoulder. "No secrets," Lovely confirmed.

"Well, this one might not be a secret, but it's a surprise," Beck said.

"He just told Nick tonight before you came over, to be honest. Right after you talked to him, apparently. Must have been quite the convo, Mom."

She felt that warmth spread to her cheeks again.

They'd laughed, talked, and practically admitted how much they missed each other.

"What did he say?" she asked instead of sharing all that.

"Just that it's almost winter down under, so he's thinking about spending the season here in the sunshine."

"Ooh, maybe he can rent your townhouse, Pey," Callie suggested.

"Nope." Savannah leaned closer and tapped her glass with her nail. "He was very specific about wanting to stay at Coquina House again."

"Really." Beck gave in to the butterflies in her stomach. "Well, we could use a nice long-term guest, right, Lovely?"

Her mother chuckled and tapped her head. "Something's buzzing."

Beck laughed with the rest of them, but as they talked and joked and laughed for the next few hours, she wondered if maybe there wasn't something to that "lovedar" that her mother claimed to have.

Because something sure was buzzing.

CHAPTER TWO

KENNY

Ava practically threw herself into the front seat of the truck, dumping her backpack with a sigh so dramatic, Kenny knew exactly why his daughter had been cast in the high school production of *Mary Poppins*. But then he'd known that while he was backstage sawing wood, half-listening to the rehearsal.

"Starving," Ava announced without preamble. "Exhausted. Overworked. Need food. Behind on biology notes. Mrs. Packman made us watch some boring video instead of practicing dance steps. Also, did I mention I am famished?" She managed a grin. "So, how are you, Daddy dearest?"

He laughed softly, resisting the urge to tell her just how much she was like her mother, more every year. A little intense, a little sarcastic, a lot of fun. "About the same. And we have *nada* to eat at home. Drive-thru burgers and fries?"

"Ugh." She made a face. "Fat and grease will not look good in those incredible dresses the costume lady has picked for Miss Lark. My character is rich, you know. And a little ditzy. But definitely well-dressed. Can't you cook us some healthy chicken and veggies?"

"I could, if I hadn't been working on two new houses since six forty-five, then zipped straight to Coconut Key High School to build a chimney for Mary Poppins to dance on." He turned the ignition and started to pull out of the parking lot. "Sorry."

She blew out a sigh that could have been heard in the back of the auditorium, had she still been on stage. "You know what you need? A wife."

He snorted. "To cook? Ava, the 1950s called."

"I'm serious. We're stretched to the nines, Dad. School, the play, your new general contracting business is going great guns. We need a third leg on the stool of the Gallagher household."

"We're fine," he said as he reached the highway and checked traffic. As he turned to his right, he saw the intent expression she leveled on him. "What? I don't need a wife, Ava."

"Are you going to stay single forever?" she countered.

What the hell? "Man, you must be hungry if you're trying to marry me off. Last time I dated someone, well." He lifted a brow, remembering the tension between her and Maggie. "You weren't a fan of the idea."

"I wasn't a fan of Maggie, but..." She dug into her purse as her cell phone chimed, giving the subject a much-needed reprieve. He wasn't in the market for a wife, and if he was...

He closed his eyes for a second and the image of Heather Monroe, a permanent fixture in his brain, flashed.

"Oh my God, Dad, you are not going to believe this," Ava said as she stared at the phone. "I got news. I got big, fat, juicy news."

He couldn't help laughing. "Lemme guess. Lael Channing doesn't want to go out with Tyler McDonald anymore."

"Mc*Millan*," she corrected.

"Sorry, fast food on the brain."

"It's so much bigger than that," she said, tapping her phone.

"Umm..." He rooted around for more high school happenings that he knew far too much about. "Gabe What's His Name Big Mouth didn't get into UF after all."

She groaned. "He did, last month. But props to you for keeping up with even the seniors. This one's much closer to home and family."

Home and family? He frowned and shot her a look as he reached the light. "Is everything okay? Is that from Beck or Savannah?"

That would be no surprise. Her grandmother and aunt were constantly in touch with Ava, sometimes more than they were with him.

"Even better," she said in a sing-song voice, turning to him with so much spunk, it was clear her exhaustion and hunger and late homework were forgotten. "Maddie is moving here this week!"

"Maddie? And Heather?"

"Well, duh. She's not coming without her mother, and Marc. You know the house she bought over on Ibis Way is closing this week."

He did, all too well. He'd helped her finalize the negotiations and double-checked the inspector's report. "But she can't move here until school is out, right?"

"They're going to go back to Coconut Key High like they did last fall! Do you know what this means?"

That he wouldn't have two more months to prepare, and Heather wouldn't have two more months of being a widow.

Because surely, once she hit a year, it would be cool for him to let her know how he felt.

"Maddie will be here for the play!" Ava announced excitedly. "And you know what else?"

Yes, he knew. He'd have to hide those feelings even longer. Even though they'd be living in the same town, going to the same church, and hanging out with the same family. Well, he could make it to, say, next Christmas. Hopefully.

"Don't you think, Dad?"

Dang, he hadn't heard a word she'd said. He threw her a look, hoping he didn't appear too perplexed or lost.

"I mean, I know I just said we're stretched to the nines, but we have to help them move, right? She's getting everything in a U-Haul up in Charleston, but she'll need help unloading."

"Of course we'll help," he said. "Heather's driving a U-Haul by herself?"

"Yeah, but it's cool. She's awesome like that."'

No kidding.

"Anyway, they're like family to us."

"They're not family," he said. "Not...technically." It was bad enough he'd fallen for a woman who'd lost her husband to brain cancer a little more than six months ago. But the things he felt for Heather weren't exactly *sisterly*.

While Ava texted back a response, he let his mind drift back to the very last conversation they'd had, after her offer on a three-bedroom house in Coconut Key had been accepted, and she was heading home to sell her house in Charleston and move her life and family here.

So much had been unspoken. He and Heather had become good friends and, in a strange way, they'd led each other on a journey of faith. He'd lost his belief in God after his wife and son died six years ago, and she'd found Jesus after her husband passed.

He had accompanied her to church as a favor—because he discovered he couldn't say no to her, ever—and in the process, he reached a truce with the God he believed had let him down so badly.

He and Heather talked easily about faith in their lives. They talked about a lot of things easily—their kids, especially because their daughters were best friends. And their mutual friends and family, since Heather was Jessie and Josh's younger half-sister. They talked about how life on Coconut Key was so different from his in Atlanta and hers in Charleston, and how much they loved it here. They talked about their jobs, their pasts, even their late spouses, but never about their *feelings*.

And yet they bubbled under the surface, always there, undeniable and—

"Dang!" Ava exclaimed, face in phone. "We have a problem."

"What?"

"Marc. Oh, that kid." She groaned. "I love him, you know, but he's needy as all get out."

"What's wrong?"

"He doesn't want to quit his baseball team."

Kenny understood that. He'd worked hard with Marc over their spring break to persuade the fourteen-year-old to go out for the JV team at his high school, and he'd made it. They'd texted a lot these last few weeks, and Kenny had been coaching him by FaceTime as best he could.

But the Coconut High team was deep into practice and might have even started playing games already. Tryouts for that team were held two months ago.

"Yeah, he's bummed. Maddie's obviously so happy because not only do we get to be besties in school together, she'll get to see Levi Carter who is literally waiting for her to come back. Like, he hasn't looked at another girl since she left."

He frowned. "Who's Levi Carter?"

"Hottest human alive who is, no surprise, totes into Maddie, but, gah! Marc can't ruin this because of stupid baseball." She turned to him and shook the phone with frustration. "Can't you talk to him or something?"

He blew out a long exhale, not sure he wanted to tell Marc to forget about baseball. The boy had had some problems with not-so-great friends, and Heather had counted on Kenny for guidance. So, he took it as a personal victory that Marc made the team at his school in Charleston and was going to play this spring.

And what did "totally into Maddie" mean? Did her mother know about this "hottest human alive"? Should he mention it?

"Dad?" Ava pressed.

"Thinking."

"Could you help him get on the Coconut Key team?" she suggested.

"It's kind of late in the season, honey. The teams are practicing now and games start soon. I doubt he could walk on, but..." He frowned and glanced at her, his mind whirring for a solution. "Isn't that play director, Mrs. Packman, married to the coach?"

She rolled her eyes. "The curse of a small high school. The teachers are all married and they all do everything. But, yeah, Mr. Packman, the chemistry teacher, is the baseball coach. Do you know him?"

"Nope." He grinned. "But I know his wife, and I'm making her a chim-chim-i-ney, so she owes me a fave-favory, don't you think?"

"Hah!" She punched his arm. "Good one!"

"And you're right. It's a small school. Maybe we'll get lucky and the JV team'll take a walk-on. When they see his arm, they will."

Her smile grew bigger. "You're so awesome, Dad. I love how you want to take care of my friend's family."

"Well, they're my friends, too."

"So you're happy they're moving here?" she asked.

Happy? That was one way to describe it. Terrified, optimistic, tense, and a little like a kid who'd been handed a ticket to Disneyworld would also work.

"Of course I'm happy," he replied.

"'Cause you'll have your church buddy again."

His smile grew just thinking about it. "Yeah, it's nice when she's there."

When Ava didn't answer, he glanced at her, feeling the intensity of the look she was giving him and suddenly really regretting that last comment. "You know what, A? I can totally cook. Let's zip into Coconut Market and get chicken to grill. And a salad? Would that work?"

But she still stared at him with that same expression she wore the moment she cracked an algebra problem. And he did not like the problem she just cracked. Well, he liked the problem, but not that she cracked it.

"No chicken?" he asked.

"No...Savannah's right," she whispered. "I should have known. She has a sixth sense and is always right."

"About what?" *Damn it, Savannah.*

"You do care...about her."

He faked a look of confusion. "About Savannah? Of course I do. She's my biological sister and your aunt." And in fat trouble for gossiping about this.

"I mean, it makes sense but..." She drew back. "How did I miss this?"

Because he hid it like a pro. Except not from Savannah, apparently. "Miss what, Ava? Do you or do you not want grilled chicken? Please." He put an edge in his voice so that maybe she'd let the dinner decision distract her.

"Does Heather know you like her?" she asked.

Dear *God.* She was exactly like her mother—annoyingly direct.

"Ava, I don't know what you're—"

"Don't lie, Dad."

"I'm not lying," he fired back. "But I am hungry, and so are you as you whined about numerous times, so what do you want for dinner?"

But she bit her lip, a little glint in her eyes. "How did we miss this? Maddie and I should have—"

"Ava!"

She closed her mouth at the reprimand in his voice.

"Don't, okay? Don't go there. Don't start...spinning things because...that's how they get out of control." And the one thing he needed with this relationship-that-wasn't-a-relationship was control. "You just worry about... being Miss Lark and Maddie and Levi what's-his-name and the things that are important to you."

"*This* is important to me."

He let his eyes close as he pulled into the market parking lot under the giant coconut.

But Ava was still staring, still processing, and still looking a little amused and amazed. "Dad. You and Heather."

"Are friends," he insisted. "And we go to church together and that's all."

Still holding his gaze, she lifted her phone, her thumbs starting to move without even looking at the damn thing.

"Don't." He pushed the phone down before she could type anything. "Don't drag Maddie into this—"

"Into what?" she demanded.

"Whatever you are..." He flicked his fingers by his temples. "Fantasizing about."

"Am I the only one doing the fantasizing?"

He narrowed his eyes and inched in. "Too far, kiddo," he ground out. "You are sliding into dangerous territory that is most certainly not your business. So drop the subject."

"Can I ask why?"

"No, you can't."

She angled her head, her eyes warm, and her smile... oh, God, did she have to look so much like Elise that it was like sitting here in the truck with his late wife?

"All right," she conceded. "I'll drop it. And I won't say anything to Maddie." Her smile grew. "But, man, you two would be freaking perfect together!"

He exhaled a breath, somehow managing not to say *I know.*

"So, you know what I'm going to do for you?" Ava asked.

"Stay out of my business, I hope?"

"What Mom would want me to do," she said.

"What's that?" he asked.

"Pray," she said with a smug smile. "It usually worked for her."

"What are you praying for, A?"

"For you to have...everything," she said softly, reaching for his arm. "And also that you pull out of this lot and go to Mickey D's. I'm feeling greasy fries and a milkshake to celebrate."

"Good call." He backed up, and really hoped she remembered how to pray.

CHAPTER THREE

PEYTON

Peyton awoke with a start, peering at her phone to see it was still not five AM. She fell back on her pillow with a sigh, sliding her legs over the ridiculously silky and expensive sheets that were on every bed in The Haven. She'd always liked that when she lived here during what she thought of as "The Havenly days" after the hurricane had displaced them all from Coquina House.

She closed her eyes and remembered those months, which had been such a dichotomy for her. On one hand, Peyton was learning to become proficient in the kitchen, helping Jessie with the new restaurant, wrapped up in Savannah's baby, and cocooned here on the Gulf of Mexico in a perfectly safe and wonderful...well, haven. On the other hand, that whole time she'd nursed a broken heart because Val had left to go back to Miami—where he felt he'd left so much unfinished—and rarely contacted her.

Now, she understood why he'd made that choice and

why he'd kept their contact to a minimum. And she loved that he'd gotten through his issues and come for her in February, pleading for a chance at love. And she was so happy now, as everyone kept noting.

But there was something about Coconut Key that was home, something safe about being with a group like Mom and Savannah and Jessie and Lovely. And as happy as she was with Val, she was resentful, too.

Why couldn't she have both?

She turned her head when she heard a sound from the kitchen, not too far from the guestroom. Who would be up at this hour?

Savannah with the baby? Or did Nick come down to get something for her? Whoever it was, they wouldn't mind if Peyton came in to make coffee. She used to get up at this hour every day when she was the assistant manager at the Coquina Café, and she'd already decided late last night that she was going to head over to the restaurant to see if Jessie needed help before the breakfast rush.

She slid out of bed, tiptoeing down the hall to find Savannah sleepy-eyed, holding Dylan in one arm, pressing the microwave buttons with the other.

"What are you doing up?" Peyton whispered as she came in. "Is he okay?"

"He's perfect," Savannah assured her, stroking the baby's head as he perched on her arm and turned to give Peyton a gummy smile.

Her heart just shifted. "So perfect," Peyton agreed.

"He started to fuss and I didn't want him to wake Nick. So I thought I'd come down here and get him a little mushy breakfast, but I'm up for the day so..." She tipped her head toward the coffeemaker. "Herbal tea."

"I bet you'd kill for coffee."

"With my bare hands," she said on a laugh. "I do get my one cup later. And since we started solid foods, I might wean him to formula soon. Don't judge."

"Judge? Please." Peyton came closer and put her hand on his bald little head, overjoyed when he grinned again and reached a hand out with a loving gurgle. "Yes, you know your Auntie Pey-pey, don't you?"

"Of course he does."

Peyton leaned in and kissed his head, getting a whiff of baby scent that always made her swoon a little. "Oh my God, child, I love you."

Savannah smiled, tilting her head. "Then you better come and visit often, Auntie."

"I will," she promised, turning to the selection of K-cups. "Would it be just mean of me to brew coffee?"

"Please, if you can get your jollies sniffing my baby, then I can get a whiff of your coffee. Brew away." Savannah took her tea and settled in across the kitchen in the large farmhouse table by the doors, sliding Dylan into the high-chair where he slapped the tray demanding food. "Why are you up at this ungodly hour, anyway? Are you leaving to go back to Miami at the very crack of dawn's first light?"

"I'm going down to the Coquina Café to help Jessie. She said she's been swamped. And I really miss working there."

"She misses you, too," Savannah said. "But Heather'll be here soon, so Jessie won't have to go long without an assistant manager."

"Mmmm." Peyton took the cup from the coffeemaker and headed to the fridge for cream.

"Totally nailed the Beck Foster 'Mmmm,' Pey."

She laughed. "I know. When we're old and we sound like our mom, it will be her classic non-committal, I want to say something but better not 'Mmmm.'"

"Exactly." Then Savannah leaned forward. "So what do you want to say that you think you better not?"

After she stirred in the cream, Peyton took the cup to the table and sat down with Savannah, who was already spooning something that looked like applesauce into a happy little mouth. "Heather doing my job kind of hurts."

"Heather loves that job and you're happy in Miami." She waited a beat. "Aren't you?"

"Everyone says I am."

"Peyton Danielle Foster."

She made a face. "I hate that I'm named after Dad. Someday, I'm going to drop that and just be Peyton Foster..." She didn't finish, but Savannah smiled.

"Peyton Foster Sanchez. Has a nice ring to it." She winked. "And speaking of rings..."

"Any day now," she said. "He wants to surprise me, I think."

"Will that make you happy?"

Peyton shot her a look. "What do you think?"

"What I think isn't important. You need to be sure. Are you sure?"

Smiling, Peyton rubbed her thumb over Dylan's chubby little forearm, the skin so smooth it sort of hurt her heart to touch him. "I'm sure," she whispered, lifting his hand. "Sure that I want one of these little dumplings."

"They aren't that hard to make, you know." She lifted a brow. "What are you waiting for?"

"That's going to be carved on my gravestone," Peyton said with a dry laugh. "'Here lies Peyton Foster. Died waiting.'"

"Pey, you're not waiting. You're moving to Miami, talking engagements, and soon you'll be married and poppin' out little bambinos."

On a sigh, she eased back, taking a sip of hot coffee.

"I mean, that's what I'm hearing, right?" Savannah pressed, looking concerned.

"You're hearing correctly. We're on that path and it's a good thing, but..."

"You can't blow this relationship because he won't live here," Savannah said. "I know I whined about you moving, but I would never, ever want you to miss out on love just to live near us."

"It's not that..."

"Val doesn't want a baby?" she guessed with a soft gasp. "Because that would be a disaster for the girl who had one whole closet devoted to baby dolls."

"Oh, no, he wants a baby." She gave a dry laugh. "Like, yesterday."

"Thank God. Then, yes, get home and start procreating, dear sister. You have time for two or three."

She looked over the rim of her cup at her sister. "Where's the first place and who's the first person you turned to when you found out you were pregnant?"

"Mom," she answered without a millisecond of hesitation. "But I didn't have a relationship with the baby daddy, Pey. I saw him *once*. Dylan was..." She shuttered her eyes. "I hate to say mistake, but, let's be real. He was the original one-night-stand baby."

He let out a little squawk when the next spoonful took too long, making them both laugh.

"Guess he doesn't like being called that," Peyton joked. "But my point was that even if you'd have been married and as settled with Nick as you are now, you would have wanted to raise him near Mom. And, I am kind of ashamed to admit this, but I want my family with my baby. Mine. And Val's. But mostly mine."

To her credit, Savannah didn't scoff at that. "I'd like you to be here, too. Any chance you can change that man's mind?"

"Not much of one. He's got a great job that he'd never recreate in the Keys, and he loves that job."

"As much as being the best-looking fisherman in the Keys?"

Peyton considered that. "He was here escaping a painful memory," she said. "Now that he's recovered, he's doing what he was trained and educated to do, and they love him at that company. He's thriving, getting new business, and being eyed for every possible promotion. It's very different from running a small fishing business. He's going to do very well and he's able to help his family financially, which they need."

"And you love him enough to live there with him?" Savannah asked.

"I love him so much." She felt her whole face melt into a smile. "I just want to be in two places at once, so I guess I'll be on US 1 a lot. Especially if I get pregnant."

Savannah's eyes popped. "Uh, are you just playing with fire down there..." She used the spoon to gesture toward Peyton's lower half. "And throwing caution to the wind?"

She lifted a shoulder. "I went off the pill many months ago and haven't gone back."

"You did? When Val was gone? Why?"

"I was actually thinking about going it alone, you know? Sperm bank style."

"Radically non-traditional for you, Pey. But, honey, you come from a long line of whoopsies. I'd be very careful if you're not ready."

"I'm ready...if it happens."

"Oh, it'll happen, trust me." Suddenly, Savannah's whole face lit up as she looked over Peyton's shoulder. "Daddy's here, Dyl-pickle."

Peyton turned to catch Nick amble into the room in sleep pants and a faded T-shirt, his golden hair tousled. He grunted and gave a wave in their general direction, heading for the coffee.

Now, there was a man who left *everything* for a woman and their child. And sometimes it just hurt to look at Nick and know he did that for Savannah, but Val wouldn't do that for her.

They dropped the conversation, quiet until Nick joined them. He leaned over to kiss Savannah then drop another on the baby's head, getting a big applesaucy smile in return.

"Morning, all. Why is everyone up so early?"

"I should be on my way to Coquina Café to help Jessie, but we're chatting."

"I had a hungry baby," Savannah said, bringing in the next spoonful to an open, waiting little mouth. "What's your excuse?"

"I'm going to run and then..." He let his words trail off, shaking his head. "I don't know," he said, sounding a little bewildered. "I've never not had anything to do."

"Is that fun and relaxing?" Peyton asked.

He took a slow inhale as if he needed a minute to think, then gave a tight smile. "It's both, but it's also...weird."

"Nick's restless," Savannah said, reaching out a hand to touch his arm. "I think he should write a book."

"A tell-all biography with all the dirt on everyone in Hollywood?" Peyton's brows shot up. "That would sell like crazy."

"And make me relive that personal hell? No thanks. I do have a mystery running around in my head, but I can't imagine sitting in a chair for that long and typing."

"Maybe some volunteer work?" Peyton suggested. "There's a food bank in Key West that always needs people."

"I'd do that," he said, "but...I don't know. I like the idea of doing something for good instead of money, but I'd love to work with kids. I guess I could look into being a Big Brother or something."

"My mom is friendly with that woman who organized the Bachelor Auction last year," Savannah said. "What's her name, Pey? The yoga instructor who was always hanging all over Val?"

"Gwen Parker," Peyton said with a groan. "I wouldn't want that cougar anywhere near Nick."

"Not scared," Savannah said. "We should talk to her."

He nodded and let out a sigh. "I'll figure it out."

"And speaking of helping," Peyton pushed up. "I

better go. Tell Callie I'll be back after the breakfast rush and we can head home to Miami."

Savannah made a face. "Oh, it's home now."

"Well, you know. Home is where the heart is," Peyton said with a bright smile.

"You be careful with that heart," Savannah said. "And also with...that other stuff. Remember the fertile stock you hail from, sister."

If only Peyton could be so lucky.

PEYTON WAS STILL MULLING over the baby idea when she slid the key into the back door of Coquina Café and got a wonderful whiff of eggs, pastries, and bacon even though it was just after six o'clock. The doors opened at seven, so Jessie and Linc, the line cook, were probably deep in the weeds for breakfast prep.

When she came around the corner, she spied Linc at the grill.

"There's our long-lost assistant manager!" he exclaimed. "You back for good, Peyton?"

"I wish," she replied, a little surprised at the honest answer that slipped out. "Just for the morning. You guys need help baking, or is Jess already loading up the pastry rack with her scones? Which are totally better than mine."

"She's up in the dining room, but not working on the pastries. Unless 'doling them out for good behavior' to a sugar addict counts."

She frowned. "Doling them...oh, is Beau here?"

Because Chuck's four-year-old son would be the sugar addict in question.

"Chuck's sloop is coming in this morning from St. Barts, so he had to drive up to Key Largo to get it docked and take the crew to the airport to go back, so Beau's here." He lifted his brows. "Looks like Coconut Key is going to have its first boat charter business."

"That's awesome." Since he'd arrived a few months ago—after a boating accident where he'd lost his memory and gone missing for four years—Chuck had been talking about bringing one or more of his sailing vessels from St. Barts to Coconut Key.

"Is she alone up there?" It couldn't be easy setting up for the breakfast rush with a four-year-old.

"Yes, I'm sorry to say. Desiree had a crappy night and I'm not sure she's going to make it in," he said, referring to his wife, who worked almost full-time as a hostess. "And last time I was out there, Beau had found a crayon and was coloring on every single clean placemat. And some tables. Kid's a handful, Pey."

"He is that." Tying an apron on mostly out of habit and because it felt good, Peyton shouldered the swinging door into the beverage pass-through then did the same to the one that led to the dining room.

Just stepping into the cheery area, lit by the rising sun over the Atlantic and a bank of windows that poured in light, put Peyton in a great mood. She'd worked so hard to help reimagine the high-end, upscale—but failing—fine dining restaurant called Chuck's into this bright and beautiful café that so perfectly showcased Jessie's comfort food.

But she barely had a second to appreciate it when one

very small, dark-haired creature whizzed by, a pastry in one hand, a crayon in the other.

"Hello!" he yelled at her, because Beau didn't *have* an inside voice.

"Hello," she replied, snagging his arm just as he dropped into a seat at table twelve, crayon at the ready, crumbs raining on the floor someone had already cleaned for this morning's service. "And no, you will not color that placemat."

"Thank you!" Jessie called from the coffee bar. "I can't do two things at once."

"I've got him." She took the crayon and closed her fingers around his tiny hand. "Come with me, buddy."

He smiled up at her, all baby teeth and big brown eyes. "Where are we going, Miss Pey?"

"To do something really fun." Which she'd figure out in a minute. But the distraction was enough to get him to take her hand and head toward Jessie at the coffee bar.

"I didn't expect to see you this morning," Jessie said, wiping back a stray curl with her wrist.

"I woke up missing this place."

Jessie laughed. "Well, this place misses you. And Des is feeling under the weather."

"Linc told me. I'll run the hostess stand."

Beau managed to wrest his hand from Peyton's grip and scramble up on a bar stool. "Cookie, Miss Jessie?"

Jessie sighed and shook her head. "You've had enough."

"No!" He pounded the counter like a drunk who'd been cut off by the bartender. "*Une biscuit!*" He shouted the demand in French, something Peyton rarely heard from him since he and Chuck had left French-speaking St. Barts for Coconut Key.

Jessie frowned. "Excuse me?"

"A cookie," he corrected himself.

"It was your tone, not your language," Jessie said, stepping away. "But while you're up there, Beau, I'm going to get your own picture for you to color. And if you color it nicely—"

"A cookie?" he asked.

"A...something." She sighed as she walked to the hostess stand, looking way too frazzled for this hour.

"Do not move," Peyton whispered to Beau, then followed Jessie. "Are you okay?"

"I'm fine," she said, bending down to find the kids' placemats at the bottom. The ones that were *supposed* to be colored.

"You don't sound fine."

As she straightened, she looked at Peyton, her eyes tired with shadows. "Mothering is not for the faint of heart," she whispered. "Especially if that heart is fifty-five years old. This is definitely a younger woman's game."

"So I should start ASAP?" Peyton asked, half joking.

Jessie's eyes flickered in surprise. "Not where I was going, but okay." She walked back to the bar with a child's placemat and a fresh crayon. "If you want a head start, I could use a babysitter for an hour or two even more than a hostess."

"Of course!" Peyton said. "I can take him down to the beach or to swing on Lovely's hammock."

"Hammock!" Beau picked up the word and screamed it back, shooting his fist in the air. "Now?"

"In a minute," Jessie promised, tapping the bar. "If you color me a pretty picture."

He instantly went to work as Jessie and Peyton stepped a few feet away, both of them watching him. But when Peyton looked at Jessie, she was nibbling on her lower lip and looking like she might cry.

"You're definitely not okay," Peyton said, putting a hand on her arm. "Do you want me to stay here for the week until Heather gets settled in?"

"No, honey, I want you to be where you are happiest, and we can all see that's with Val. I had everything under control until I found out I had Beau this morning."

"Miss Jessie? Is this good?" He held up the paper for her to see.

"It's gorgeous, honey. Don't forget the blue sky."

Happy with that, he turned back to his work.

"And will he ever call me Mommy?" she asked on a whisper.

"Have you asked him?"

Jessie shrugged. "I'm kind of waiting for all the legalities. Chuck is officially changing Beau's last name to Donovan. Then that same lawyer is handling the adoption. Then...I'll be the world's oldest mother of a four-year-old."

"Stop it," Peyton said. "Age is a number."

"And a really sore back that failed me at the playground. Do you have any idea the muscles it takes to push a swing or stay up on a teeter-totter?"

Peyton smiled. "No, but I'd like to find out. Can I take him there this morning?"

"I would be your slave for life." She shifted her gaze to the coffee bar and whispered, "Instead of his."

"Jessie!"

"I know. I'm awful. It's menopause, I swear, which is why I'm the wrong age for this." Her whole expression crumbled. "I love him to death, but he's never been disciplined very much. I'm scared of this challenge."

She reached to hug Jessie. "Do not be scared, Jess. You got this and you have Chuck, who is an amazing father and is *not* letting his age stop him."

Jessie just sighed. "Sometimes I'm so up for it. I mean, that kid is adorable. A ball of energy, yes, but sometimes he's so sweet, it breaks my heart and I really do love him." She waited a beat. "Mostly when he's asleep."

"Do you think just because your husband showed up still alive, you are automatically going to love the son he adopted while he was missing with amnesia?" Peyton whispered.

"Yes."

"Well, get real, Mrs. Donovan. Love has to grow, and yours will. It already is."

She let her shoulders drop with another sigh. "I know. I'm just impatient. I want to be connected to him immediately, and it's hard."

"Relax this morning. I'll take him to the playground for a while, then we'll get something healthy to eat, visit Lovely's hammock, and then I'll take him to the beach."

"Aren't you going back to Miami today?"

"I am, but with his attention span? All that will take about an hour and a half, and I'll go then." She planted a light kiss on Jessie's freckled cheek. "Go finish the pastries and coffee bar. I'll go practice being a mom."

"Well, if you learn how, let me know." She reached into her pocket and pulled out her keys. "Take my car because his car seat will make you say very bad, bad words when you try to unlatch and re-install."

"Got it." Peyton winked as she walked back to Beau. "Oh my gosh, Beauregard, look what you did! Is that a bumble bee on the flower? I hope we don't see any at the playground, which is where we are going."

"Playground!" he screamed just as the kitchen door opened and Jessie's morning wait staff appeared.

Jessie blew Peyton a kiss and headed off to her comfort zone—work. And Peyton took off for the playground to practice the job she so fervently wanted to have.

CHAPTER FOUR

BECK

When her phone flashed with the notification that Oliver Bradshaw was waiting for her to join a Zoom call, Beck immediately abandoned the pile of fresh sheets she was folding to take upstairs for the daily bed change.

The beds could wait. She only had two rooms occupied and those guests were out for the day. Calling her at nine in the morning meant it was eleven at night in Sydney. They'd navigated the time difference rather easily these past few weeks, and Beck knew if Oliver contacted her that late, then it was probably important.

Was he finally going to tell her what Savannah and Nick already knew? His decision to come for the summer had surprised—and delighted—her, but she was a tiny bit disappointed that he hadn't mentioned it to her. Well, they said he was thinking about it, so maybe he hadn't yet decided.

God, she hoped he did. Because she was starting to

understand why they call it a "crush"—this much distraction and attraction could weigh a woman down.

She headed into her first-floor owner's suite, straight to the cubby where she'd set up a desk in front of the window to create a small but functional office. Since she lived on the premises, she'd made the decision not to take up valuable space with a reception desk. Walk-ins were few and far between. She knew when guests were arriving, and she and Lovely frequently met them in person at the top of the stairs with mimosas, Coquina House's signature drink. Greeting guests with the bubbly had become a ritual.

At least it would when they had new guests arriving on a regular basis. Right now, business was little more than a trickle. So, at the very least, she hoped Oliver was going to be a season-long renter.

Who was she kidding? She wanted more than a booking out of this relationship.

Tapping her laptop, she glanced out the window next to her, seeing a few people on the beach, and puffy white clouds suspended in a blindingly blue sky that matched the water from the shore to the horizon.

Who wouldn't want to come to Coconut Key, she wondered. Just then, the video call connected and a very handsome and now-familiar face flashed on her screen.

"G'day, Grandma Beck."

She laughed at the name he frequently used, since they did, after all, share a grandchild. "Hello, Grandpa Ollie."

He rolled his eyes. "I think I've told you no one calls me Ollie and survives to tell the tale."

She laughed softly, loving the Aussie inflection that

lifted his voice at the end of every sentence. She dropped her chin on her knuckles to look at the screen. "I like to live on the edge that way."

"Ollie's dangerous ground," he teased. "How's your day going up there in the Keys?"

Sometimes it was impossible to think of the Keys as "up" anywhere. But they were to this man on the other side of the equator. "Kind of slow," she admitted. "How's your night going down under?"

He shrugged. "Quiet. I'm planning a trip to the beach, though."

"Oh, that's nice." She knew he had a beach house in Wollongong, about an hour from his home in Sydney, and that he went there frequently, no matter the weather, because he loved the place. "Will you take your boat out?"

"I don't know. How's the surf look?" He leaned closer. "I meant next weekend...and I meant your beach, not mine."

And, oh, that crush pressed harder on her heart. "Ah, so the rumors are true."

"Is my son telling my secrets to you?" he asked, his dark eyes sparking. "You know, I'm still not quite used to saying those words, 'my son.'"

"I know exactly how you feel," Beck said, remembering the day Ava had shown up on a search for her father's biological mother. "They're nice words, and your son is an extremely nice man."

"He is that. So, how do you feel about a visit? A long one, this time."

"I think it's awesome," she said honestly. "You should spend time with Nick and Dylan and..."

"You."

She laughed again, wishing she could play it cool, but pretty sure that was impossible with this man. "Well, I'll be here."

"Good. Would it be greedy of me to take the best room in the B&B again? I am a fan of that Coconut Room with the sweeping ocean view. I don't expect a discount because it would take your best accommodation off the market for a few months."

"The rates are lower in the summer," she assured him. "And for how long will you be staying with us at Coquina House, Mr. Bradshaw?"

"Long."

A little thrill danced through her.

"Will you get sick of me?"

Not for a moment. "It's a lot of money, even with the off-season discount. So why don't we—"

"No discount," he insisted. "I was going to spend the winter traveling anyway, so this is perfect for me. I'm quite excited about the prospect."

"So am I," she confessed, then tried not to bite her lip for saying too much. "I mean, it's great to have that room occupied and..." She let out a nervous laugh. "I'm looking forward to it."

"So, how's our ad doing?" he asked, referring to the Facebook ad they'd developed together, although Oliver had created the graphic and drafted the copy. Beck wouldn't have known where to begin.

"I just checked the numbers this morning and it has a...fourteen cent CPC?" She wrinkled her nose because interpreting the results was as foreign to her as creating the ad. "Is that good?"

"That's fantastic," he said. "We'll work on another when I get there."

"Oh, you don't have to work. I'm sure you'll want to spend time at the beach with Nick and Savannah and little Dylan."

"I'm not coming there to be a fulltime grandfather," he said with a warm smile.

"Well, you're not coming here to rekindle your advertising career, either." So why exactly was he coming?

He eased closer to his screen, giving her an even better look into his dark, dark eyes, which never failed to take her breath away. "I'm two glasses of brandy into my night and you've had nothing but coffee and, if I know you, half a scone while you washed the day's linens. Am I right?"

"Well, you make me sound a little like a scullery maid, but yes, you're right. And why are you telling me about the brandy?"

"To rationalize what I'm about to say."

She tried to swallow, but failed. She did manage a breath, though. "What's that?"

"I can't wait to see you again," he said softly.

"Oh." And now she was lightheaded, damn it.

"And with that, I'm going to say goodnight and I'll see you...soon."

She darn near shivered. "How soon?"

"In a week. I arrive a week from Sunday, and Nick will pick me up. I should be there for that lovely Sunday gathering you all have, a little jetlagged but ready to start...my holiday." He gave in to a smile that told her he already knew he'd said more than he should have.

She nodded, choosing her words just as carefully. "I'm looking forward to it...Ollie."

He narrowed his eyes in warning. "Dangerous ground, Beck."

Dangerous, indeed. And she kind of couldn't wait to fall.

"SOMEONE IS HUMMING like a happy little bird."

Beck turned from the stove where she was carefully melting some chocolate—following Peyton's directions but with so much less cooking confidence—to see her mother coming in the sliding doors. "I *am* a happy bird, Lovely."

"Ooh, does that mean we have more reservations?"

"As a matter of fact, we've booked the Coconut Room...open ended for Oliver Bradshaw."

"Ohhh." She wiggled her eyebrows. "Well, isn't that nice and convenient and perfect?"

"Stop it."

"Why?" Lovely asked as she set her bag on the kitchen counter and slid off the sunhat that protected her face on the short walk from her cottage to Coquina House. "You admitted you have feelings for him the other night at The Haven."

"Well, my daughters plied me with mimosas and questions. I don't know how much I truly *admitted*. That was more like the Spanish Inquisition."

"And you managed to avoid most questions, turn the tables to talk about your girls, and sidestep the truth."

"I never lied."

Lovely came closer and put her arm around Beck's waist. "We did have a pact that we would not have any secrets ever again, didn't we?"

She smiled and nodded. "We did."

"So I'll share if you will," she said.

"You have a secret?" Beck asked.

"You first."

"Okay." She took a breath. "But to be honest, I haven't kept anything from you, Lovely. I'm just figuring it all out myself."

"Then allow me to figure it out with you, sweet girl. I understand not telling your daughters everything, but me?" She leaned in. "Your mother gets to know all the deets, as our darling Savannah would say. I missed the first time you fell in love, so I want to enjoy this one."

"*Love?*" She practically choked. "I've spent a week with the man and a few hours—okay, a few more than a few—on video calls. You are pushing it with love."

Lovely raised a dubious brow. "You're different. This is different. I pronounce this different."

Beck had to laugh. "From Josh, you mean?" She knew how much Lovely—and everyone else in their tight circle—had been rooting for Beck and Josh. "It *is* different," she agreed. "You know Josh and I will always be friends, and only friends, but you can't..."

"Manufacture chemistry?" Lovely guessed when Beck didn't finish.

"Exactly."

"And you have chemistry with the dashing Mr. Bradshaw?"

"There's definitely something bubbling," she said. "But not this chocolate, no matter how hard I try."

She let go of the spoon and turned from the non-melting chocolate to look Lovely in the eyes. "I don't know what it is, or why it is, or how long it could last, but..." She took a slow inhale. "I can't stop thinking about him."

"Oh!" Lovely pressed her hands together, barely able to cover her smile. "That's so wonderful."

"Is it? It's also a little scary."

"Why?" Lovely frowned, a few creases deepening on a face that didn't quite look its full seventy-four years.

Yes, her mother had some tiny scars as a reminder of an accident that nearly took her life over a year ago, but she didn't have the leathery skin one might expect on a woman who lived in the Keys for her entire life. Probably because she was so beautiful on the inside, it made her skin glow.

"You shouldn't be scared. Unless he wants you to move to Sydney, then you should be very scared because I will kill him with my own two hands."

She laughed and held up two "Scout's honor" fingers. "You have my word I will not move to Sydney. I *promise*. But distance is one reason I'm scared." Falling flat on her face in love like a schoolgirl when she was fifty-six and supposedly mature was another.

"Pffft. If it's real, he'll move here."

"Tell that to Peyton."

Lovely grunted under her breath. "Why can't that boy move back here? I get that he loves his job, but if he loves Peyton?"

"She isn't going to give him another ultimatum," Beck said. "She's done that, and it cost her eight months and —" She whipped around at the bitter smell and light smoke rising from the melting chocolate. "Oh, darn it all!" She yanked the pot from the stove so hard the metal bowl slipped from the top, spilling chocolate on the stove with a hiss.

Flipping the burner dial, she stepped back, shaking her head. "How is it I never learned to bake anything?"

"Your mother," Lovely said. "Well, the one who raised you. Olivia was terrible in the kitchen."

"She hated to cook anything," Beck agreed. "She always made me feel that a woman stuck in the kitchen was a loser, but I *gotta* up my baking game," she admitted. "I know we're only responsible for a light breakfast, but I just feel like we should have more treats and sweets on hand for guests and I can't keep siphoning off the Coquina Café supply."

"And a good B&B wouldn't serve store bought," Lovely said.

"But I wanted to have something for the Davidsons when they come back from their tour of Key West, which could be within the hour. The Halbergs are swimming with the dolphins in Key Largo, so they'll be back much later. They might want an evening dessert, too."

"How about fruit kabobs?"

"That's what I was going to make, but Peyton always adds a chocolate drizzle that looks so festive."

"I have a bottle of Hershey's syrup in my pantry from when Ava slept over and we made sundaes. Relax, Beckie." She patted Beck's face, then turned to the fridge. "I'll start the kabobs, but you have to tell me about Oliver's visit. When does he arrive?"

"Next Sunday."

"I'm a little surprised he's not staying in the guest house at The Haven, aren't you?"

"I think he senses that Nick and Savannah are still in the honeymoon phase. No one wants to intrude on that, plus it's only a ten-minute drive. And he really liked it here, specifically requesting the Coconut Room, which does have such a glorious view."

"The Haven has a glorious view, and the guest house is separate, and I think what he really liked is the owner." She lifted a skewer and slid it into a chunk of cantaloupe. "The fun, attractive, delightful one."

Beck sighed at the dismal failure of chocolate and took the bowl to the sink. "You're fun, attractive, and delightful," she said.

"Okay, the *young*, fun, attractive, and delightful owner."

"Not that young," Beck sighed. "But, Lovely, I can't lie. He does make me feel...younger. Is that wrong?"

"Wrong? This is everything right, dear girl. This is... life. And you want to squeeze every drop out of it! Nothing is wrong about these feelings."

Beck thought about that for a few minutes as she rinsed the metal prep bowl and slid it and the rest of the too many utensils she'd used into the dishwasher.

"Okay, maybe not wrong," she finally whispered. "But it feels...unsteady. That was the thing about Josh. After being knocked to the ground by my cheating husband, there was solid-as- a-rock Joshua Cross ready to hold me when winds blew. And he did." A tweak of guilt squeezed. "He literally did—through Kenny's arrival, and a hurricane, and Dylan being born prematurely and redoing this B&B and even the celebrity wedding, he held me. But he just wasn't...magic." She sighed noisily. "I wanted it to be and I kept waiting for it to be and I knew it should be, but..."

"When did you know?" Lovely abandoned the watermelon, coming closer to Beck.

"That it wasn't magic? Probably sometime during—"

"That Oliver was," she interjected. "When did you first feel the magic?"

Beck didn't even have to think about it. "When he walked up the stairs out on The Haven's deck and announced he was Nick's father. My knees went a little wobbly. My throat was dry. My heart hammered. And..." She bit back a laugh. "Well, that wasn't a hot flash I felt."

Lovely giggled. "Your poor hormones are so confused."

"No kidding." She leaned against the counter and crossed her arms, still thinking of the early days when Oliver arrived. "At Savannah and Nick's wedding, he came with me to give the baby a bottle and...I don't know, Lovely, something happened."

"Yet another biological response?"

She shook her head. "It was emotional and indescribable and...real."

Lovely blinked, her eyes moist.

"Not something you need to cry about, Lovely."

"Oh, I know. I'm old and I weep easily." She put her arms around Beck. "I'm happy for you the way you're happy for Peyton and Savannah."

"I'm glad you are," Beck whispered, hugging back. "Because if I fall and hurt myself, even this old menopausal lady might need her mommy to pick up the pieces."

"You are not going to, but if you need me, I'm here."

Beck inched back and snapped her fingers. "Almost forgot. Your secret?"

"My...oh, that was..." She gave a sly smile. "Just my way of getting you to tell me yours."

"You really think I'm going to fall for—"

They both startled at the sound of a car door from the small B&B parking lot downstairs.

"Our guests are back," Lovely said. "And we are having mushy moments instead of making afternoon mimosas and fruit kabobs."

"But you said you had a secret and I—"

"Beckie!" She notched her head toward the veranda, the footsteps on the stairs getting louder. "We have a business to run, money to make, and...a life to live to the fullest, sweet girl. No time for idle chatter!"

Beck laughed and was still smiling as she popped the champagne, so grateful to have her mother—the real one, not the one who hated life in general and the kitchen in particular—to share these days with her.

CHAPTER FIVE

PEYTON

"You know what I want to do the minute I get home?" Peyton glanced at Val's handsome profile as he drove through the dark Miami night.

"I hope it's the same thing I want to do," he replied with a very sexy smile that never failed to thrill her.

"Is that why you're taking us toward Brickell Avenue? Your apartment instead of mine?" she asked. He almost never spent the night in the two-bedroom Coral Gables apartment Peyton shared with Callie. His high rise was more private, and she suspected he didn't want to give her little sister a bad impression—not that what they were doing when they spent the night together was any big secret.

But she liked that he was protective of Callie.

"Nope, that's not why I'm going this way. That's a surprise. What do you want to do when you get home?"

She tapped the Tupperware container on her lap.

"Eat the flan I was too full to devour at Papi's birthday party."

He laughed. "Did you get the recipe out of Abuelita yet?"

"Not for lack of trying. I promised to teach her all my best secrets that I learned from Jessie, and she just rolled her eyes and said something in Spanish that I didn't quite get."

He threw her a look. "You don't remember?"

"Ummm." She squeezed her eyes shut and tried to remember the sound of the thick accented word his grandmother had whispered. "El...biznado? Biz knee-ay...something."

He snorted a hearty laugh. "*El bisnieto?*"

"Yeah, that might have been it. What does it mean?"

"What did you say?"

She shook her head. "I said I didn't speak Spanish but I would learn if she'd teach me how to make that flan. What does *el biznieto* mean?"

"It means..." He laughed again. "God, I love that woman."

"All right, I'll get out my translator." She reached for her bag, but he put his hand on her arm. "It means that my family loves you. Especially my abeulita, which is really wonderful because she doesn't love everyone."

"I love her, too. I love them all." And she did, too. Every one of his family was as warm, colorful, and fun as hers, and they'd made every effort to make her feel welcome. How could she not love that clan?

"And me?" he asked.

She leaned closer, reaching for his hand. "The Sanchez I love the most."

For a long time, he didn't say anything, but seemed deep in thought. That didn't bother her. He told her frequently that he loved her, but it was clear something was on his mind. In fact, he frowned a little, glanced at her again, then threaded his fingers through hers.

"And you're the Foster I love the most," he said softly.

Smiling, she turned from him and looked around as the sound of the road under them changed and she realized they were on the Rickenbacker Causeway, the road to the beach. "This isn't the way to either of our apartments," she said.

"I know. I want to take a detour. Kind of like I did when I went to Coconut Key."

She angled her head, splitting her attention between their route and his expression, not able to figure out either one. "What do you mean?"

"Well, you know my life had fallen apart when I moved there."

"So had mine. It's a place to put broken lives back together, I guess."

"And start"—he squeezed her hand—"a new path on the long journey of life."

"Aren't we poetic tonight, Valentino?" Laughing, she dropped her head back, peering under her lashes at the road ahead. "Also, where are you taking me?"

"The best place to make fish puns," he said.

"The ocean?" she guessed.

"Yep. Because I met the gill of my dreams." He brought her knuckles to his lips as she moaned at the joke. "Let's take a walk on the beach, Pey. It's a gorgeous night and I want to share something with you."

"Okay." For a moment, her heart dropped a little, wondering what it might be. The last time they walked on the beach at night it was after a Bachelor Auction in the Keys, and she'd laid her heart on the line and he'd... shared "his truth" about his fiancée's sad passing. A few days later, he moved back to Miami.

She pushed the memory aside as he pulled into a well-lit beach park she recognized, with a few cars in the lot. The moon was nearly full, shining on the surf and the white sand, visible through palm trees that swayed in the night breeze.

"I love this beach," she said. "It reminds me of the Keys."

"That's why I picked it."

For what, she wanted to ask, but instead they climbed out of the low-slung sports car that was so different than the truck he'd driven when he was a fisherman. Now he was a successful CPA with a Brickell Avenue high rise apartment and a sports coupe.

But he was still fish-pun making Val, so she happily slid her hand into his as they crossed the parking lot and found a beach entrance between some trees.

"Think it's safe?" she asked.

"We're not going far." He guided her toward the sand. "But I do want a certain vibe for this."

"This...what?" she asked.

"Just trust me, Pey."

"I do." She followed his lead, slipped off her sandals, and felt cool sand under her bare feet.

They didn't walk far, just close enough to hear the waves and see the white surf sparkle in the moonlight.

Another couple was down there, and they passed a family toasting marshmallows over a bonfire, giving her a sense of security.

He led them a little closer to the water's edge, then turned to take her in his arms.

"How's this for romantic?" he whispered.

"Um...*ro*-mantic...like r-o-e, Val?"

He looked skyward. "Do you only love me for my puns?"

"No," she said, squeezing him tighter. "I love you for your good heart, and your incredible intelligence, and your passion for doing all or nothing. Also..." She ran her hands up his back and squeezed his shoulders. "You're a stud."

"Is that all?"

She laughed. "Is that why you brought me out here? So I could count the ways I love you?"

"Nope. So I could." He eased her back a little and only then did she realize his hands were trembling ever so slightly. "But I wanted to do it on a beach. Do you know why?"

Right then she knew nothing, so she shook her head.

"Because we were on a beach that night that you told me what you wanted."

She swallowed. "The ultimatum that cost me everything."

"Oh, no, Peyton. Don't think of it that way, please. It wasn't an ultimatum at all. It was a wake-up call. You gave me the incentive to heal." He brushed some hair back from her face, lightly grazing her cheek with his knuckles. "And I did. And now I'm ready."

Her heart rate kicked up as she searched his face for a clue to what he was going to say, but she didn't get anything but lost in the depths of eyes the same color as the midnight sky.

"Ready for what?" she asked.

"For you. For us. For the future." He thumbed her lower lip and looked as if he might kiss her, but he didn't. Now she was vibrating a little, too, with anticipation and nerves and, oh God, so much love for this man. "Peyton, on that beach that night, you told me you were 'playing for keeps.' You told me that there was an end-game for you, that you didn't care when it happened, but you weren't...I can't remember the exact words."

"Window shopping?" she supplied.

"Something like that. And I'm not going to lie, it scared me. I knew then that I loved you. Hell, I knew the first time I walked into Jessie's restaurant kitchen and flirted with you."

She gave a low chuckle. "I kinda did, too. I could barely talk. And you were making crab jokes."

They both smiled at the memory, the humor breaking the tension she still didn't quite understand.

"And every time I was with you, even when you had that stupid boyfriend and I had to keep things platonic, I could feel myself falling harder and faster."

She frowned. "Why did you run away? Really?"

"Because I knew I wanted to marry you."

"Oh." Not that he hadn't said as much since she'd moved here, but never quite that...straight out.

"I knew," he continued, "that there was no other way to go with you. All or nothing, as I am. And I wasn't healed yet, I wasn't ready or good enough for you. I can only hope that I am now."

She reached up and touched his face. "I think you are."

"Good." Stepping back, he slowly lowered himself to one knee, making Peyton suck in a soft breath. "Because I am here, on this beach, to finish the conversation we had on that other beach, in the Keys."

Chills exploded over her arms as she pressed her fingers to her lips. "Val..."

"Peyton Danielle Foster." He reached up and took her hand in his. "You made me believe in love again," he said simply. "You saw something in me I thought was gone forever, making me laugh, and love, and hope for a future. I want that future with you, Pey. I love how nurturing you are, and kind. I love how much you care about your family and mine. I love how you tackle every challenge in life with low-key determination, even if you don't see those things in yourself. I do. I love the woman you are today and the one you're going to be decades from now."

She absolutely couldn't breathe, think, or speak.

He let go of her hand and reached into his pocket, producing a small black box.

The box. The moment. The *proposal*. She fought tears and watched as he flipped it open.

"I want to be by your side, as your husband, and the father to our children. Forever and ever."

Every word floated over her like fairy dust, dreamy and sparkly and as bright as the diamond in his hand. All she could do was close her eyes and revel in the moment.

"Say yes!" someone from the bonfire called, adding a hoot, making Peyton let out a nervous laugh.

"Please, Pey," he whispered, sounding nervous, too. And a little scared. "Say yes."

When she looked down at him, she saw the trepidation in his eyes, as if he thought she might not say yes. And, for some reason, that touched her to the soul.

"Yes," she whispered, finally taking her eyes off him to get a good look at the oval-shaped diamond resting on a satin bed. "Oh, my." Her eyes popped. "That's beautiful."

"So are you," he said when he slid it on her finger with shaky hands, slowly standing to kiss her. "I love you, Pey."

"I love you, Val."

He leaned back, looking into her eyes, and tapped her on the nose. "And now, it is o-*fish*-al."

She groaned and laughed, and over the sound of the surf, she could hear the little family cheering, so they turned to walk back, passing them to wave as they yelled, "Congratulations!"

"Thank you!" Peyton and Val called back as he held up her hand in victory.

They stopped to kiss a few times, getting even more heated the closer they got to the car. In it, they made out like a couple of teenagers until the windows fogged.

"Val, I have a question."

He drew back, looking like he might be a little afraid of what she'd ask. Did he think she was going to ask him to move to Coconut Key? Because part of her wanted to, but part of her didn't want to change anything about this moment.

So she took the safe course. "What did Abuelita mean when she asked for *el biznieto*?"

He laughed softly. "It means great-grandson."

"Oh."

"And I think we should give Abuelita whatever she wants." He kissed her one more time before taking her home to his apartment.

CHAPTER SIX

KENNY

"Please, please, please let me skip school and help them move in, Dad."

Kenny shot Ava a look. "I don't know what that means, 'skip school.'"

"Come on! Maddie is here! Do you know how excited I am?"

Yes. He knew exactly, because if Maddie was here... her mother was here. And Kenny's whole body hummed in anticipation of seeing Heather again.

"I'm sure the move's gonna take all day," Kenny said, thinking of the text exchange he'd had with Heather last night. Even that little bit of contact had made it impossible for him to fall asleep. "She has to go to the real estate office and sign papers, which takes forever, then get the keys, then we'll drive the U-Haul to the house."

"We'll drive it? Are you taking her?"

"Yeah, that thing's a beast. I can't believe she drove a truck that big twelve hours from Charleston with two kids, a dog, and everything she owns." He felt his lips lift with a proud smile. "That took a pair, I gotta say."

When Ava didn't answer or amp up her argument whine, he glanced at her, meeting her rather accusatory gaze. He tried to dismiss it with a harsh Dad look, but she just smiled.

"What?" he asked.

"I think you know what."

Oh, man. "I don't know what you're talking about."

She gave a soft snort. "So you're skipping work, but I'm not allowed to skip school?" she asked, with that conspiratorial gleam in her eye. "That doesn't seem fair." Like she might...blackmail him into letting her skip school.

He could just imagine it: *Let me, Dad, or I'll tell Heather you get a moronic grin on your face every time her name comes up.*

He had to nip this in the bud. "If you skip school, then you can't go to rehearsal—Mrs. Packman's rules, not mine."

"I can't skip rehearsal! We're doing the first walk-through of act two staging, and hardly anyone knows their choreography except Joelle, and Mary Poppins better know her dance steps. I'd be behind the whole cast if I missed, and Miss Lark is in so many scenes. You realize my character's whole purpose is to distract the audience while the cast is changing costumes? I can't miss timing of costume changes."

"Exactly," he said as they reached the high school, happy he knew how completely distracted she got by the play. "Then I'll see you tonight after rehearsal."

"Grrr." She curled a lip and hoisted her backpack on

her lap. "Please try not to have too much fun without me."

"Oh, yeah, hauling furniture is so much fun."

"It is when the whole gang is there," she said as he pulled into the lot. "And everyone's going to be there. It's like a party and I'm missing it."

"Ava." He used his best Dad voice when he pulled up to the curb. "I'll pick you up tonight after play rehearsal. Be sure to let Mrs. Packman know I'll finish the stairs tomorrow but, for God's sake, don't let any of the kids climb them until I put the railing on. After that, we finish the chimney, the pedestals for the statues, and the sets are completely done."

She answered with a typical Ava-not-getting-her-way face, but then it melted into a smile. "Okay. Be sure to give Mrs. Monroe a big *kiss*...for me."

He narrowed his eyes. "Out. Go learn. Hush your mouth, little girl."

She giggled like she *was* a little girl, and threw open the door. In a split second, she called to a classmate and disappeared into the sea of denim shorts and T-shirts that barely covered a bellybutton. He watched her walk away, and his heart twisted like always. Truth was, she wasn't a little girl anymore. And when he realized he'd raised her alone for a full third of her life, it kind of took his breath away.

Man, he hoped he was doing a good job. And that Elise was still watching out for both of them.

MANY HOURS LATER, Kenny finished setting up a shelving unit and dresser in the bedroom he assumed would be Maddie's, then headed back into the living room, hearing the sounds of laughter and activity. As Ava had predicted, the Monroe family move-in had become a party.

Jessie waved him toward the kitchen counter where she was uncovering a selection of sandwiches. "Everyone needs to stop and eat," she said. "Starting with you, Kenny Gallagher."

Heather turned from the refrigerator the second she heard the name, her gaze meeting his. "Yes, please eat, Kenny. You haven't stopped since early this morning."

"I will, I promise," he said. "I got the dresser finished in Maddie's room if she wants to unpack."

"Oh, she took little Beau for a walk," Jessie said. "He was getting into everything."

"And she wasn't helping anyway," Heather added. "She's got her face in her phone, reconnecting with all her Coconut Key High friends."

"Any of them named..." He dug into his memory for the kid's name. Something...biblical. "Levi," he said as it came to him.

"Levi Carter?" Heather looked skyward. "Yes, I've heard of the famous Levi Carter." Then a frown formed. "Should I worry about him?"

"I don't know him, although I understand he's—and I'm quoting now—the hottest human alive."

Jessie snorted but Heather's eyes widened. "The hottest human alive?"

"Hey, I thought that was me," Nick cracked as he walked by with a dining room chair over his head.

Behind him, Savannah poked his back, risking having that chair fall.

"That was the sexiest man alive, in *People Magazine*."

Nick turned and stuck out his tongue, proving that fame and fortune did not always mature a man, and making them laugh.

"I really wish everyone would take a break and eat," Jessie said, trying to snag Josh, who was hustling back to the truck.

"Almost unloaded, Jess," he said. "Where's Marc? He was going to tell me where he wants the bed in his room."

"Did you set up the X-Box in the den?" Heather said. "I'd look there."

"He is *not* playing X-Box," Kenny choked, turning toward the den. "We need—"

Heather reached over the peninsula and snagged his arm. "Let him go, Kenny. He's super moody. I don't think he said ten words on the way down."

"Really? I'm so sorry, Heather." He blew out a breath. "I tried, but Coach Packman said absolutely no walk-ons."

"I know you tried," she said, her blue eyes holding his gaze and making it impossible for him to look away. "He'll be fine. There's always next season."

But so much could happen in a year. "Next season he might lose interest, but I'll play ball with him this summer, I promise."

She smiled and, of course, his heart rate kicked up like he'd been the one carrying the chair over his head.

"I just want everyone to take a ten-minute food break," Jessie said. "Everything is easier when you're not hungry."

Heather cleared her throat. "How about we stop and eat?" she called out, but her voice just wasn't loud enough to be heard by the eight or nine people scattered about hauling boxes and furniture.

She sighed when no one responded.

"I got this," he said, with a quick wink. He put two fingers in his mouth and let out a high-pitched whistle and everything stopped. "Chow time!" he yelled. Then he slid a look to Heather. "We learn that in first responder's training."

Her cheeks flushed a little as she blinded him with a smile. "Good technique to have."

"With this crew it is," he agreed.

Within seconds, the "movers" let go of what they were doing and congregated around the food and drinks that Jessie happily doled out, and everyone talked, laughed, and ate. Except there was no sign of the kids.

After waiting for a few minutes, Kenny slipped around the corner to the den, and sure enough, he found Marc. Not playing X-Box, but he was looking at his phone, a miserable expression on his face.

"Food's out," Kenny said.

"I heard." Marc spared him a look. "So did the whole neighborhood."

It wasn't like Marc to be too sullen, especially when they were alone together. The two of them had played hours of catch, and Kenny had taken him to the batting cages on a number of occasions, so he wasn't used to getting a surly teenaged mouth from the kid.

"You don't want to eat?"

He shook his head and thumbed the phone.

"That's a first," Kenny noted, trying to make light and

joke about Marc's voracious appetite. But when he didn't smile, Kenny added, "You need protein to play, bud."

That got him a dark look. "I *wanted* to play, Kenny," he said. "You got me so psyched over spring break and when I went for late tryouts and made the JV team at my school —my *old* school—I was stoked. I knew I could get the outfield, too."

"With your arm and precision? And your eye for a fly ball? Absolutely."

"Not if I'm living here," he scoffed. "I might as well be in East Bum—"

"Don't." Kenny marched closer, knowing he was looming over the kid, but not caring. "Your mother hates that word."

"She hates everything except…" Marc looked up, and for one heart-stopping second, Kenny thought he was going to say *you*. "Coconut Key."

"It's not such a bad place, you know," Kenny said. "This house is great. You can fish right off that canal, and I bet you guys can get a small boat or borrow one of Beck's and…" His voice trailed off as he saw the raw misery in Marc's eyes. And the distant threat of tears.

Instead of finishing, he sat down next to him. "It won't be so bad, man, I promise."

"It's not bad," he said. "I liked it here. But I wanted to play baseball so much. You have no idea how hard it was for me to go to those tryouts without my…"

Father. He didn't have to finish for Kenny to know who he really missed.

"But you did it," Kenny said. "And I'm damn proud of you, kid."

He shook his head, closing his eyes, definitely fighting

tears. "'sokay," he said, trying to be as tough as a fourteen-year-old could be. "It's fine."

"It's not fine," Kenny ground out. "What the heck is wrong with that school that they won't take a JV transfer student on the team? It's not that big a school."

"I heard the coach is cool, but the assistant coach, that Mazz...whatever guy? He's trying to get a coaching job and thinks the only way to do it is to win, so he's a grade A...you know."

"Well, the coach barely talked to me, but he said Coach Mazzeraldi would be the one to ask. But he wouldn't even take my call," Kenny groused. "But I'm not quite ready to quit, Marc. There has got to be a way."

"Doesn't sound like it."

He slid a look to Marc. "God *always* provides a way."

"Yeah, like some guy up in the clouds cares about whether or not I play baseball."

"Actually, He does."

"Yeah, well, I'll believe that when I walk on the team."

"Hey, you two." Heather stepped into the den, her eyes suspiciously bright. "You talk much longer and the sandwiches will be gone."

Kenny stood and lightly yanked at Marc's T-shirt sleeve. "Up and at 'em, kiddo. Eat and help me finish that truck."

He stood and slipped the phone in his pocket. "Yeah, I could eat." Marc walked out, passing Heather who leaned against the door jamb, her arms crossed. She didn't say a word, but wore an expression Kenny couldn't read.

"Something wrong?" he asked. "Should I not have told him God provides a way? Then when it doesn't happen, he's lost?"

She gave a tight smile. "I love that you told him that, but...listen. Maddie's gone to get Ava at school—"

"Half an hour after rehearsal started?"

"Well, something happened."

He could feel his whole body ready to run, imagining her falling off those steep stairs he'd built. It killed the EMT in him not to finish the railing, but they'd run out of time. "Why didn't she call me?"

"She did." She held out his phone to him. "Your cell was on the kitchen counter. But she's fine, absolutely fine, don't worry. But I'm afraid you have to go from one disappointed kid to the next, Kenny."

"What happened?" Kenny asked, taking the phone.

"They're canceling the play. Come on and get food, Kenny. We'll tell you what we know."

"Canceling it?" While they walked back into the kitchen, he skimmed the stream of texts from Ava that she probably thumbed out in lightning speed, each one a mix of devastation, worry, and heartbreak.

Everyone was talking, many of the group looking at their own phone as the news traveled.

"Ava said the director's daughter was in a terrible car accident in Seattle," Beck told him. "She's been airlifted to the hospital, but the director is leaving today and staying indefinitely."

"That's awful," he said, closing his eyes and sending up a prayer.

"Poor Ava," Savannah groaned. "She was so excited about this play. She must have had Nick run her lines with her twenty times."

Next to her on the sofa, Nick was holding Dylan's hands and trying to get the baby to stand up on wobbly legs. "They don't have another teacher to take over that job?" he asked.

"It's a big commitment," Kenny said. "Singing, dancing, music, major sets...that I built." He groaned. "Maybe they can use them next year."

Savannah leaned over and whispered something in Nick's ear, pulling his attention.

"Ava is wrecked," Heather told him, putting a hand on his arm. "Maddie said she wanted to go get her 'cause you were busy, so she took Jessie's car. Is that okay?"

"Yeah, yeah, it's fine, but..." Something was humming in his head, something working on his heart, and for once, it wasn't his reaction to Heather's light touch. It was...something else.

God always provides a way.

And then it clicked into place. "The director is Marybeth Packman."

Marc looked up from his sandwich. "That's the coach's name."

Kenny nodded. "They're married. And my guess is he's going to Seattle, too."

"So no baseball coach, either?" Beck asked.

"The assistant will probably step in," he said to Marc. "Which means they'll need a *new* assistant." He couldn't resist a smug smile. "And I bet the new assistant coach'll take a walk-on transfer student," Kenny added.

"Holy..." Marc managed to stop before he slipped. "Can you do that?"

"Can you?" Heather asked, her whole face brightening. "And would you?"

"Of course I would." He put a hand on Marc's shoulder. "I always wanted to coach a high school ball team. I'll start with JV if you will."

Marc's expression mirrored his mother's, the same blue eyes growing wide with happy disbelief. "Are you serious?"

"Oh, heck yeah."

A small cheer went up in the group, but Beck put her hands on her cheeks as if she didn't want to be too happy with this turn of events. "But meanwhile, Ava—"

"Doesn't have to worry." Nick handed the baby to Savannah and stood slowly, looking at Kenny. "My brilliant wife had the same idea Kenny did."

"To coach the JV baseball team?" Jessie asked.

"To volunteer our skills." He added a grin that the camera—and most women under seventy—loved. "I know a little bit about acting and directing."

This time, the cheer that went up was even louder, especially from Marc.

"That would be sick!" he exclaimed.

"And amazing," Beck added.

"Same thing," Savannah informed her. "And Ava will be so happy!"

"Do you think they'll let you?" Heather asked. "I mean this play is kind of a big deal."

"Are you kidding?" Josh choked. "He's Nick Frye!"

"They'll sell out of every ticket," Lovely, who'd been unusually quiet all day, finally chimed in. "They might have to add a show."

And Ava would be so happy, Kenny thought, not to mention the savior of the play for having a famous uncle.

"That's awesome, man." He walked over to shake

Nick's hand. "This probably isn't how you want to spend your early retirement from acting."

Nick gave an easy laugh. "I don't hate the idea," he admitted. "I've been looking for something to throw myself into, and this could be fun. And you sure you have time for coaching? Ava's always telling Savannah how busy you are."

"I'll make time," he said, turning to Marc, who looked excited about life again. "And I think it'll be a blast."

They heard a car door outside and Beck peeked out the window. "The girls are here. You want to tell her, Nick?"

"I'd love to."

Just then, the front door opened and Maddie came in first, making a face like she'd gotten an earful. Ava was well behind her, walking slowly, the weight of the world on her narrow shoulders. Oh, how Kenny wanted to save her from every disappointment, but also let her know that life is full of them.

But in this case, he just got to watch the pain disappear.

As she walked in, they were all very quiet, the anticipation thick.

She stopped, looked around, and her gaze landed on Kenny. "You heard the news?"

"Yep."

"I'm so upset," she said, her voice reed thin. "This was the most fun thing I've ever done and now it's—"

Nick stepped forward, closer to her. "Now it's supercalifragilisticexpe...what's the rest?"

She narrowed her eyes. "Not funny, dude."

"No, I really need to know. What's the rest of that word?"

She blew out a sigh. "You're not going to make me laugh right now, if that's what you're thinking." She inched around him to look at Savannah. "Can't you rein him in?"

"Alidocious?" Nick finished. "I gotta learn that song."

Ava blinked at him. "Why?"

"Because I'm going to step in and direct the play," he said. "If that's okay with you, of course."

Her jaw dropped as she processed this, her mouth opening to a little 'o' that got wider with each second. "You're...you are...you? Nick Frye? Directing *Mary Poppins*?"

He shrugged. "Good idea, or the worst you ever heard?"

"Oh my God!" She launched at him, throwing her arms around him with a high-pitched squeal. "That's... are you serious? You would do that? You would direct a high school play?"

He laughed and patted her back, easing her away. "I'd love to."

She screamed again, turning to Maddie, who looked just as excited. They hugged and jumped up and down and everyone talked at once while Kenny just stared at his daughter, drinking in her joy.

Suddenly, two slender but strong arms reached around him from behind and gave him a light squeeze.

"Your sacrifice is lost in the excitement," Heather whispered.

His whole body tensed at the feel of her, the gentleness of her voice, the light garden-like scent that clung to her. For a split second, he simply froze and took it all in.

"Not a sacrifice at all," he assured her, turning his head toward her, but not his body. He didn't want to move, didn't want this unexpected hug to end. "I love the idea of coaching." He finally turned, his heart thudding when she didn't drop her arms. "I'm pretty excited about the idea."

She smiled up at him, that light in her blue eyes seeming even more intense. "Thank you," she said softly. "You can't imagine how this makes me feel."

Neither could she.

"Just hope they'll let me do it," he said, knowing he should step out of her light embrace, but everyone was so busy celebrating Nick and the play that surely no one noticed them standing there, inches apart, staring at each other like this.

After one more glorious second, he stepped back and she dropped her arms, but they didn't let go of each other's gaze.

"We'll go to the high school together, Kenny," Nick said. "They can't say no to us."

"Not a chance," he agreed, shifting his attention to the other man. But just past him, he could see the look on Ava's face and knew she hadn't missed one minute of his exchange with Heather.

Oh, well. That hug was worth it.

CHAPTER SEVEN

LOVELY

She'd been through worse, right? So much worse.

Lovely Ames had once hovered over her natural body, nothing but a spirit or soul or something, dead as a person could be. How much worse could it get?

And, as she'd told anyone who'd listen in the almost year and a half since that Christmas Eve accident, nothing about death had been scary or painful.

In fact, nothing about death was nearly as hard as many parts of life could be.

Giving up a child to let her sister take the honor of being that child's mother was hard. Watching her sister drive away when Beck was ten years old and crying in the back seat because she didn't want to leave her "Aunt" Lovey—and not seeing her for another forty-five years—that was extremely hard. There had been storms and losses and disappointments and plenty of rough years in the seventy-four that Lovely had lived.

So, in the scheme of things, sitting in her doctor's

office, mindlessly skimming through a *Good Housekeeping* magazine, silently patting herself on the back for figuring out how to get an Uber—since she hadn't driven a car since the accident—wasn't that hard.

She took a deep breath and slowly exhaled.

But if she had cancer? *That* would be hard.

Dying wouldn't be bad, she knew from first-hand experience. But having the dreaded disease and putting her beloved family through it? So very hard that—

"Ms. Ames?" A pretty nurse came out to the waiting room holding a clipboard.

Lovely stood slowly, not that age made her move that way. Fear did.

"Hi, I'm Kaitlyn, Dr. Chang's nurse. Can you come with me?"

As Lovely walked closer, she nodded, vaguely aware of how hard her heart was beating.

"Are you alone today, Ms. Ames?"

"Yes, today I am."

But the last time she'd come to this office, for her annual appointment, Beck had been with her. She'd asked all the questions Lovely forgot, gotten the information and changes in medications, and managed all the healthcare business that wonderful daughters did for older mothers. They'd gone to lunch afterwards, celebrating Lovely's good health, and spent the day planning for the opening of the B&B.

"My daughter was...busy," she explained, trying not to flinch at the lie. Beck would have dropped everything and carried Lovely here if she'd known about this appointment. But Lovely had kept it a secret.

"Oh, don't worry about the scale," the nurse said,

misinterpreting Lovely's expression when they stopped for the standard weigh-in.

"I don't," Lovely assured her. "Life's too short to get caught up in a number." But not *too* short...right?

"Absolutely," Kaitlyn said enthusiastically. "And you're very fit. But if you like, close your eyes and I'll write down the number."

"I don't care," Lovely assured her, stepping on the scale.

A few minutes later, her blood pressure taken—no surprise it was up a bit—and her clothes off in exchange for a paper robe, Lovely sat in a now-familiar doctor's office, staring at a chart about osteoporosis on the wall.

Her heart still thumped hard enough to feel it against her ribs and her palms were clammy against the cool leather of the examination bed.

Taking a deep breath, she tried to think positively, but there was nothing positive about the lump she'd noticed a few days ago in her breast.

"Lovely Ames." The door popped open and Dr. Amy Chang greeted her with a huge smile, sliding her clipboard to the side to offer a hug. "How are you feeling?"

"Better just looking at you," Lovely admitted.

Dr. Chang had been a huge part of Lovely's recovery after the accident. Yes, there'd been dozens of specialists from every walk of medicine throughout the ordeal. But this fifty-something steady rock of common sense and natural warmth had been there throughout the entire ordeal. Lovely trusted her completely.

"I understand that B&B you and your daughter opened is beautiful," she said lightly, always starting a medical conversation with something personal to put Lovely at ease. Except today, it didn't work.

"It is," she replied. "How did you hear that?"

"One of three general internists in Coconut Key?" She laughed as she walked to the sink to wash her hands. "I hear everything. And just looking at you, I'm guessing that going into business has been good for you."

"It has," she agreed. "But..."

"You've found a lump." Pitching a paper towel in the trash, she tapped the clipboard on the counter. "I read the nurse's write-up. First of all, don't panic. It could—and most likely is—nothing to worry about."

"At my age?"

"At any age," she said reassuringly. "It could be a cyst, it could be a benign mass, it could be a little harmless ball of fat."

"Or it could be cancer."

She narrowed dark eyes at Lovely. "You are not a defeatist, Lovely. I knew that from the minute I went to see you in the hospital and your Time of Death certificate was in the file, and you were quite literally awake and breathing."

"But it could be cancer. I know that. I Googled."

She rolled her eyes with a smile and put a gentle hand on Lovely's shoulder to ease her onto her back. "Then you've attended the worst medical school in the world. Let's have a feel, shall we?"

Lovely nodded and looked straight up at the ceiling where someone had replaced one of the panels with a picture of the beach that looked very much like the one she'd been looking at her whole life.

Comforted by that, she stared at the two-dimensional horizon while Dr. Chang gently examined her breasts.

"That's it," Lovely whispered when she touched the spot on her left breast.

"Does that hurt?"

"No, it doesn't. Except I know it's there."

"And you imagine it's burning."

Lovely's eyes widened. "Yes, exactly."

Frowning, the doctor softly pressed, then closed her eyes and concentrated on the size and shape. "This doesn't alarm me, frankly."

"So it's nothing?"

"I'm not saying that, but it's not misshapen or sharp-edged. But it wasn't on your last mammogram four months ago, either. I'm going to schedule you for another."

Lovely's eyes widened. "So it's not...nothing."

"It's not anything yet," she said. "It's very small, which is always good, but let's get a peek at it and make a decision whether we want to biopsy it or not."

"Should I do anything in the meantime?"

She shrugged. "If it's a cyst, you could try warm compresses, no caffeine, and a supportive bra. But we can get you in for a mammo fairly quickly. Early next week or so."

"I can manage that, I suppose."

"Not alone, I hope." Dr. Chang closed the paper robe and patted Lovely's shoulder. "Talk to your daughter. I'll never forget your wonderful story about reconnecting with her after your accident."

"I want to, but..."

"You don't want to worry her," the doctor finished. "I

understand, but, Lovely, this isn't something you want to go through alone."

"Everything's so good in her life," she said. "The business is a challenge, but we're having fun. And there's a new man..."

"You think dropping a lump-in-the-breast bomb will ruin everything." It wasn't a question.

"I love her so much." She gnawed on her lower lip, a little surprised that tears sprung to her eyes. "And I don't want to have secrets from her, but this is such a burden."

"One that you shouldn't bear alone," Dr. Chang said, the slightest edge of caution in her voice. "Please let her support you and help you. If you're willing to drive a bit to Marathon or Key Largo, I can get you in a little bit sooner."

But driving meant bringing Beck—or *someone*—in on this. She didn't want to burden anyone with her secret. "Can't I get it at the place where I got the last one? It was close." She could get another Uber, now that she knew how.

"Yes, it'll take a little longer. But I'll authorize that."

"Okay, yes. I'll do the closer location," she said quickly. She didn't see any reason to tell anyone yet.

Dr. Chang nodded as she made some notes. "You change back into your clothes; Kaitlyn will be in shortly and the front desk can set it up." Looking up, she smiled. "It's too soon to worry. Most lumps—the vast majority—are nothing but cysts."

"I know." Her voice cracked and the doctor instantly reached for her hand.

"But don't do this alone, Lovely. Promise me."

She gave a tight smile and nodded, not wanting to make a verbal promise she might break.

When the doctor left, she sat at the edge of the exam table for a long time, her gaze on her bare knees poking out from the robe. There were still scars visible from the accident, and memories of the months her legs didn't work...until she walked into Beck's arms.

She closed her eyes and let out a little whimper. On Sunday, Oliver Bradshaw would arrive. Lovely couldn't throw a damp blanket of worry and fear over what was about to be Beck's next great season in her life. Lovely joked about lovedar, but she knew those two were... special. Call it intuition, sixth sense, life experience, or lovedar. She *knew*.

If Beck spent the first few weeks of Oliver's time here fussing over Lovely and worrying about her health and diving into researching cancer and...

No. She shook her head vehemently as she placed her bare feet on the floor.

There was no way she'd ruin this glorious time in her daughter's life. If she had to, if the news was bad, if she needed the support, of course she'd go to Beck. But not now. It was too soon and the doctor said not to worry. So, for now, she wouldn't. And neither would Beck.

CHAPTER EIGHT

BECK

Having the Sunday party at Coquina House instead of The Haven had been a good idea, and one that Beck had to thank Lovely for suggesting. Yes, Savannah and Nick's Gulf-front home was more spacious, but Beck and Lovely wanted to be here, at the B&B, when Oliver arrived, to greet him like any other guest—with a mimosa. The kids could still play on the beach, and the adults could gather on the veranda, so the weekly event wasn't too different.

The friends and family were the same, which was all that mattered. Ava was in heaven now that Maddie was here, and they'd set up a volleyball court on Beck's beach, just like they always had at The Haven. Heather and Kenny had gone to church and would be here soon, but Jessie and her family were here, and Lovely, of course. Even Josh had come, which made Beck feel so good, since she didn't want any awkwardness between them.

If Peyton were here, as she had been for more than a year, it would be perfect. They could celebrate the engagement—news that still had Beck smiling every time she thought about it. But Val had just been assigned to a huge business development deal and had to work yesterday, and it seemed like a long drive for them to make for one day.

Even though Peyton had said they'd make that drive as often as they could...would they?

Beck tamped down the thought. She couldn't have everything in life, and right now, she already had an embarrassment of riches. And she really needed to concentrate on building the B&B, not worrying about how often Peyton visited.

At the moment, they only had one room booked—a fact that Beck was trying not to dwell on—and that couple had rented a boat for the day and wouldn't be back until this evening.

She looked up when the veranda door opened and Jessie came in, letting out an audible sigh.

"You okay?" Beck asked, looking up from the artichoke dip she was scooping into a bowl.

"I am now." Jessie made a face and took a peek into the living room. "Are we alone?"

"Everyone's down at the beach, I think. Except for Savannah and Nick and Dylan, who are at the airport waiting for Oliver."

Jessie's dark eyes twinkled. "Are you excited to see him?"

"Yes, for the fourteenth time, I am." She slid a cracker through the dip and held it out for Jessie. "I know you made this, but taste it anyway and tell me what's wrong."

"With my dip? It might need more pepper."

Beck laughed. "Nothing is wrong with your dip. With

you. You're tense, and you look like you were coming in here to...hide."

Jessie didn't answer but took the cracker and ate it, closing her eyes as she tasted. "I'm right, it needs more pepper. Maybe I'll just stay in here and whip up a new batch."

"And I'm right—you're hiding." Beck eyed her. "From Chuck?"

"God, no." She snagged the pepper grinder and twisted just a little too aggressively. "Beck, can I ask you a question?"

"Anything, hon."

She stirred the dip and grabbed another cracker to taste and nodded with her eyes closed again. "Better."

"Jess."

She looked at Beck. "I don't know how to be a mother, that's what's wrong."

Beck opened her mouth to dismiss the silly statement, but shut it quickly. Nothing was silly if it was how she truly felt. "Why do you feel that way?"

"Every time I think I've connected with Beau and we kind of have a moment and I do the right thing, wham—he either ignores me, or disobeys me, or clings to Chuck like he's a lifeline and I'm an ogre."

"Honestly, I think you just described parenting a toddler. They are...capricious. You never know what to expect from one minute to the next, and no matter what you do, it could be wrong."

"I doubt that was the case with your firstborn," Jessie said, leaning against the counter.

"Peyton? She was easy as pie, that's true. But Savannah?" she snorted. "I still have bald spots, she made me tear my hair out so frequently."

Jessie snorted and nibbled on a cracker, listening.

"And Callie—"

"Was perfect."

"Not in every way," Beck said, thinking back on her "surprise" baby and how different raising her was from the first two. "For one thing, I thought I was done. Peyton was twelve, and Savannah was ten, and I was getting all geared up for the teenage years when, wham. Infant. So maybe I was a teeny bit resentful. Or maybe I was just put off by the fact that she always seemed to prefer Dan to me."

"Not anymore," Jessie noted.

"True, we're much closer now. But I couldn't...what was the word you used? Connect. He did, I didn't. Please don't worry about Beau. He's not even five. By the time his personality and your relationship are set in stone, he'll have gone through about six hundred different stages." Beck smiled. "That's kind of the fun of being a parent."

She blew out a breath, shaking her head. "I don't know what's wrong with me, Beck. But it's...not fun. It's an incredible amount of work."

"Most of it thankless," Beck added.

"Yes! And Chuck and I are never alone, which is important because we're like newlyweds now. And on top of all that, I feel absolutely awful confessing this because I spent at least ten years of my life wanting one thing, and one thing only: a child. Now I have one and I feel..."

Beck waited, knowing that it was better for her friend to figure it out rather than try to make suggestions.

"Let down," she finally said. "Like...disappointed. And, oh my goodness, that makes me the worst human alive."

"It makes you human, period," Beck said. "You don't just suddenly get handed a four-year-old at fifty-five and get all maternal inside."

"Seriously. Those hormones have left the building."

Beck rolled her eyes. "Tell the woman who just had her third hot flash. But you have to grow into motherhood with Beau. And you will. I know you will."

Jessie looked doubtful, but didn't say a word.

"Have you talked to Chuck about it?"

"Not really. I want him to think I'm the Mother of the Year. And I want to be worthy of that."

"You are worthy of that!" Beck insisted, reaching out to her. "And Beau's a high-energy, brilliant, challenging kid. Don't be so hard on yourself, Jessie. Give yourself some time. You've been 'married' for a few months and you only met Beau less than six months ago. Relax, okay?"

She smiled and closed the space between them with a hug. "I love you, Beckerella."

"I love you, too, Messy Jessie."

She felt Jessie chuckle at the childhood nicknames, but then Jessie drew back and looked concerned. "Are you quaking? You're literally trembling. New menopause symptom I haven't experienced yet?"

She laughed. "No. I'm just...you know."

"Excited about Oliver?" Jessie made a silly face and tapped her fisted hands under her chin, suddenly looking very much like that little girl from their younger days. "What do you think is going to happen?"

"I don't know. I'm going to take my own advice and give it time and relax," Beck said. "You know, I may have imagined this whole thing. He may just think of me as a co-grandparent, mother of his son's wife, and the nice lady who owns the B&B where he's staying."

"*Right*," Jessie groaned. "Or he might want to jump your bones."

"Jessie!" Beck playfully jabbed her elbow into Jessie's arm. "I don't even remember *how* bones are jumped."

"Trust me, you'll figure it out."

"Like riding a bike?" Beck asked on a laugh.

"Oh, honey, it's *nothing* like riding a bike." Jessie grabbed one more cracker, but froze and cocked her head. "I just heard a car door."

Beck's eyes widened. "Oh, I better get Lovely and pour that welcome mimosa."

Jessie frowned. "Lovely went home."

"What? She did? Why?"

"I thought she told you. She had a headache, and she took the dogs home to nap with her."

A little ping of disappointment hit her chest. "She's not here to greet our

guest? Why wouldn't she even say goodbye to me?"

"She seemed a little distracted, and didn't want to make a big deal, but I thought she told you."

Beck shook her head. "Is she okay? How bad a headache? She doesn't get those frequently."

"It's hot out there," Jessie said. "I'm sure she'll be back after a rest."

"Hello?" Savannah called from the living room and Beck grunted.

"And I don't have the mimosa ready."

Jessie gave her a nudge. "He ain't here for the mimosas, Beckerella."

"Can you *please* be cool?"

"Like a cucumber. And you better tell me every detail after you ride that, um, bike."

"And don't make me blush, Jessica! You know it brings on a hot flash."

"So will the bike."

Beck was still laughing when she went around the corner to greet her guest, and as soon as she did, just about everything else was forgotten.

THE ONLY DOWNSIDE of an otherwise dreamy afternoon with family and friends was that Lovely had missed it. Beck had exchanged quite a few texts with her mother throughout the day, and understood her desire to rest rather than socialize. Even though it was completely out of character.

Was she avoiding Oliver for some reason? That made no sense at all. Lovely had been as giddy as Jessie at the prospect that there might be something romantic between Beck and Oliver, and it wasn't like her at all to stay away when he got here.

As sunset neared and people were gathering up to head home, Beck slipped into the kitchen—which darling Ava and Maddie had cleaned to a shine for her—to make a plate for Lovely. She said she wasn't hungry, but Beck knew what her mother loved, so she added a generous amount of the steak that Kenny had grilled and a mountain of Heather's potato salad, and two—no, make it three—of the oatmeal raisin cookies that Peyton had taught Savannah to make.

"Still hungry?"

Beck turned at the now-familiar accent, smiling as Oliver came in from the living room. "Not a bit, but I'm going to take this to my mother. All settled in up there?"

"I'm unpacked and ready to experience summer in the Keys." He walked closer, and Beck noticed for the billionth time that day how gracefully he moved, carrying himself with such elegance and confidence.

"Brace for heat and humidity," she warned.

"And stunning ocean breezes." He gestured toward the closed French doors. "Don't you open these?"

"Usually only mornings and evenings in the summer, but, please feel free." She covered the plate with plastic and stole a glance at him as he spread the doors wide. He was tall, like Nick, and no stranger to the gym, with a dark gold version of his son's golden hair, plus a few silver strands. His face showed his sixty-some years, just a little weathered from sun and laughter, so the best kind of lines.

"Has everyone gone?" he asked, looking out at the veranda. "I know Savannah and Nick took Dylan back. And I said goodbye to Josh."

"My guess is the kids are taking one last swim or playing volleyball, along with Heather and Kenny. And I'm headed on a two-minute walk down Coquina Court to Lovely's house."

"May I join you?"

Her smile widened. "I'd love that, if she feels well enough for company."

"I heard she was a bit under the weather, so I can stay outside while you visit."

She nodded, grateful for his thoughtfulness. "We'll see how she's doing." She lifted the plate but barely had it off the counter before he gently took it from her, their fingers brushing lightly as he did.

"I've got that."

"Thank you. We can take the street or the beach route. Which do you prefer?"

"Let's head down on the street and back on the beach. How does that sound?"

"When you say it, it always sounds delightful." At his flicker of surprise, she added, "The accent. It's absolutely melodic."

"Oh, that. Well, I don't hear it, but I suppose after a bit of time here, I'll *speak like a Yank.*" He flattened the last few words and removed every trace of his lovely accent.

"Please don't ever do that again," she joked.

Laughing, he held the plate with one hand and stepped over to close the French doors he'd opened, once again touching her with how considerate he was.

"Don't tell me," he said. "It's like Samson and his hair. The accent's gone and so's my appeal."

"I think he lost his strength, but might have still been appealing."

"I'm not going to risk it," he said. "I'll just slather on some Aussie every time I feel like I've lost your attention." He winked. "Mate."

She laughed lightly, the flirtatious banter making her whole body tingle. Or maybe that was just another hot flash. Either way, she was feeling warm as they walked down the front stairs of Coquina House and stepped onto the crunchy broken shells that the street was named after.

For a few seconds, neither of them spoke, and Beck suddenly tried to dig for some small talk. They never had a moment of silence on their video calls, but now, inches apart, face-to-face, under the last rays of warm sun...she had nothing.

He glanced at her, humor in his eyes. "You're feeling awkward," he said softly.

"So much for small talk, huh? Just go right to the heart of the matter."

"We've done plenty of small talk," he said. "However, with you, even separated by a screen, it's not very small. But now I'm here and you're wondering what it all means, I imagine."

"I don't think it means anything other than...you're on vacation, visiting family, enjoying the Keys."

He chuckled. "Yeah, yeah, yeah. I am delighted to spend time with Nick, I won't lie. But please don't for one moment think that's the only reason I'm here."

"I know," she said, feeling a little uncharacteristically coy. "You said you were looking forward to seeing me, and I...like that."

"What about me? Do you like me?"

She slowed her step and blinked at him. "I do, but... you know we're not quite that direct in this country."

"Ahh." He nodded, adjusting his hands around the plate of food he held. "You want a bit of a courting dance."

"I don't want...anything."

He slid her a look. "I do," he said simply.

"Okay," she swallowed. "Why don't you tell me what it

is?" Because if he was going straight to that bike ride Jessie was talking about, Beck would have to plead...not ready yet. Not by a long shot.

He stopped walking just as they reached the bright pink hibiscus trees that marked Lovely's property.

"I *will* tell you," he said. "Because if there's one thing life has taught me, it's that it's far too short for small talk, awkward moments, or wasted words. Expect blunt honesty. Is that all right?"

She nodded, looking up at him. "I think that'll work."

He smiled and angled his head. "Okay, then. Beck, I like the way you make me feel," he said softly. "Haven't had this feeling in a long time."

"Me neither," she admitted.

"So what I want is to get to know you. Not on a superficial level, but to know your heart. To know what matters to you and how you handle a crisis and what music you like and what puts that light in your eyes."

The declaration danced all over her like a shower of sweetness. "That's...nice."

"It could be," he said. "I will say there's something about you that..." His voice trailed off and he shook his head. "I'm simply drawn to you."

The uncomplicated confession nearly melted her heart. "I...feel the same." She laughed. "Not quite as poetic, but..." She felt her cheeks warm. "Real."

"Real is good," he said, leaning down an inch. "Just tell me what you're thinking, keep it honest, and I'll do the same."

"Okay. I'm thinking...that...I'm having a little trouble breathing right now."

He laughed softly. "Maybe I can help." He closed the

space between them and placed the softest, lightest, sweetest kiss on her lips, lasting a fraction of a second. "Did that help?"

"It might have made things worse. Now I can't breathe *and* I'm dizzy."

"I'll catch you if you fall, no worries."

She managed a laugh and gently guided him toward Lovely's house. But would he catch her if she fell too hard, too fast, and...he disappeared to the other side of the world?

One thing at a time, Beck. One thing at a time.

"Come on," she said. "Let's go see my mother."

CHAPTER NINE

KENNY

Ava looked at Kenny from the passenger seat of his truck, her green gaze narrowed over the giant to-go cup of coffee she'd poured before they left the house. "I got a bad feeling about this."

"Why? We're going in as a group, with the Monroes and Nick." Kenny looked around the parking lot for the white Porsche Cayenne, the closest thing to a "dad" car Nick Frye could bring himself to buy. But there was no sign of him. "Plus Mike Elliott knows me."

"It's not Mr. Elliott I'm worried about. He's a great principal and a cool dude. But they don't call Agnes Torrent 'Agony and Torment' for nothing."

"His admin?" He nodded, remembering the time he had to bring Ava a book she'd forgotten, and Mrs. Torrent had given him an earful. "The one who launched into a ten-minute lecture on how kids should pay consequences for their dumb choices?"

"The very same. God forbid a parent bring someone a lunch they forgot. Agony and Torment would rather that kid fall over dead from malnutrition and learn a lesson."

"We're coming to help the school out of a jam," he said, parking in the back—away from the crush of kids getting out of cars—and scanning the lot for Heather's SUV.

"Maddie said they'll be here in two minutes," Ava told him, tapping her phone. "She's so psyched about re-enrolling and finishing the year here. I can't say I'd be happy about transferring twice in a year, but she's fearless."

"I'm just glad the schools are so flexible like that," he said, looking at his own phone and thumbing through some morning messages from the two crews he had working on renovations.

"And Savannah just texted me," Ava said. "Nick's running really late. Teething emergency."

He shot her a look. "A what?"

"I dunno." She shrugged and held the phone up, reading. "'Dylan the Devil decided all twenty-six teeth should break through his gums at four in the morning. Nick will be there in half an hour or so.'"

Kenny groaned. "I was kind of counting on his star power to help us seal the deal. I know they'll want him to direct the play, but we have to convince them this is a package deal so I can coach Marc's JV team."

"It's really nice of you to do that, Dad."

"I like coaching."

"That's not the only thing you like," she muttered, looking at her phone. Then her head shot up. "Speaking of, Heather's pulling in now."

"Ava." He ground out the word in warning.

"Oh, come on, Dad." She gave him a playful punch. "You two are perfect for each other. Maddie thinks so, too."

"Maddie?" He choked the name. "Why would you even mention something like that to her?"

"Um, because we'll be sisters." She grinned at him. "So, we might be schemin'."

"Sisters?" That word he could barely get out. "*Schemin'*?"

"We think a Christmas wedding would be cool. Or at least an engagement."

And now he just stared at her because saying anything was impossible.

"What? Two Christians like you are probably going to want to wait to—"

"Too far!" he barked, making her startle at the rare use of the full power of his voice. "Stop it, Ava," he added, softening the tone. "I get that you and Maddie think this is some kind of fun game or crush...thing...like Levi Carter."

She made a face, trying not to laugh at that.

"I'm serious," he said and leaned a little closer to really lower his voice and make his point. "Heather Monroe is a grieving widow and a single mother, trying to put her broken life back together. And if you two start giggling and making suggestions and...and...*schemin'*, whatever that is, you're just going to make both of us really uncomfortable."

She swallowed and nodded, making him feel bad for the mini-lecture when she obviously only wanted him to be happy.

"So just cut it out, okay? I can help her but that

doesn't mean I want to go out with her. Or that she would want to, in any universe, under any conditions."

He was completely aware of the SUV that pulled in right next to them, but didn't take his eyes off Ava just to underscore how much he meant this. Behind him, he heard a car door slam and Maddie call out.

With one more exhale, he reached for his seat belt.

"Except that she does," Ava whispered.

"Excuse me?"

"Want to go out with you."

"What?"

"In this universe, too," she added, flipping her belt off. "But I promise, Dad. I'll respect your wishes. No *schemin'*." She flung the passenger door opened and greeted Maddie as she always did, with a hug like they'd been apart for a decade.

She did? He gripped the steering wheel with both hands, staring straight ahead, almost afraid to look to his left and see her. She *wanted* to go out with him? Was Ava sure? What had Heather said? Had she told Maddie? When was *he* going to find out? Could he—

"Hey, Coach." Knuckles rapped on his window. "You okay up there?"

He turned and looked down, his truck far enough off the ground to make Heather look petite. Her silky blond hair was pulled back into a ponytail, which just showed off her beautiful bone structure, and her big blue eyes were bright and happy even without any makeup.

She lifted a to-go coffee cup from Coquina Café in a mock toast. "Don't be scared of Agony and Torment," she teased from the other side of the window. "She likes me."

Yeah? Who doesn't?

He smiled at her and unlatched the door, opening it slowly when she stepped back. "I wasn't worried until I heard the nickname." He pocketed his keys and gave in to the urge to just smile at her. "But maybe you'll butter her up, since you're seeing her first."

"That's the plan. Where's Nick?" she glanced around. "I thought you two were going in as the dynamic duo."

"Teething emergency. He'll be here soon."

Marc came around from the other side of her SUV, popping out earbuds to nod at Kenny.

"Hey, kid," Kenny said. "How ya feelin'?"

He shrugged.

"He's not a morning person," Heather said. "Also, I think first day at a new school, even if he went here in the fall, is stressful."

"I'm sure they'll be fine," Kenny said. "And with luck, he'll be able to come to practice this week and make new friends on the team."

"You think it's going to be that easy?" Heather asked, lowering her voice to a whisper as they fell behind the kids on the way across the parking lot.

"I don't know," he said honestly. "It's a little bit of a long shot, but I still think with the package deal of two dads willing to volunteer and fill in for two teachers' extracurricular responsibilities...I'd take the deal if I were the principal."

"Well, I'll try to put him in a good mood when I go in to do the transfer meeting. While I'm in there, you can butter up Agony and Torment to get an audience with the king," she said.

"You think it'll be that hard to see Principal Elliott?" he asked.

She gave him a look. "It can be, but don't worry." Her whole pretty face softened into a wide, warm smile. "I prayed for you this morning."

And his heart just folded in half. "Thanks, Heather."

Twenty minutes later, he kind of wondered if those prayers had been ignored.

"You know what I don't like about Mondays, Mr. Gallagher?" Agnes Torrent looked over tortoise-shell reading glasses perched on the end of her long, narrow nose.

"I'm sure the teenagers you deal with daily are in rare form," he joked, glancing at Ava sitting on one of the chairs behind him.

She ignored him and followed his gaze. "Miss Gallagher, do you or do you not have chemistry lab right now?"

"Oh, I do, Mrs. Torrent, but Mrs. Brindle said it was okay if I came in late, since I'm escorting a transfer student." She added a charming smile that didn't soften anything on the hard-set features of the admin.

"A transfer student who attended last fall and needs no escort." She pointed a finger to the door. "Get to chem lab this minute."

Ava's jaw started to drop as an argument brewed in her eyes, but she instantly thought better of it, looking at Kenny. She knew how important this was, especially if she wanted a director for the play. Who still wasn't here.

"Okay, that's fine." She stood up and took a few steps closer to Kenny. "Bye, Dad. You're the best, you know," she said with way too much enthusiasm. "Oh, and I just got a text that Uncle Nick is pulling in, so..."

So he'd have back-up.

"Have a good day, honey."

She made more of a show by giving him a big, loving hug that Kenny was sure was all for the purpose of impressing A&T. Good little actress, his girl.

When she walked out of the small reception area, Kenny turned back to the woman. "We'll just need a few minutes with the principal."

She took a slow inhale as if digging deep for patience. "Principal Elliott's schedule has been set in concrete for weeks," she said. "You will have to follow the rules and make an appointment like everyone else does."

But the office was empty. Behind her, a few teachers walked around, making copies or chatting. Classes had started, and, for the moment there didn't seem to be a crisis.

"This is very important, Mrs. Tor...rent." Damn, he'd almost called her Torment.

"Everything that happens here is important," she fired back, turning from him to her computer screen, tapping a few keys. "I can get you in early next week, Tuesday, around two in the afternoon."

Not only was that the middle of his workday, but next week, the baseball team would be one week further into the season. The assistant coaching position might be full. And the play would be torn down and forgotten.

He wanted to tell her all that, but he really wanted to save the idea for the principal. She might not get it, but he would.

"I'm here now," he said. "I need fifteen minutes when he's done with Ms. Monroe."

She pursed her lips, staring at the screen. "Tuesday at two o'clock," she said. "Going once. Going twice..."

"I'm here!"

Kenny whipped around to see Nick blow into the office, looking like, well, wow. Yeah, bad night. He hadn't shaved, his hair was tousled, and a faded T-shirt and khaki shorts was the best he could do.

Oh, man. That wasn't going to impress Principal—

"Oh. My. *Gawd.*"

Then he turned to Mrs. Torrent, who was literally rolling back her seat as the color faded from her face. She stared at Nick, her eyes slowly widening to giant saucers.

"Hi," Nick said easily, pouring a lifetime of boyish charm and that subtle 'yeah, I know I'm good-lookin' and famous' into one syllable. "Sorry I'm late." He came over to Kenny and put a hand on his shoulder. "Did I miss the big meeting yet?"

"You?" Mrs. Torrent squeaked out the word, her whole body seeming to tremble. "Are you...Uncle Nick?"

Nick shifted his gaze to her, that Hollywood smile blinding.

"To a few," he said. "Just Nick to you." He reached over the desk and offered his hand, glancing at the name plate as he did. "Ms. Torrent, is it? Pleasure to meet you. I hope you're taking care of my brother-in-law here."

"Miss...Mrs....Call me Agnes." She was literally breathless. "I'm such a fan!" After she shook his hand, she looked at hers for an instant, and Kenny half expected her to declare she'd never wash it again. "Nick Frye!" she raised her voice a little, snagging the attention of two teachers behind her.

Immediately, their faces lit up with shocked surprise.

"Hey," Nick said, giving them a quick wave, somehow managing to carry off complete humility.

Kenny fought a smile, and then realized just what he'd been handed.

Mrs. Torrent was still staring with her hand over her mouth. "Can I get a picture?" she rasped.

"Sure—"

"Uh, just a sec." Kenny put his hand up, ready to negotiate. "First we need to secure an appointment with Principal Elliott. Mrs. Torrent was just explaining to me that it will be impossible to see him until next week."

"What?" Nick looked stunned. "That's not gonna do. Next week, Agnes?"

"Oh, well, I don't...he's so...I can't..." She blinked at him. "I can't believe it's *you*. I've watched every episode of *Magic Man* twice."

Nick leaned over to get closer. "I need to tell you a secret," he whispered, slathering every word with...whatever magic was in the title of his hit show.

"Okay," she managed, gripping the armrests as she tried to swallow.

Too much more of this, and Kenny would have to perform CPR.

"We can't reveal everything now, but trust me. We're here to change your life and put this school on the map. All we need is ten minutes with the powers that be." He waited a beat, letting the effect of whatever he was selling hit her hard. "Could you do that for us, Agnes?"

"Yes." She barely breathed the word, nodding. "Yes, Mr...Uncle...sir." She gave a soft laugh as if she realized how inane she sounded.

Just then, the principal's office door opened and Heather, Maddie, and Marc came out.

"Hi, Uncle Nick," Maddie said, and Kenny remembered that she loved to use the moniker whenever she could. "Welcome to our new school."

He reached out and hugged both the kids and gave Heather a warm smile. "You guys all settled into the new place?"

"Thanks to you!" Maddie was definitely going to make the most of her famous "uncle." She turned to the admin and added, "He helped us move in. Isn't that cool?"

"So...cool." Mrs. Torrent blinked, then stood. "You just stay right here for a moment. Let me talk to Principal Elliott." She added an apologetic smile to Kenny. "We'll just see if we can squeeze you in."

"Now that I brought the keys to the kingdom," he joked under his breath. "She had no intention of giving us a meeting until Hollywood showed up."

Nick laughed. "Happy to help the cause, and sorry I was late."

"We have to get to class," Maddie said. "Bye, y'all." She gave her mom a kiss and tugged at Marc, who was on his phone. "Put that away, ding dong. You want her to take it away from you?"

"She can't do that."

"I wouldn't test it. Bye!" As Maddie headed off, Marc hesitated a minute, looking up at Kenny.

"Good luck," Marc said. "I really hope this works."

"Me too," Kenny replied, giving his shoulder a squeeze. "Pretty sure we got this." Because right that moment, he didn't want anything as much as he wanted that kid to be on the team, and to be his coach. If all the tables had turned, and different lives had been lost, he'd want somebody to do it for Adam.

As they left, he turned to Heather. "How'd it go in there?"

"Good. They're all enrolled. Well, re-enrolled. It was easy. I hope your meeting is, too."

"If it happens."

Nick gave him an "are you kidding" look, and turned as Agony and Torment came out smiling.

"Give him ten minutes to take one call with the superintendent, then he'll see you." She beamed at Nick. "And I'll take that picture now."

While they snapped a few selfies, Heather and Kenny sat on the chairs in the waiting area.

"Marc's counting on this so much," she said. "And I know Ava is, too, for the play. I really hope it works."

He jutted his chin toward the suddenly effervescent Mrs. Torrent. "We have the secret weapon for the play. I doubt they'll say no to him. I don't bring much except I played ball in college. Plus, I'm not an actual team dad, which is what they want for volunteers."

"You haven't been around high schools much," she said. "What they want is time and money, because they're out of both. Are you sure you have the time to do this, Kenny? I know your business is booming and you're a single dad."

"I've only got two renos right now, and they're in good shape. And Ava's pretty self-sufficient," he assured her. "We're good."

"Thank you again." She put her hand on his arm and added the slightest amount of pressure, drawing his gaze down to where her narrow fingers pressed against his forearm.

She does...want to go out with you.

He looked up and met her gaze which felt like it climbed right into his soul and took up residence.

Suddenly, he knew exactly how Mrs. Torrent felt.

"I just want you to know how grateful I am for the interest you've taken...in him."

He nodded, rooting for the right answer and all the sanity that seemed to disappear whenever they had a moment like this.

"He reminds me of my son, Adam, I guess," he said, a little surprised at the honesty, but sometimes he said things without thinking and knew in his gut they were right. His late wife would tell him that was the Holy Spirit doing the talking for him.

"I imagine he does," she said, tapping her hand over his arm in a tender, sympathetic gesture. "So if helping him gives you any measure of comfort, then I'm glad." She added a smile which, of course, just made her prettier. "He's crazy about you, you know. He'd never say it because he thinks it's not cool, but you've just stepped right in and filled a void in his life and...wow. You might not realize just how much you mean to him."

So, maybe Ava was wrong. Maybe she imagined the whole "she wants to go out with you" thing when she heard Heather raving about how much Marc liked him.

"He's a great kid," he said, slowly easing his arm away from her touch to cross it and assume a much safer posture. "And, honestly, I'm psyched to coach baseball. Ava certainly wasn't going to give me the opportunity."

"Well, thank you."

"Wait until we get the job, though. Principal Elliott has to say yes."

"And when he does, we're going to celebrate." She bit

her lip and lifted a hopeful brow. "Maybe just the adults for a change. I could use a grownup night out."

Wait...what? Did she just—

"Principal Elliott will see you now."

Heather popped up and pressed her hands together as Kenny slowly stood.

"You know what I'm going to say, don't you?" Her eyes twinkled as she asked the question.

That you want to have dinner with me, he thought, still processing that. "That you'll pray for us," he said instead.

She gave a sweet laugh. "With all I have. Now, go get 'em, Coach."

But if he needed a prayer, it wasn't so that he'd get a volunteer job at the school. It was so he'd know how to decipher some seriously confusing messages.

CHAPTER TEN

PEYTON

"I don't know why, Jess, but I'm a total nervous wreck." Peyton navigated the hectic Coral Gables traffic as she talked into the speaker in her dashboard. "I wasn't nearly this nervous when I interviewed in Key West. Oh my God!" She slammed on the brakes when a Publix truck cut her off, leaving the big green logo blocking her view of the road.

"Well, your shopping might be a pleasure," she muttered, "but your driving isn't."

"What's that?" Jessie asked.

"The usual Miami question: where did these people learn to drive?"

"You got spoiled by Coconut Key traffic," Jessie said. "And you're nervous because this is a bigger, more comprehensive program than that culinary clinic in Key West. This is the Miami Culinary Academy. I know I'm a graduate, so I'm biased, but this program has produced some top chefs."

Another wave of nerves rolled over her. "You're not helping."

"How about your mother? Would she help? She just strolled into my office. Here, let me put you on speaker." After a click, she heard, "Talk to offspring number one, Beck. She's a hot mess for today's interview."

"Hey, Peyton!" Mom's bright voice came floating into the car and immediately, Peyton felt better. "You're going to wow them, baby girl."

"Momma," she said, feeling the kick of missing everything about Rebecca Foster, including her eternal wellspring of sunny optimism. She could use a bucket of it today. "I'm okay," she assured her. "Callie helped me get ready, which means I'm an hour early."

"That's my sister," Savannah said.

"Oh! You're there, too?" A punch of envy hit. "What are you doing at Coquina Café, Sav?"

"Drinking coffee, eating omelets, what customers do here." Her always just-this-side-of-sarcastic tone both warmed Peyton and made her a little sad. "Dylan and I needed a little Mom and Jessie time. Getting Peyton is just a bonus."

"She's on her way to the interview," Mom told her. "Nervous."

"You'll slay it, Pey," Savannah said with all her oodles of confidence. "Do you get to cook for them?"

"Not this time," she said. "They'll give me a tour of the kitchens and classrooms, then I'll sit down with two chefs and the MCA admissions officer. If I pass muster today, then they whittle to twenty candidates who come in and cook, and then they pick eight for the next semester." She reached a light and tapped the brakes, letting her head fall back and realizing that the nerves and traffic had her feeling dizzy. "I really want this, you guys."

"I'm not the least bit worried," Jessie said. "You talk to them about your passion for food and your vision for a restaurant. That's what they want—graduates who open restaurants."

These days she could barely remember her vision for a restaurant, she'd been so wrapped up in Val.

"So, how's the fiancé?" Mom asked with a smile in her voice when she used Val's new and official title.

"He's great," Peyton told her. "He practiced the interview process with me last night and woke me up with a 'good luck' phone call and promised to take me out tonight to celebrate. He also got called in on a major new business pitch for a shipping company. He said they liked that he knew his way around a boat and a spreadsheet."

"He's a keeper," Savannah said.

"Jessie?" she asked, trying to get her head back in the interview game. "Do you think they'll want to talk specific recipes or something more esoteric?"

"Oh, you know, your signature dish, your voice on a plate, how your childhood affected your cooking."

"Uh oh." Mom moaned. "Wait until they find out your mother's great culinary moment was chocolate chip pancakes."

They all laughed, but Peyton couldn't even think about chocolate chip pancakes.

"Gah, you guys, I'm so stinking nervous."

"You know what I always say," Savannah chimed in.

Peyton knew. "What's the worst that could happen? I remember that was your go-to before any risk-taking adventure, of which you had many."

"It's a question that has gotten me through life," Savannah insisted. "So, what's the worst that could happen today?"

"I could screw up this interview and not get selected as a finalist and end up living in Miami with no real purpose."

"Pffft." Savannah scoffed. "You'll find a purpose."

"If it's not this road, then another, honey," Mom said.

"Plus, they're totally picking you," Jessie added. "You're my protégé!"

Peyton wasn't sure that counted for much considering how long ago Jessie had graduated, but she really appreciated all the support. "Thanks, you guys. You're the best. I have fifteen minutes until I get there, maybe twenty in this traffic. Get my mind off this by telling me what's new in Coconut Key."

"I'll start," Savannah volunteered. "My husband is directing the school play, so file that under 'how the mighty have fallen.'"

"Or 'how could Nick be any more awesome,'" Peyton countered, already knowing the story of how Ava's teacher had to drop out of the play from their mother.

"The principal is beside himself," Mom added. "And they were so excited, they also let Kenny step in as assistant coach, like some kind of package deal to replace the married teachers who had to go to Seattle for a family emergency."

"Oh, and Heather and fam have moved in," Savannah added. "So we're all trying to sit on our hands and not push Kenny into her arms."

"Anything happening there?" Peyton asked, barely noticing the traffic as she was transported mentally back to the place where she wanted to be. The thought of it was like a little paring knife stabbing at her heart.

"If it is, she isn't saying," Jessie piped in. "I've danced around it with her, but she's very coy and cool. Oh, and she starts tomorrow in your old job."

And now it was an eight-inch chef's knife twisting through her chest, making her feel physically sick.

"That's nice." She could swear she could feel the bile rise as she said the lie.

"Not exactly your old job," Jessie added quickly. "She's really more of a front of house person, and you know she kills it at the coffee bar. No one can replace you as my sous chef."

Which they all knew was a lie since Linc, the line cook, was brilliant.

"Okay, is that it?"

"Well, there is one other thing..." Savannah said. "Not reported in the *Coconut Key*

Weekly Standard, but Rebecca Foster has been seen holding hands with a tall, handsome Aussie who looks like he wants to put her shrimp on the barbie, if you get my drift."

"Savannah!" Mom choked while Jessie and Savannah laughed.

But Peyton just had to push down another rise of... jealousy. "I hate that I'm missing all this, Mom."

"You're not missing anything," her mother insisted.

But the truth was, she was missing *everything*. "Well, thanks for the update and pep talk, guys," she said as she spotted the turn at the next light. "I think I'm going to sign off and practice my speech about my vision and passion and..." She couldn't even remember the rest, making her palms sweat against the steering wheel.

"Just remember, big sister," Savannah said. "What's the worst that could happen?"

She could get chosen, sink deeper into Miami, and never get back to Coconut Key.

"I could mess up this interview," she said. "Which I refuse to do."

After they said goodbye, she pulled into the parking lot and found a spot. She was fifteen minutes early, so she spent the extra time sitting in the parking lot taking deep breaths—which somehow didn't calm the nauseous jitters she shouldn't have, but did.

THEY SWITCHED the order of events and started with interviews instead of the tour. To Peyton's great relief during the meeting with the admissions officer, one of the Academy deans stopped in, and she remembered Jessie Donovan as a classmate.

Of course when Peyton shared Jessie's story about how Chuck had been presumed dead at sea for four years, then returned, alive but without his memory, the dean was astounded. That took up most of the hour, but even more importantly, Peyton felt like she'd made a great connection with the dean and left a good impression on the admissions officer.

Next up were two chefs, one an experienced general chef named Miguel, the other, Renee, a pastry chef as sweet as the delights she made. Peyton connected easily with Chef Renee, and they talked desserts and baking for a good half hour.

But the other, Chef Miguel, wasn't as warm or charming. In fact, he was cold and distracted and spent the whole time Peyton and Chef Renee chatted looking at his phone and giving the vibe that he'd rather be anywhere but here.

Peyton turned to him at a natural break in the conversation, looking expectantly at the slightly graying man with deep lines around his mouth and eyes.

"Let's do the tour," he said abruptly, pushing up.

"Oh, sure, of course." Peyton stood, too, sliding her purse on her arm. "Chef Renee, will you join us?"

"I'm afraid I can't, Peyton." She extended her hand. "I've got a class to teach, but it was wonderful to meet you. I look forward to baking with you."

Peyton smiled as she shook the other woman's hand, but the smile faded as she followed Chef Miguel down a hall, the silence between them churning up her stomach again. Had she said something that offended the man, or was he just surly?

When two students passed them, nodding to Miguel, and both looking visibly terrified, she sensed it was the latter.

You can do this, Peyton. He's just a chef with a little power and a sour puss.

"This is the test kitchen," he said, pushing open a door to a large kitchen where three students in blue jackets worked, watched by a chef in white. "We test students here, not recipes."

She nodded, not sure if she should go closer to the stainless prep table where a student was skinning and deboning a beautiful salmon filet...and making a bit of a mess of it.

"Ooh," Peyton murmured when the knife dug too deep under the skin of the salmon.

"You see what she's doing wrong?" Chef Miguel asked, loud enough that everyone looked up at the new arrivals, a soft flush over the cheeks of the woman with the fish.

The students looked a little scared, and even the teacher didn't seem thrilled to see Chef Miguel.

"We're in the middle of an exam," the instructor said, which easily translated to *Please leave*, but Chef Miguel just walked further into the kitchen.

"And someone's failing."

The student's shoulders dropped as the utility knife in her hands shook a little. "Chef Miguel," the woman said, then returned her attention to the fish.

"Can you skin and de-bone salmon, Ms. Foster?" the chef asked her.

"I can, but..." She put her hand up. "Don't want to interrupt the exam."

He tapped her on the back, nudging her closer. "Show Hannah how it's done, please."

Seriously? He wanted her to walk into another student's test and show her up? Her gut tightened as she looked at him.

"Now?" she managed to ask.

"Yes, now." He gestured toward Hannah. "She has the knife skills of a four-year-old."

Peyton blinked at the jerk, but he just angled his head and lifted a challenging brow. "This is part of your interview," he informed her.

Still, Peyton stayed frozen in place, torn.

"It's fine," Hannah said with a weak smile. "I'm making this poor salmon even deader than it was." She lifted her knife, handle out, toward Peyton. "Skin and debone."

With a shuddering breath, she stepped forward, looking into Hannah's blue eyes, hoping her own gaze effectively communicated how sorry she was for this awkward moment.

"'sokay," Hannah whispered, assuring Peyton that she'd gotten the message across.

As she took the knife and rounded the counter, she glanced around for an apron, since she'd chosen winter white trousers and a silk top for the interviews.

"Just work," Chef Miguel barked.

Okay, then. Hell's Kitchen, not the MCA.

Peyton closed her eyes for a moment, then opened them and looked at the salmon. Just as she positioned the blade under the skin—the way she had a hundred times working for Jessie in the Keys where seafood was the staple of so many recipes—a whiff of the fish wafted up and nearly knocked her over. And the knife slipped.

The smell of fish had never bothered her. But today, with strangers looking on, the knife felt unsteady and the scent was overpowering.

She blew out a breath and forced her fingers to follow her brain, feeling the flesh so she knew exactly how quickly to pull as she slid the blade between the body and the iridescent salmon skin.

Once again, the briny smell permeated into her brain and made her stomach turn.

"You see how she does it, Hannah?" Chef Miguel

urged. "The balance between the knife and her wrist? You see that?"

"Yes, Chef," Hannah whispered.

Across the kitchen, the instructor—fairly useless, if Peyton had to say—did nothing but sigh with the resignation of someone who knew their power had been usurped and that fighting for it was a waste of time.

She finally got the skin just about off the fish, but once more, a powerful, pungent odor that she usually enjoyed made her head light. *How was this possible?* Fish reminded her of Val, of cooking, of Coconut Key, of everything she loved.

She looked up and caught the stern stare of Chef Miguel. "Give her boning tweezers, Hannah."

"Yes, Chef." She reached for one of the tools laid out on her prep table and handed them to Peyton with the speed and efficiency of a surgical nurse. She didn't deserve this, Peyton thought. This nice girl named Hannah who was just taking her fish prep exam did not deserve this humiliation.

Peyton reached for the tweezers but suddenly her lightheadedness felt more like actual dizziness and her stomach clenched. One more whiff of the fish made her throat tight, and a light layer of perspiration stung over her whole body.

She'd never been a victim of nerves but this situation was awful.

Her hands were trembling as she clutched the tweezers and dragged them over the pink flesh feeling for a tiny bone. She'd de-boned plenty of salmon, but this one...this one was making her sick.

Truly, truly sick.

Bile threatened to rise and strangle her, and all of a sudden, Peyton realized that she was going to throw up.

She dropped the tweezers and took a horrified step back, blinking at the surprised Hannah.

"Bathroom?" she managed to ask.

The young woman pointed to the door they'd just come through. "Turn left, second door."

Without any explanation, Peyton sailed through the kitchen, whipped the door open so hard it hit the wall, and tore down the hall to the ladies' room, barely making it in front of a stall before she blew out the entire breakfast Callie had insisted she eat.

What the hell was wrong with her?

She pressed her hand against the cool metal as she regained her balance and spit one last time into the toilet. Wiping her mouth with toilet paper, she tossed it, flushed, and slowly made her way out to the sink.

There, she stared at the white porcelain and her hands under cold water, her brain utterly blank as the waves of nausea passed. Fish never made her sick. Nerves never made her sick. Truth was, she had a steel stomach and nothing made her sick.

Very slowly, she lifted her gaze to the mirror, taking in the shadows under her eyes and deathly pale complexion.

Had she been done in by an arrogant chef and a smelly salmon?

Or...she sucked in a soft breath, as Savannah's voice suddenly echoed in her head.

What's the worst that could happen?

The worst...or the *best?* Was it possible she was—

"Hello?" A young woman's voice came through the door. Hannah, she was certain. "Are you okay?"

She let out a breath and put her hand on her stomach. "Way better than okay," she whispered. "I'm..." *Not sure yet*, she reminded herself, trying to do some mental math.

It could have been the stress and the fish...or it could have been something else.

CHAPTER ELEVEN

LOVELY

She should call Beck. She should just pick up that phone, text her daughter, and say, *Hey, I gotta tell you something. Gotta get a mammo today. There's a lump.*

How hard would it be? For Lovely, it would be easy as pie. For Beck?

For Beck it wouldn't be easy at all.

Lovely blew out a sigh and stared at the phone on the table next to her, picking up her tea instead, even though it had turned cold, sipping while she stared at the horizon. The ocean had turned twenty different shades of blue since the sun rose over Coconut Key, maybe an hour or two ago. Lovely had lost track of time, knowing only that she had to be somewhere at noon.

Somewhere she didn't want to go, but had to.

She reached down to scoop up Sugar, sensing the presence of her needy little Westie without actually looking at her. The dog instantly curled into her go-to position, pressed against Lovely's chest, whimpering with satisfaction.

"You don't feel anything wrong in there, do you, Sug?" she whispered, stroking the dog's white fur. "You'd sense it, wouldn't you?" She turned to Pepper, her little Cairn who was, of course, staring at the beach, ready to bark a warning at anyone who passed by. "How about you, Peppie? You're always on the alert for anything wrong."

Pepper's stubby tail rocked, but she didn't turn to offer even a look of curiosity at the question. Of course not. She was guarding the perimeter.

Lovely smiled and glanced around for Basil, but her Jack Russell was no doubt perusing the kitchen floor, cleaning. If she called him, he'd look put out. *There's work to be done, Lovely! No time for lounging or thinking or feeling bad for yourself.*

And Basil would be right. This was crazy, this wallowing in fear and self-pity.

But she couldn't help it. A lump in her breast was cause for that and more. Why did things have to go bad just when everything was so perfect? After a lifetime of waiting and longing and missing the child she'd given to her sister to raise; after cheating death in an accident that took her to heaven and back; after all the various challenges life had thrown Lovely Ames, she was finally happy. Bone-deep happy. Beyond content, well beyond.

This was like peace and joy and glory and ecstasy and everything...shattered in the shower when she lifted her arm and did a self-exam more out of habit than fear.

Now, she had to—

The phone buzzed, lighting up with the name Beckie.

This was the universe or the Creator or karma or something...this was her chance.

Clearing her throat, she picked up the phone and tapped the green button, then the speaker the way her granddaughter had taught her.

"Beckie!" she said, not having to fake brightness in her voice because just imagining that wonderful woman on the other end of her phone made her smile.

"Hey, you. I just wanted to check in and let you know we have the Adamson family arriving from Jacksonville today."

And she'd be getting a mammogram! What kind of business partner was she? "Oh, that's right. I didn't think they'd get to Coquina House until late this afternoon."

"Oh, they don't. Five o'clock, I think, is the ETA. But I just wanted you to know I'm all set here, so you can take the day to do whatever you like. No need to rush over and help me clean out the last guests."

"Oh...I wouldn't have minded." But she couldn't have done it.

"Today, you're free. The guests have checked out and laundry's done, and rooms are spotless. I've even got the hors d'oeuvres planned."

"Beckie! You've been busy."

She laughed softly. "I've had help, I have to admit. Who knew Oliver Bradshaw could whip up artichoke dip, fold towels, and has no fear of cleaning a bathroom?"

Speaking of joy, ecstasy, and kinds of happy. Every word Beck spoke was laden with so much of that.

"Anyway, I called because I thought you said you had something you wanted to do this morning," Beck said. "I know you told me, but I forgot. I'm sorry, Lovely. I seem to be so distracted these days."

"I just said I might be busy, so don't feel guilty for not knowing. And..." She lowered her voice. "Distracted sounds good on you."

Beck let out a happy sigh. "It's fun," she whispered. "We're having fun."

Lovely couldn't help smiling, but then knew that no matter what, she couldn't tell Beck where she was going today. Not yet, not now. Her daughter deserved to enjoy these early, exciting days of what Lovely had a gut feeling could be something real and perfect for her.

"But not so much fun that I can't take you wherever you need to go," Beck added. "Was it a haircut?"

If she said yes, then Beck would want to drop her off at the salon, and expect her hair to be shorter when she picked her up. What could she say?

Think, Lovely. Think. She stroked Sugar's fur and the answer suddenly came to her.

"Actually, you're off the hook for fulfilling my chauffeur needs today," she said, the little white lie forming in her head just perfectly. "It's the vet. For Sugar's check-up, and since Dr. Reston is two doors away from Josh's shop, he said he'd take me."

It was a safe bet that Josh and Beck wouldn't talk about this, or much else these days...not while she was so wrapped up in Oliver. And now she knew how to get an Uber, so the ride would be easy, and the radiology lab wasn't that far from Josh's, actually. So the white lie was... yeah, it was a lie.

She pressed Sugar a little harder, who responded with a loving lick of Lovely's collarbone.

"Oh, okay," Beck said, sounding a little disappointed. "I really could take you anywhere you want to go. You know that."

"You're my favorite driver," Lovely assured her. Not that she couldn't drive—she probably could, easily. With her daughter, granddaughters, great-granddaughter, and, of course, Jessie and Josh, who were like kids to her, she never had to drive again, which was normally just fine.

But today she wished she could.

"You just enjoy getting ready for that family," Lovely said. "They're here for a week, right?"

"Five days. Three rooms. Oh, and Lovely, Oliver helped me work up an ad we can run in some travel magazines. It's not cheap, but he knows the media people and can get us a deal. I can sit down with you and show you the budget, but I think it would be nice to broaden our reach."

"You don't need to show me the budget."

"You're my partner," Beck said. "I want to show you everything."

Lovely smiled. All she'd contributed was the house, which was obviously important, but

Beck had paid for the extensive renovations to turn a home that had been in the Ames family for generations into a desirable B&B on the beach. She'd have given the house to Beck anyway, but this way, they had their passion project to do together.

"You're the real boss, Beckie, and you know that."

"It's a fifty-fifty partnership," Beck replied. "So you need to approve marketing expenditures."

"I approve," she said on a laugh. "Now go and have

fun and buy ads and make money and stay happy, sweet girl."

"Aww, Lovely." She heard the smile in Beck's voice. "I really am."

And nothing—certainly not a mammogram that was probably going to show nothing anyway—would make Lovely change that.

"Call me after you get home from the vet, okay? I do want you here to greet our guests."

"Count on it, honey."

After they hung up, Lovely finally rose, dressed in her lucky purple flowered maxi dress, and braided her long hair.

"I look like the aging hippie I am," she told Sugar who, as always, sat in the bathroom door staring up at Lovely. "But not so old that I can't get myself an Uber and take care of my own business."

Sugar barked. Pepper came running in case something was wrong. And Basil went to the door at the word "business."

"All right, you three. Let me get this stranger to pick me up and I'll take you out. Then I will go get my girls smooshed." She patted her breasts, feeling, somehow, like they'd betrayed her.

She followed the three wagging tails to the door, still feeling a little bad about lying to Beckie, but knowing it was the right thing to do. And what would she say if and when this "trip to the vets with Josh" came up?

So, just as the driver pulled up to her cottage, she grabbed Sugar—much to the little nugget's joyous surprise—and brought her along. She'd stop at Josh's on the way back and…cover for her lies. Which was also lying, but Lovely was in a little too deep now.

Oh, that was cold.

"I'm so sorry." The nurse put a gentle hand on Lovely's shoulder and helped her get a little closer to the mammogram machine. "This only takes a minute if you're still, Mrs. Ames."

"Lovely," she corrected. "Mrs. Ames was my mother."

"Oh, sorry, I…" As she positioned Lovely's rather tiny breast on the plate, the woman frowned at her. "Lovely? From Coquina Court?"

"Yes." She searched the other woman's face, seeing sweet golden brown eyes surrounded by a fringe of dark bangs, enough creases to put her in her fifties, but very pretty in a Linda Ronstadt kind of way. "Do I know you?" she asked, not seeing anything familiar in the attractive woman.

"A long time ago," she said. "Julie Gurley, although my last name is Ellis now."

"Julie…" She narrowed her eyes and dug into her memory. "You…"

"Dated Joshua Cross before he could drive, and you were his neighbor, and used to take us to the movies in Big Pine Key on Saturday afternoons. You teased me by singing 'Julie, Julie, Julie do you love me…'" A soft flush deepened the color of her cheeks. "And now I'm gonna smash your pretty breast, so how's that for payback?"

Lovely sucked in a breath and let it out as a happy

laugh, hardly noticing the cold plate on the top of her boob. "Julie Gurley. I do remember you!"

"Hang on, now, Lovely. I'm going to take the picture." She stepped away and Lovely made a face, not even thinking about that lump in her breast but the cute little fourteen- or fifteen-year-old that Jessie had called "that Gurley girl" when Josh liked her.

"You're just as pretty now," Lovely said.

The woman came back over and loosened the panel with speed and grace. "Thank you, but I'm what? Forty-some years older."

"I recognize the bangs," Lovely said, studying the woman and letting the memories flood. "Everyone else your age had curtains, with that part and straight hair. But you had bangs and a sweet giggle."

"I've always liked my bangs," she said on a laugh that Lovely actually remembered.

"I don't think I knew you lived in Coconut Key. I seem to recall your family moved."

"We did, and I left Florida for years," Julie told her. "I married and had two kids and lived in Boston, but I got divorced two years ago and my kids left Boston. There was no reason for me to stay, so a few months ago, I moved back here because I loved growing up here." She winced a little. "And now I'm sorry but I need a side view, Lovely. Turn for me, please."

"Oh, of course." She did, but barely thought about the cold this time, still sliding back to those days when Josh would ask her for a ride to Big Pine Key. His parents were busy and he liked this girl, Julie, and wanted to take her to the Saturday matinee. "Have you seen Josh since you've been here?" she asked.

Julie leaned back, one hand on Lovely's breast. "Josh? No, I haven't. But I saw the name on a woodworking shop where his father's bookstore used to be. I meant to stop in, but I haven't."

"You should. He's divorced, too, you know."

She nodded, her attention on the machine. "I'm going to slide this plate down, Lovely. Please don't sing that Bobby Sherman song to me."

Lovely laughed, remembering the girl had had a quick wit and an easy-going attitude. And so pretty!

Closing her eyes and staying very still as instructed, Lovely didn't think once about the ordeal she was going through.

"That's it, Lovely," Julie said as she released the machine and let Lovely step back. "If you stay in here for just a few minutes, I'm going to do a preliminary check of this mammogram."

Lovely's eyes popped, her whole being yanked back to the present. "You'll be able to see if anything's wrong?"

"No, no. This will be read by a radiologist and the results given to your doctor, then you'll get a call. I just take a look to make sure it's clear and readable, in case I have to do another set."

"Oh, okay."

"Just have a seat and I'll be right back." Julie patted her arm in a reassuring way that Lovely imagined she did many times a week with worried women.

"Can you check on my dog while you're out there? I left her with that nice receptionist."

"I sure will. Hang on." She slipped out of the room, while Lovely tucked the cotton robe tighter around her and sat down. *Julie Gurley*, she thought with a smile. She'd always liked that girl. And so had Josh.

She had no recollection how or why their young friendship ended—maybe when her family moved? She didn't know, but she did know one thing. They'd liked each other once, so maybe they would again.

"Lovely?" Julie tapped on the door and pushed it open. "We have a clean image. You are free to change and get your dear little dog, who is currently curled up in our receptionist's lap."

"Sugar loves a good lap," Lovely joked, standing up and holding the other woman's gaze. "It was so nice to see you after all these years, Julie."

"And you, Lovely. Please tell Josh I said hello."

"Tell him yourself. He's single, you know. Just out of a relationship and looking for..." Her voice trailed off as the other woman's eyes grew. "Whoops. Overstepped."

"It's fine," she said on a laugh. "I'm single, too."

"Well, can I give him your number?"

Her mouth opened to a little 'o' which made her heart-shaped face even prettier. Lovely leaned in. "Since I'm here in this room, it's safe to say...life can be short. Why not seize a chance when it's handed to you?"

She tipped her head with sympathy. "You're going to be fine, Lovely."

"Did you see anything? Can you tell me?"

She shook her head. "I am not qualified to read anything, but you have such a wonderful spirit about you, I'm just sure you're going to be great."

"And Josh?"

She sighed. "I'll write my number down when you leave."

Lovely put her hand on the other woman's arm. "Just don't tell him why I was here, okay?"

"We are one hundred percent confidential."

"Let's just say we, uh, bumped into each other...on the street."

Her eyes flickered, then she frowned. "Whatever the scan says, Lovely, you shouldn't go through this alone. You know that, don't you?"

"I won't...if there's anything to worry about."

"Promise me?" She covered Lovely's hand and squeezed. "I want to know you're not trying to tackle anything like this alone."

Lovely's heart shifted around as she looked into the soft brown eyes and easily saw the young girl she remembered from those car rides to the movies. A sweet, kind, spunky girl who'd grown into a beautiful—and tenderhearted—woman.

"I'll promise...if you go out with Josh."

She dropped her head back and laughed. "I will if he asks."

"Oh, he will."

A few minutes later, Lovely was dressed and walking Sugar down the sidewalk toward the strip shopping center where Josh's shop was located. The whole time she hummed that old song...*Julie, Julie, Julie, do you love me?*

As she strolled along with Sugar, she felt remarkably light considering what she'd been through that day.

CHAPTER TWELVE

BECK

Beck dropped her head back and leaned on her arms, face to the sun, fingers in the sand.

"I never sit on this beach," she admitted. "I stare at it for hours, watch everyone else run around, and I've even painted it with Lovely. But I don't ever remember sitting on it."

Oliver slid her a look, but his expression was unreadable behind sunglasses. "What good's the beach if you don't put your bottom on it?"

"It's part of the view, not the furniture," she replied. "But I should take advantage of it more often. I like it down here."

Well, she liked it down here *with him*. Especially after a long day of preparing the B&B for guests, including a family of five arriving later today, and another couple tomorrow. The ads were starting to kick in—she'd taken a surprising number of reservations for the typically slow summer months—and the future felt as bright as the sky above. All day, Beck and Oliver had cleaned, cooked, organized, and planned together and it had been...wonderful.

She'd missed Lovely's deft touch, but her mother had definitely seemed a little slower this past week, and Beck had worried that the work and stress of starting and running a B&B had gotten to her. So, Beck was glad Josh took her to the vet, and they probably had lunch together.

In the meantime, Beck had as much fun as she could remember having in a long, long time. Oliver was funny, energetic, full of great ideas, and extremely comfortable in the kitchen.

All that was left to do was to shower and dress, then put out the welcome trays for the guests.

It had been his idea to clear their heads with a walk on the beach, and then they'd just kind of settled in front of Coquina House on the sand, their endless, meandering, light but always personal conversation still going strong.

"Next you're going to tell me you've never been swimming in the ocean," he said.

"The Gulf, yes, up at The Haven. This ocean? I don't like the seagrass in my toes." She made a face. "It tickles."

He leaned in, like he might tickle her, but not touching her. "Go get a suit on, Ms. Foster."

Just the way he said it gave her chills despite the sunshine. "Not a chance. Guests arriving in two hours. Lovely will be here soon, and you, my friend, are expected at your son's house for dinner. Jessie told me Savannah has texted her twenty times in her attempt to cook for you and impress her father-in-law."

He sighed slowly, as if he didn't love being turned

down for a swim. "She shouldn't worry. For one thing, I'll eat whatever she makes. For another, I'm already impressed. She reeled in Nick Frye, and that makes her special."

She smiled. "He settled the ultimate tumbleweed," she added. "And that makes him special."

"And together they made the world's most perfect grandchild." He gave her a sly smile. "Am I right?"

"Well, I also have Ava, but Dylan is the world's most perfect grand*son*."

He tipped his head, conceding the point. "I still can't believe I have a grandson, or a son." He shook his head. "How different would life have been if I'd have known? But I forgive his mother," he added quickly. "You know I do."

"I don't doubt you. I told you when I found out my mother—the one that raised me, not Lovely—had kept the truth from me for fifty-five years, I wanted to kill them both. But life's too short."

He didn't answer that, swallowing hard, no doubt thinking of his late wife. He rarely mentioned her, Beck thought, except for the occasional reference when telling a story. All she knew about the woman he was married to for thirty-two years was that her name was Margaret, she was quite good at tennis, loved to travel, and she'd died after a long battle with cancer. That was two and a half years ago, but in Beck's unprofessional opinion? He was still mourning. She wasn't sure how she knew that, but she did.

She also wasn't sure how she knew they couldn't get too serious about their budding romance until he was completely done grieving, but she knew that, too.

And one other thing she knew—Oliver valued directness and honesty, so she decided to try a little of her own.

"Do you want to talk about Margaret?" she asked.

"No." The abrupt reply must have surprised him, too, since he punctuated it with a self-conscious laugh. "Not to you," he added.

"Why not to me? I'm a good listener."

He took his sunglasses off and looked right into her eyes, squinting a little, which deepened the crease around them and—rather unfairly, she had to admit—made him better looking.

"I don't want her between us."

Yes, exactly as she'd thought. "How is talking about her getting her between...anything? I think it would be healthy and important."

For a long time, he looked at her, thinking, silent. He took a deep breath and she braced herself for him to launch into a speech about Margaret. That she was delightful and smart and perfect and he ached with how much he missed her. She knew it was there, under the surface, so...*here it comes.*

"You're the first woman I've met since I've been widowed who's interested me," he said, making her draw back in surprise. "You haven't figured that out yet, Beck?" he asked on a laugh. "I came halfway around the world to see you."

"To see Nick and Dylan."

He shrugged. "Yes, of course. But mostly to see you."

She wasn't sure how to respond. "You sure are...blunt."

"I'm Australian. Don't mix us up with the Brits who love a good euphemism and skirt the emotional stuff.

Aussies are bold, and we say what we think. And I'm honest." He turned and lifted his hand, stroked her bare shoulder with a touch so light it almost made her shudder. "You," he whispered, the one word as powerful as a speech. "I came for you."

"Well, that's...flattering." And a lot to accept.

His dark gaze scanned her face with such slow intimacy it made her fingers slightly fist the sand under her hand. "It's not meant to be flattery," he said. "It's the truth. And it scares the bloody hell out of me."

She blinked, surprised again. "Why are you scared? The distance? The shared grandchild? The fear of the unknown?"

"No, no, and maybe." He grinned at her. "There's no distance issue if I move here, and, assuming I could do so legally, I will."

Once again, the bluntness of that stunned her. He'd *move* here? "Of course you would. Your son lives here."

"And you."

She swallowed and listened, trying not to lose herself completely in his brown eyes and candor.

"And nothing about our shared grandson is scary," he said, "save his nuclear waste diapers."

She snorted a soft laugh. "They can be bad." Then her smile faded. "So, fear of the unknown, that's it?"

"I guess," he said. "I don't do things...easily."

"Not sure I know what that means," she admitted.

"It's a rugby thing. I play hard. I play to win. I'm not scared of getting hurt, because any good rugger has his own parking spot outside the hospital emergency department, but..."

She waited, listening, hanging on his every word.

"But if I go all in, will you?" he asked, his voice little more than a breath.

"I...don't know." He was being honest, so shouldn't she? "It's awfully soon to know. And I...I'm more guarded than you are."

He searched her eyes, quiet for a moment, the tension and electricity so powerful she could feel it arc between them.

"Do you want to know what I think?" she asked.

"That's all I want to know." He smiled and leaned closer. "Especially if you tell me you could be all in, too."

She stared at him for a while, then swallowed. "I think you're still grieving enough that before I go all in, I'd want to be sure you're ready."

"Oh, I'm ready."

"Are you?" She lifted a brow. "Tell me about Margaret."

He sort of froze, deer-in-headlights style. "I told you, I don't want her—"

"Until you do"—she put a hand on his arm—"she *will* be between us. So avoiding her isn't helping."

"Well, I'm not...I don't...I'd rather not."

"I understand," she said. "I really do. However, I've told you everything that happened with Dan. But if you haven't dealt with your grief, it could come up and bite you at any time, and strangle you and kill...us."

"Sounds...violent," he said, attempting lightness but neither of them smiled.

"It could be. And it could send you running back to Australia just as I've fallen...all in."

He didn't respond to that, but didn't look away, either.

Holding her gaze, she could see those wheels turning as he considered all that she was asking.

"I'm not ready for that," he finally said.

"Then I'm not ready for...this."

"Really?"

She took his hand. "We have plenty of time," she assured him. "We'll get where we're supposed to go."

"But what if—"

At the sound of a car on the coquina shells behind them, they broke apart, and Beck spun around, letting out a little whimper at the sight of a family van.

"Oh my God, the Adamsons are early. Dang it!" She brushed the sand off her hands. "I'm not ready. I'm not showered and there is no welcome committee with drinks."

He laughed. "It's the Keys. Showers are optional, drinks are not. Come on. I'll help you."

As he rose, she wiped the sand from her backside and started toward the house, getting two steps before he snagged her hand. "Hang on, luv."

She slowed her step and turned to him. "They're getting out of the car."

"I just want to say one thing, okay?"

She nodded, torn between how much she wanted to hear whatever it was, and the sound of kids already coming from the drive.

"Life is short, and unknown. I don't want to waste time."

Did he think grieving was a waste of time? She started to answer, but heard a woman's voice calling, "Hello and welcome to Coconut Key!"

She turned to see Lovely step out of the front of the

B&B with a tray, as cool, calm, and prepared as any owner.

"Lovely's here? I had no idea!" Relief washed over her as she started speed walking toward the house. "I wonder why she didn't tell me."

He didn't answer, but put a light hand on her shoulder and kept up with her as they headed up to greet the guests, neither of them saying but both knowing that the conversation wasn't over.

It was early evening when Beck and Lovely really had a chance to talk. The rest of the afternoon had been taken up by hosting duties, and the family that seemed to fill the B&B with a whole new level of excitement. Beck had helped them get a light dinner from a local restaurant that delivered, settled them in the three rooms on the second floor, and said a quick goodbye to Oliver, who was spending the evening with Savannah and Nick.

But now that the sun was setting behind them and the Atlantic Ocean had turned silver-blue in the waning light, Beck saw her mother deep in thought on the veranda, staring at that water like it held the answer to all the questions of life.

She walked to the French door, about to open it and offer a cup of tea, when she paused and took a good long look at Lovely Ames.

As always, her heart swelled with love. The sense of goodness and kindness that emanated from her mother always touched something deep in Beck. It made her hope that some of that had been transferred in the gene pool, and that maybe, in twenty years or so, Beck would be a wise and compassionate woman, like her mother.

Oh, her daughters would insist she was, but Beck knew that there was something extraordinary in Lovely, something truly virtuous. A woman grew into a goodness like that, and it could take many decades.

Lovely leaned forward at the railing, as if she saw something in the water, frowning, her lips moving as if she were talking to herself...or praying. She stroked her long gray braid, as she often did when deep in thought, and her narrow shoulders seemed sunken with...defeat.

That was odd. And so was the sort of sad expression Lovely seemed to wear today. The past couple days, if she were being honest. What could have changed to put that almost intangible aura of sadness around her?

Just as she reached for the doorknob, ready to take the quiet moment while their guests soaked up their last few minutes on the beach, Beck realized what it could be. What it had to be.

Oliver.

His arrival changed everything...including Beck. Just look at today. If Oliver hadn't been here, how would today have been different? Josh wouldn't have taken Lovely to the vet, Beck would have. And Beck would have spent hours preparing the B&B for new guests *with* Lovely. They'd have worked side by side, stopping for lunch at the Coquina Café, laughing and talking the day away, just like she had with Oliver, only...

Oliver wasn't her business partner. Lovely was. And Beck had essentially ignored her today. Since he'd arrived, really. Lovely had to feel that, deep inside, though she'd never say anything. And it had to hurt.

Guilt punched as she twisted the handle and opened the door. Immediately, Lovely turned and forced a happy face. Yes, forced. Beck saw that, and felt just awful.

"I was just coming to offer you some tea," she said. "A little of that herbal citrus you like?"

"No, sweet girl." She pushed away from the railing. "I'm going to walk home and tuck myself in. I'm exhausted and the dogs need to go out."

"You can bring them here when we have new guests, Lovely. They're part of our life."

"I always want to check for allergies, but this sweet Andrea Adamson said they love dogs. I'll bring them by in the morning, although you probably don't need my help."

Beck walked across the veranda to her. "And that's where you'd be wrong, partner."

She smiled, her green eyes, the very same color as the ones that greeted Beck in the mirror every morning, warm with love. "I did save your butt this afternoon," she teased.

"Big time." Beck reached for her. "I never got to ask you why you didn't call down to me when you arrived."

"You were busy, and it was easy to see all the heavy lifting had been done."

Busy with Oliver, Beck thought. Exactly what she thought might be bothering Lovely. "But you should have—"

"I had a lot on my mind, Beckie," she said, breezing by her. "And now I'm ready to head home before it gets dark."

"I'll walk with you," she said quickly.

"The Adamsons might need you. I'm fine. I'll see you

tomorrow." She leaned in to give a kiss, but Beck inched back.

"Something's bothering you, Lovely, and I think I know what it is."

Her eyes popped. "You do?"

"Of course. I know you. I know your looks and your sighs and your…distant expression." Beck's throat grew thick with emotion. "Please don't ever think I'm picking him—or anyone—over you. I love you so much…" Her voice cracked as she reached for her mother, whose slender frame folded right into her. "I'm sorry, Lovely. I feel like I hurt you today."

"Beckie! I'm fine!" But she could hear the same thick emotion in Lovely's voice.

"Not true," Beck insisted. "I just don't want you to think I'm going to turn into some…some teenage girl with a crush just because he's pursuing me."

Lovely drew back. "He is pursuing you, then."

"It would seem so." She looked skyward. "With a bit of…determination." She almost added that he'd mentioned moving to Florida, but that could send an already worried Lovely spiraling even more. "But I'm not sure, not at all."

"Why not? You like him, don't you?"

"Very much," she said without hesitation. "But it's my opinion that he's not done mourning his wife. He barely mentions her, and when he does, it's like he's almost not comfortable admitting he's a widower."

"He probably thinks you wouldn't be comfortable."

"Why? I told him about Dan, and we were married just about the same amount of time."

"But you don't love Dan anymore, and he will always

love his wife and the memory of her." Lovely took her hands. "Your job is to help him get over her, not hold back until he does."

"Is that my job?" Beck asked. "Or is my job to be your daughter and partner and the one person you can count on when you need anything?"

Lovely's face fell and she covered her sadness by pulling Beck into her. "Oh, my sweet, sweet Beckie."

Beck patted her back, sure she was absolutely right about what was bothering Lovely. "I'm not picking him over you."

"That's not..." Lovely straightened her back, the way she did when she was determined not to let life get to her. "I will not..." she said slowly, "...come between you and love. You deserve it, and I like Oliver. I like him very much."

"You do?"

"He's a sixty-year-old version of Nick," she said on a laugh. "What's not to like?"

"The fact that he takes my time away from you?" Beck asked.

"Pffft!" She flicked off the comment. "The very last thing I want is for you to pick me over him. Anyway, it's not a contest. Now, I have to get home before Pepper does a protest pee."

"I'll walk with you."

"If you insist," she said, gathering her bag and the light sweater she wore in the evenings. "But you're shirking your B&B duties."'

"They know the way to their rooms and I've given Mrs. Adamson a tour of the kitchen. Now tell me about the vet," she said as they headed out. "Is Sugar perfectly healthy?"

Lovely was quiet as she navigated the stairs that kept the stilt house off the ground. But once she got her footing on the shell drive, she let out a breath and gave Beck a huge smile.

"Yes, she's fine, but wait until I tell you about the woman I met. I actually already knew her from many years ago." She slid her arm into Beck's as they walked, as much for support as love. "Her name is Julie Gurley, well, Ellis now, but you'll never guess who she used to date."

"Who?"

"Josh!" She squeezed Beck's arm with a giggle. "And she's divorced and he's going to call her!"

"Really? Tell me everything."

And as they gossiped all the way to Lovely's cottage, arm-in-arm, Beck felt her world get a little right again. She tucked Lovely close and made a mental promise not to let anyone come between her and her mother. Even a man who made her feel things she couldn't remember feeling.

Especially that man.

CHAPTER THIRTEEN

NICK

"Well, I'm off to rehearsal. Send me good vibes, babe, because I've never been in deeper doo-doo in my life." Nick leaned over to plant a kiss on his wife's hair and stroke the bald head of the world's greatest child, currently in his highchair waiting for his next spoonful of something disgustingly green. "Except for that diaper this morning."

Savannah snorted a laugh as she brought the goo to his mouth. "And the next doo-doo is gonna be such a *pwetty bwight gween…*" She tapped the baby's nose to underscore the baby talk. "After we finish *all* da beans!"

Dylan opened his mouth like a chubby-cheeked bird, taking the spoon and mushing and moaning as half of the bite slid down his chin. But Savannah caught it with the spoon like a practiced pro. A wave of affection for her rose up, making Nick drop into the chair across from her, even though he didn't have a ton of time to get to the high school.

Truth was, he hated to leave her. Hated to leave this

domestic perfection and the balance of love and laughter that he never knew he needed but now couldn't live without.

"You'll be fine," she said, looking at him as if she sensed the stress stretching across his whole body.

"I don't know, Sav. I'm in...chimney deep. Deep and dirty."

"You'll figure it out," she assured him. "I never saw anyone do so much research for a high school play. Is there anything about *Mary Poppins* on the internet that you haven't read?"

"I just wish I knew a great choreographer. How is it that I don't? All those years in show business and I don't know one hoofer."

"Hoofer? And doo-doo in the same conversation?" She directed the question to Dylan. "Daddy thinks he's eighty now."

Dylan responded by batting the tray and opening up for the next bite of green glop.

"You tell her, D-man," he said. "Hoofer is an accepted term for a dancer and doo-doo? Well, real men don't use uncouth words in front of their infant son."

She smiled at that. "You've never been in a show about dancing, Nick. So of course you don't know anybody in that end of the business."

He leaned closer to whisper, "They didn't even want me on *Dancing with the Stars*."

She laughed again. "You told me your schedule was full when your agent ran that by you."

"That was the PR spin Eliza put on it...because I *couldn't* spin." He fell back on the chair, unable to resist lingering a few minutes longer. "I really thought with just a few weeks before production that stepping into the director's role would be a piece of cake."

"You've had two rehearsals," she said, doing an airplane dive with the spoon much to Dylan's drooly delight.

"Enough for me to know these kids do not know any of the dances yet," he told her. "They know their lines and the song lyrics, and some of the basic staging, but that director was also a choreographer and she took all her knowledge and steps with her. No wonder she said the play would have to be canceled."

"Have you tried to reach her?"

"Completely off the grid," he said. "Her daughter is out of the woods, thank God, but still in ICU and Mrs. Packman has checked out of Mary Poppins-land."

"Understandable. But don't be so hard on yourself, Nick. It doesn't have to be Broadway. It's Coconut Key High School."

"But I don't want to let Ava down," he said. "Or the whole family. Or the school. Or the town. That lunatic Agnes Torrent in the principal's office has basically told the free world that I'm doing this, so they're adding a third performance just to accommodate the people calling for tickets." He ran his fingers through his hair and groaned. "Even when I watch the videos of this production at other places, I can't figure out how to tell those kids where to be and at what point in the music. It's a part of the business I know nothing about."

"I say be honest with them. One of the seniors might step up—no pun intended—and know more than you realize. And give them some time. They're all getting used to having a celebrity in front of them and they might be intimidated."

He nodded, considering that. "The lead is very good, and thank God she knows her steps. I just wish she knew everyone else's."

"And lean on Ava. She's smart and helpful, and not the least bit intimidated by her Uncle Nick."

"She's also a natural on stage," he said, inching closer to kiss her again. "I'll be home after rehearsal. Should I pick something up for dinner?"

She lifted a brow. "Mama's cooking tonight."

"Really? Look at you knocking the job out of the park."

"Just call me Savannah the SAHM."

He made a face. "What the heck is that?"

"Stay at Home Mom. Which, I'm beginning to think, is exactly the job I was destined to do. And do you fully understand the irony of that, Nick? My actual job description has the word 'stay' in it—the one thing I used to think I couldn't do."

He watched her finish off the jar of baby food with a flourish, get the last spoonful in Dylan's mouth, and pat his little chin clean like she'd been doing it for years.

"I think you can do anything," he said, making no effort to hide the admiration and love in his voice.

"Well, the jury's out on my banana stuffed chicken, but Peyton said I could FaceTime her if I get stuck." She smiled up at him. "Break a leg, honey. Isn't that what they say for stage stuff?"

"Usually, but with my dancing and choreography skills, it might be terribly close to the truth."

He was still mulling over how to approach the

dancing dilemma when he cruised into the auditorium and saw Kenny lying on the ground under the tall stairs he'd built for the set.

"I didn't expect to see you here today," Nick called out to the other man who'd become such a good friend these past few months.

Kenny pushed up and nodded a greeting. "Director Frye."

"Please." He looked skyward. "Not sure I'm going to earn the title. What's going on with those stairs?"

"I want to be sure they're secure." He lifted a screwdriver. "The construction worker in me wants them to roll fast and easy. The EMT in me has visions of kids falling to their death in the middle of a dance number if they don't lock."

Oh, great, he hadn't even thought about safety. Gazing up at the steps, which went up to the "second floor" door of the backdrop, he shook his head. "They dance up there, too, don't they?" Nick asked.

"Hell if I know, but they do walk up there." He twisted a screw, grunting as he tightened it, then pointed the screwdriver at the top of the stairs. "Run up to the top and move around, Nick. I want to see if these are secure."

"So it's okay if I fall to my death?" he joked as he jogged up the stairs.

"I'm here to catch you," Kenny said dryly, stepping back and studying the movement of the structure under Nick's weight. "It looks good. Now dance a little."

"Dance."

"Yeah, you know. Hop around. Whatever you expect these kids to do."

"If only I knew."

Kenny inched back and peered up at him. "You're kidding, right?"

"Kind of. Yeah. Not really." Nick shook his head. "Dance. Okay." He moved a little, lifting one foot, then the other and even from up here—way up here—he could hear Kenny chuckle. "I'm not a dancer, okay?"

The chuckle grew to a belly laugh as the other man bent down to adjust one of the wheels. "No kidding, Hollywood."

From his perch, Nick sighed and looked out at the empty auditorium, which would, in so very few weeks, be filled with parents and friends and classmates and...critics. He'd never cared about negative publicity. He'd laughed all the way to the bank. But this mattered for his niece and her school and the town. Now he cared. A lot.

"All right now. I think these'll hold." Kenny popped to his feet and checked his watch. "Baseball practice starts in fifteen minutes and I'm trying to time it so that Heather and Marc arrive after I've had a chance to talk to the coach. Today's my big push for Marc to walk on to the team and this guy is not going to be easy."

Nick groaned and came back down the stairs. "Tell me again how drunk we must have been when we had this great idea to become school volunteers."

"Drunk on furniture-moving adrenaline," Kenny said on a laugh. "We did it for the kids, or did you forget?"

Nick gave him a skeptical look as he reached the bottom of the stairs. "I did it because my wife whispered promises in my ear. And you did it so..." He snorted softly. "Someone would whisper them in yours."

Kenny flinched a little, like Nick had hit a nerve. "I'm coaching for Marc," he said. "To get him on the team.

He's a transfer and that won't be easy, so I want to help him out. Plus, I like coaching. Played ball in school and it's fun."

It was Nick's turn to chuckle as he turned to the empty auditorium, stood a little straighter, and called up his deepest stage voice. "Methinks thou doth protest too much." He threw a look at Kenny. "Hamlet," he said. "That Bill Shakespeare was smart, don't you think?"

Kenny just shook his head.

"Not denying it, are you?" Nick pressed.

"Denying what? That I love baseball and care about Marc?"

"And Heather."

Kenny blew out a long breath, but again, no denial.

"You should make your move, dude," Nick said, leaning on the large table decorated with ruffles and letters for a dance number he didn't even want to think about right then. It was more fun to razz his friend and watch him squirm.

"There's no move to..." Kenny's voice trailed off and he looked Nick in the eye. "Don't you think it's too soon?"

He shrugged. "That's for her to decide. Does she know?"

"Kind of. We've danced around it." He added a smile. "I was about as graceful as you."

"Shut it," Nick warned with a smile. "And, hey, I'm just offering unsolicited advice, but if it were me? I'd be straight with her."

"And say what?"

"How you feel."

Kenny let out a mirthless laugh. "She'd go running back to Charleston."

"That bad, huh?" Nick grinned.

"Pretty bad," he said with an expression that showed how much it pained him to admit that. "But I'm handling it."

"I just think you should be up-front with her," Nick said. "That's all women want."

"Really? Then why'd you rent a yacht for Savannah's birthday and make your big move in a helicopter? Seems like you think they want...grand gestures."

"I do like me some drama."

"Just no dancing."

"Amen, brother." He glanced around the set. "Don't think they'd want to change it to *Death of a Salesman* or *Cat on a Hot Tin Roof*? I've been in both of those. Not a two-step in any scene."

Kenny gave him a long, sharp look. "Are you really worried about this play? Because, man, you got some serious responsibility now."

The words punched. "I know, but this..." He huffed out a breath. "Might not have been my greatest idea."

"You've only had a few rehearsals," Kenny said. "Ava told me everyone was so starstruck they did a terrible job. Once they get used to you, it'll be fine."

Nick stuck his hands in his pockets and took a few steps closer, needing to confide in more people in a desperate effort to get advice.

"I know how to act," he said. "I've watched a hundred people direct. But there's so much music and dancing. It's not a play, it's a full-scale production. And I just don't think these kids are ready. I think if I'd have known that, I might not have been so fast to volunteer. I don't have a clue what I'm doing."

"You *don't*?"

They both whipped around at Ava's small and stunned voice.

"Hey, A," Kenny said quickly, covering for Nick. "I didn't think I'd see you. Rehearsal doesn't start for forty-five minutes, right?"

"Yeah, I thought I'd come over here and do some homework. See if Uncle Nick needed me." She lifted her brows as she walked down the center aisle. "Kinda sounds like he does."

"You shouldn't have been listening," Kenny said.

"Um, it's an auditorium." She gestured toward the empty seats. "Sound carries, like it's supposed to."

"It's fine she heard," Nick said. "So now you know I'm in a whole lot of trouble here. I don't know diddly about dancing."

"He ain't lyin'," Kenny joked as Ava came up the side steps to the stage.

"Mrs. Packman had this clipboard with a lot of staging notes," she said. "Did she give that to you?"

"Nope. She and her husband were already gone by the time the principal met with us on Monday. I found a production handbook in the back and a musical summary. I know the order of the scenes and the numbers, and the actors. I don't know how to make the dancing look good." Which was the understatement of the day.

"Well, Mrs. Packman was so upset when she got that call," Ava said. "But you'll figure it out. You have to tell the kids, Uncle Nick. Everyone thinks you know this stuff."

"Then everyone's wrong," Nick said, putting a hand

on Ava's shoulder. "Kid, I do not want to let you down. You're my niece and I don't want to embarrass you."

"Or himself," Kenny muttered.

"Truth? I don't give a rat's ass what people say about me," he said. "But Ava? I care."

"Oh, Uncle Nick!" Ava gave him a hug which made Nick grin like a loon. Savannah had told him that at one time, Ava was the biggest non-hugger on the planet, so the gesture meant even more.

"You couldn't embarrass me," she exclaimed. "I'm like the queen of the school just for being related to you and then you come in and save the play? My street cred is at an all-time high."

"Take it from one who knows," Nick said. "Nothing crashes faster than street cred in show business."

She laughed, and so did Kenny, but he wasn't joking.

"Ava, how can you help him?" Kenny asked.

"Well, I know exactly which scenes are really worked out well. I'll go over them with you. And Joelle, our lead? She's a natural dancer so she'll help." She gave him a warm look. "It'll be okay, Uncle Nick."

He laughed and shook his head. "I'm supposed to tell *you* that."

"Hey, have you not read the script? What's the theme of *Mary Poppins*?"

"Umm...supercalifragilistic...ness?" he guessed.

She rolled her eyes. "Read the script, Uncle Nick. What does everyone say?" She put her hands on her hips and lifted her chin. "'Anything can happen if you let it!'"

"Yeah, I read that. And good accent, too."

"Blimey, Uncle Nick! We got work to do!" She slid her arm in his. "We'll be 'practically perfect in every way'!"

He laughed at the other line from the play that got tossed around constantly.

"We'll do it, right, Dad?"

Kenny nodded to his daughter with the same love and pride Nick imagined he gave to Dylan at every possible chance. "You got this, A. Just help him however you can. But I have to see what I can do about getting Marc on the JV team."

"You know what, Uncle Nick? I know where Mrs. Packman stashed a lot of her stuff. Let me go look in the dressing room for that clipboard."

As she took off backstage, Nick pointed at Kenny. "That's a good kid you raised."

"Thanks," he said, hopping off the stage. "She's one hundred percent her mother. I just watch and pray."

"I think you do more than that. And I also think"—Nick raised his brows—"you and Heather would be stronger together than apart."

"Gotchya." Kenny started off down the aisle.

"Lay it on the line, man," Nick called. "You know you want to."

Kenny didn't turn, but held up his hand, making Nick smile.

"I found the clipboard!" Ava called. "I told you anything can happen if you let it."

"Listen to that girl, Gallagher. *Listen*."

He gave a thumbs-up over his shoulder, and that made Nick smile even more.

CHAPTER FOURTEEN

KENNY

If anything could happen, then all Kenny wanted in the next ten minutes was to get Marc a spot on the team. Which looked more and more like it might not happen. But he had to try, and today was the day.

But he wasn't looking forward to this conversation with the newly promoted coach at all. Gut instinct told him he was going to get rebuffed, but it was important, and he had to try. He had to lay it on the line, as Nick said, although he'd been referring to Heather.

That was a whole different conversation, one he still couldn't imagine happening. Maybe if he got Marc on the team, he'd start the ball rolling with her. Geez. As if he needed even *more* incentive to persuade the coach.

As he walked from the parking lot to the field, he eyed the back of the dugout painted with the school logo and the "Coconut Crocs" mascot. He took a deep breath and sent up a "bullet prayer" as Elise used to call them. Simple, fast, and direct.

God, help me get this kid on the team.

Kenny spied Dave Mazzeraldi lining up bats along the third base line as he came around the large block and stucco walls that enclosed the dugout. The kids called him Coach Mazz, and seemed to fear, if not respect, the man. In the few days Kenny had been coming to practice, he'd felt the chill from the other man, enough to deduce that he'd hoped for another parent, a personal friend, to be named assistant coach.

No doubt Mazz was none too happy when the principal told him Kenny Gallagher, who wasn't *any* player's parent, just got dropped on him.

So Kenny had played it low key for the first two practices, taking direction and running drills with the kids. But he wasn't here because he had a passion for coaching high school ball—although he actually did. He was here to get one lone transfer student to walk on to the JV team as a second-string outfielder. How hard could that be?

He was about to find out.

He'd definitely beat Heather to the ball field, since he didn't see her SUV anywhere in the adjacent lot. None of the kids were here yet, either, so this was his chance.

"Hey, Coach," he said. "Give you a hand?"

"Sure." He gestured toward the lining device on the bench. "You can chalk the base lines and finish these bats. I gotta make a quick call."

"Will do, but can I talk to you first?"

The other man, maybe forty, kind of reserved and stilted, dropped the last bat and strolled toward the dugout. "Yeah?"

"It's about a walk-on."

The only reply was a frown.

"A transfer student I know. Good kid. Great arm. Perfect for the outfield. I was coaching him in the fall and—"

"Where? I thought you never coached before."

"Not at a school, just privately. It's a family friend," he explained. "This kid, Marc Monroe, he's got a lot of potential for a freshman and made his team up in South Carolina, but then his mother moved here and—"

"His mother? God save me from the ones from broken homes."

Was he kidding? "They're the ones that need sports the most," Kenny said quietly.

"Yeah, they're also the ones who are late to practice, don't show up for games, and never have any money for extras."

Kenny felt his eyes narrow. "This kid won't be late for anything, will be here for every game, and money's not a problem."

He stared at Kenny for a minute, then shook his head. "No. I got more outfielders than I know what to do with."

"I think if you give this kid a chance—"

"I already got you shoved down my throat," he said, then eased the insult with a laugh. "I mean, it's fine, but there were a few guys with experience who wanted the slot. Now I got some kid you want to help, and I've never seen him play? It's too late for that."

"Why?" Kenny pushed, irritation zinging up his spine. "Put him on second string for infield, then. You won't regret it and you'll be really helping a boy who needs it."

The other man huffed out a breath. "Save your guilt trip, man. I got a full roster, a full bench, and too many players already. I don't want another one."

"Look, it's one kid. I'll vouch for him. If he does anything you don't like, you can throw him off the team, but this is a good young man, from a good family, and his arm will knock your socks off."

He just shook his head as he jogged down the dugout stairs, grabbing the chalker. "Never mind. I'll do this myself." He spun around to go back to the field and as he did, Kenny reached out and snagged his arm, getting a vile look.

"Please," Kenny said softly. "Marc needs the team."

Mazz searched his face. "Decision's made, Gallagher. You don't like it, leave."

"If that's what you want, I will. But give him a chance."

For a moment, he didn't say anything. Then, he angled his head with distrust. "Why does it matter so much to you? He's not your kid."

He swallowed, not wanting to pull the pity card, but willing to do whatever it took to help Marc.

"His father died six months ago, Dave. His mother decided to move here and start over, and Marc is lost and grieving and buried in video games and pain. Do you even have a heart, buddy?" He hated that his voice cracked, and really hated that the other man's lips threatened to lift in a smile that he found Kenny's weakness. "He just wants to play ball," he finished. "And I want to help him."

Finally, after a good, long five seconds of silence, he nodded. "All right. He can start—"

"Tonight," Kenny finished. "He's on his way."

The guy gave a soft laugh and headed to the field level, chalker in hand.

Not wanting to push it, Kenny walked around the

dugout to take another look at the parking lot and practically walked right into Heather.

"What are you—"

She put her hand up. "Don't let him know I heard that."

"You did?" Did she hear Kenny's voice crack, too? See the grief in his eyes? Know that it was because he'd do anything for her?

"You fought for Marc."

"Yeah, well, the guy was being a—"

She put her fingers on his lips. "You fought for him, Kenny. I can't tell you what that means. How much..." She lowered her hand, unintentionally grazing his chin as she stepped back and let her eyes shutter. "Thank you," she whispered, her voice taut with emotion.

"It's okay." He fought the urge to hug her and hold her against him, his whole body still humming from the discussion and wanting...her. He purposely stepped back and looked toward the parking lot. "Where's Marc?"

"Waiting in the car." Once more, she gazed up at him. "You really care about him, don't you?"

"Yeah, I do." He studied her for a long time, lost in her blue eyes.

"What time should I pick him up after practice?" she asked.

"I'll bring him home for you," he said. "There's something I want to talk to you about anyway." The words tumbled out and he wasn't sure if he wanted to kick himself or fist punch the air. But it was a step.

"Okay. Is everything all right?" she asked.

"Yeah, yeah, I just..." He swallowed. "I kind of want to ask you something serious."

She blinked at him and held his gaze for a second or two more, then slipped into a smile. "Okay. I'll be home. And..." A little bit of color rose on her cheeks. "Now I'll go get Marc."

He watched her walk back to the parking lot, trying not to stare at how perfect she was, even in her Coquina Café khaki pants uniform. But he failed because...she was perfect. And all he had to do was let her know that he felt that way and...

He closed his eyes and said one more bullet prayer.

Please don't let me make a complete fool of myself.

"THANKS FOR THE RIDE," Marc said as Kenny drove up to their house. Then he added, "Coach."

"Thanks for being the ultimate team player today," Kenny replied as he pulled into the driveway and parked. He wasn't leaving without some kind of conversation—even if it was to make a date for another one. Because, during practice, he'd decided that he wouldn't spill his guts tonight...but he would ask her on an official date. That would open the door to a more natural conversation.

"I like the guys," Marc mused. "Especially that catcher, Leyton? He's cool. But Coach Mazz is a hard ass." At Kenny's look, he rolled his eyes. "Sorry. Pain in the butt? Is that okay?"

Kenny had to laugh. "Yeah. He's both."

Just then, the front door opened and Heather stepped out, wearing white shorts and a pale purple tank top which just got moved up to his favorite outfit ever. She looked fresh, liked she'd spent the time since he'd seen her at the ballpark taking a shower and doing something to make her hair flow even more, and maybe put a little makeup on.

For him?

The very thought gave him a much-needed confidence boost.

In the time it took to stare at her and get that boost, Marc had opened the door and hopped out of the truck with his backpack.

"Thanks again, Coach!" He grinned like the new official name pleased the heck out of him.

"Take a shower, honey," she said, giving Marc a quick kiss in the driveway that he didn't want but accepted. "And start your homework. Dinner's almost ready." She transferred her smile from Marc to Kenny, coming to the driver's side of the truck to Kenny's open window.

There, she blasted him with another smile and the faintest scent of a flowery perfume, locked her hands on the door and popped up on the running board so they were face-to-face.

More confidence rolled through him, or maybe just a shot of testosterone because when he looked at her, he felt...strong and protective and determined and every other thing a man should feel.

"Did you see that smile on his face?" she asked, looking bright and carefree and as happy as he could ever remember seeing her since they'd met.

"He played well," he said. "Followed every instruction, was respectful to the coach, made some friends with the other guys, and helped clean up afterwards. You can be proud, Mama." He tapped her on the nose because she was close and cute and he couldn't help himself. "Give that boy dessert tonight."

A soft pink rose in her cheeks and he took that blush as a very positive sign.

"You want to stay for dinner?" she asked. "We have plenty."

And that was another extremely positive sign.

"Tempting, but my daughter would kill me for hanging with the Monroes without her. She's still at rehearsal until seven or so, helping Nick figure out how to be a director."

She leaned back with a frown, still holding the door. "He doesn't know?"

"The dancing part is a challenge," he said. "But my daughter has promised to help. Not sure if that's the blind leading the blind, but I was proud of her."

She laughed a little. "I love the kids having extra-curricular activities. It's too late in the year for Maddie to do much, but speaking of pride? Your wonderful daughter got Maddie to help with costumes for the play. Wasn't that sweet?"

"Yeah. She didn't even tell me that." He held her gaze for a beat, both of them smiling. "We got great kids, Heather."

She sighed. "They're great together. I honestly don't know what we'd have done without you and Ava, who've made this move so easy. And Jessie, of course. And Beck. Just...everyone. But you..."

He waited, giving her a chance to finish, but she didn't. The color in her cheeks deepened though, and he took that as a *really* good sign.

"Well, while you're feeling all grateful and warm," he said, "I'm going to dive right in and ask a question."

She let that lower lip slip under her teeth and looked down for just a second, and he knew that she knew exactly what that question was. So why put it off one more second?

"What's the chance of me getting you out to dinner without our wonderful kids sometime?"

She waited one heartbeat and then the smile in her eyes was replaced by something he couldn't quite interpret but wasn't sure he liked. And all that confidence just fizzled.

"I don't know," she whispered. "I've been praying about it so much."

"You have?" He didn't mean to sound quite that surprised, but he just hadn't imagined her as fixated on the possibility as he was.

"Of course I have," she said. "I'm...not sure."

Okay, well, that wasn't a no. "What aren't you sure about? It's too soon?"

She searched his eyes, gnawing on that lip. "I don't think it's too soon," she said. "But it might be...too much."

He just stared back, silent, and totally uncertain what that meant.

"It's not just you and me, you know. We have three kids and they have...feelings."

"You think your kids would hate the idea of you...of me...of us...having dinner?" 'Cause he already knew Ava and Maddie loved the idea.

She smiled as he stumbled over his words, breaking the tension and making him reach out to put a hand over the arm resting on the open window.

"You can probably tell I'm nervous," he said. "Heather, I don't want to put you on the spot. And I don't want to upset our...our friendship, especially because our kids are close. I don't want to do anything, but I—"

Her eyes filled just enough to shock him.

"Don't cry!"

"I'm not. I mean..." She brushed a finger under her eye. "I am, but only because the whole thing is kind of overwhelming."

"It doesn't have to be," he said, leaning a little closer to the window and wishing like hell he could get out and hold her. But she looked like the truck door was supporting her right now, and he didn't want to push it.

"I know, but I'm so in love—"

He inhaled a soft breath.

"With Jesus," she finished, with a soft laugh. "You know that."

"I do know that." And how did he tell her that her faith had become one of the most attractive things about her? It would just sound...opportunistic. "Does that mean you can't date?"

She laughed again, shaking her head. "Quit being so adorable, will you?"

"Only if you will."

They looked into each other's eyes for what was probably three seconds but felt like the rest of Kenny's life as he waited for her to explain why being in love with Jesus meant she couldn't have dinner with him.

"I have to follow His will," she finally said.

"Did He tell you I'm not a safe bet? Because if that's true, I better go talk to Him."

But her smile wavered at the joke and she stepped

down from the running board, back to the ground, losing ten inches of height and suddenly looking tiny and far away.

"You *should* talk to Him, Kenny," she said softly. "We both should. I have to know that...that anything I do is what He wants me to do. And I'm not sure how."

"Hey, we took a class on that, remember? That Stanley guy on God's will. Three things: ask people you trust, read the Bible, and pray. Although maybe not in that order."

"I do read the Bible," she assured him. "It says a lot about widows, but nothing about when they can date again."

"When it feels right," he said.

"And I do pray, but I'm not...I'm just not sure." She leaned into the door a little bit. "The thing that scares me is somehow tarnishing my late husband's name."

He frowned, slowly shaking his head. "How? Because you should be in mourning for a defined period of time? Because I'll wait."

She let out a soft groan and wobbled back a little, like the words had melted her. "Truth?"

"Nothing but."

"You, Kenny Gallagher, are everything Drew wasn't," she whispered.

What did that even mean? "How so?" he asked.

"He wasn't patient and kind," she said very softly, as if the words hurt to speak. "He wasn't a man of faith in any way, as you know. But it was worse than that."

"You told me he was an atheist," he said. "But you shouldn't compare—"

"How can I not?" she asked. "He had so much anger

all the time, even before he got sick. He was short-tempered, and you're so easygoing. He was...rough around the edges and you're so..."

"I get the idea," he said, shifting uncomfortably in his seat. "He's also not here to defend himself."

"Like that," she said. "You're so...perfect."

"And you're wearing rose-colored glasses, because I'm far from perfect." And he never thought that would be his way of persuading her to go out with him—trying to convince her that he wasn't perfect.

"If I'm with you, I'm afraid that Drew would...disappear."

"I wouldn't let that happen, Heather. Just like I would never let Elise or Adam disappear."

"But I worry it's inevitable with you. You'll wipe out his memory just by being you." She smiled. "You're basically the best man I ever met."

He just stared at her for a long time, loving the compliment, but hating what it meant. "Of all the reasons for rejection I imagined—and I imagined a few—I never even dreamed it would be...that."

She gave him a sad smile and stepped back up to eye level. "This isn't a rejection," she finally said. "I have given this to God. I'm asking for guidance, for open doors, for signs in the road that show me exactly what I should do. What's best for me and for the kids, and what honors Him. Can you understand that?"

Not only did he understand it, in some ways, he could hear his own late spouse saying those words, with the same intonation, same fervent belief, and the same goal of honoring God.

Which was probably why all this conversation did

was make him fall a little more in love with Heather Monroe.

When he didn't answer, she whispered, "What are you thinking, Kenny?"

That he'd just realized he loved her.

"Oh, nothing," he lied. "Just that we better crack that Bible and find some answers."

Her smile grew wide, but it faltered again and tears welled.

"No?" he guessed.

"You're just...everything," she said. "Everything I want and didn't know I needed. But the shadow you'd cast over Drew would be...hard on my kids. And hard on me."

"I don't want to cast any shadows," he said. "But will you keep thinking about it?"

"I'm not thinking about much else."

He leaned very close and put a hand on her cheek. "I'll wait while you think and pray and read."

"Thank you." Her eyes fluttered closed as she pressed her cheek into his hand with a sigh. "God bless you, Kenny."

He did, when He sent Heather Monroe into his life. And for that reason, Kenny knew he'd wait for her. He had no choice.

CHAPTER FIFTEEN

PEYTON

Before she knocked on Val's office door, Peyton took a moment to look at him as he tapped the keyboard, working a spreadsheet with his shirt sleeves rolled up, but a tie securely around his neck. The difference between this young and ambitious executive versus the khakis-and-T-shirt guy who reeked of fish she'd first met never failed to surprise her.

Not that CPA Val wasn't just as hot as Fisherman Val. The man was simply a feast for the eyes. But the tie...the computer...the short hair and uber-professional surroundings were just so not who she'd thought he was. But apparently, she was wrong. And it didn't matter—she loved him in khakis and with bait remnants on his "eat-fish-sleep" T-shirt, and she loved him in an expensive Brooks Brothers ensemble. Either way, it was Val.

Her fiancé...and the father of her baby.

"Knock, knock." She tapped the door jamb, and he instantly turned and broke into the biggest smile.

"Who's there?" he volleyed back, spinning his chair toward the door.

"I fish."

Laughing, he shook his head. "Okay. New one for me. I fish who?"

"I fish you would ditch work and come with me to Coconut Key."

"Ah. Got me." Still smiling, he got up and came around the desk, arms out. "I fish I could, too. But..." He blew out a breath. "Somehow I became the lead accountant and am now in charge of the whole presentation."

"Wow." She lifted her brow. "What does that mean?"

"A ton of work in the next few weeks, but if a company the size of Onaway Shipping wants me to manage their account, it would be amazing." He pulled her closer to whisper, "And possibly a promotion with more money for diapers."

A shiver ran down her spine, still not used to the dizzying fact that she was six and a half weeks pregnant and they were going to be parents in early January.

"Well, since you're booked with work, I'm going to take off early so I can make Thursday night with my girls."

He inched back, his smile fading. "You sure that's a good idea, Pey?"

"I won't touch a drink, if that's what you're worried about."

"No, I'm not worried about that, but you'll...let out our secret." He put a finger over her lips. "Remember, mum's the word...*Mum*."

She nodded, knowing what they'd agreed. The night she'd taken the test and called Val to come over, they'd both just sat on her bed grinning like loons. It was too much to even comprehend. And, maybe, a little too soon.

Yes, he wanted kids, and no, they hadn't been *that* careful. Then reality hit Val and he wanted to control just how, when, and where they broke the news to either family. Especially his, the uber-traditional Catholic Cubans.

"You can trust me," she said. "I haven't even breathed a word to Callie."

"But your mother?"

"Oof." She grunted at the thought of *not* telling her. "That's going to be a challenge. Are you sure I can't just whisper? She won't tell a soul."

Except Savannah. And Lovely. And Jessie. And Callie. And...she knew why she couldn't tell anyone.

"Peyton, listen." He glanced into the hall, then drew her deeper into his office, nudging the door closed. "I have to do this right with my parents. You pregnant before we're married is going to be a huge deal. I still want to have a plan."

"I get that." Although, she didn't get it completely. "But my family's different. I don't think we Foster women know how to get married before conceiving," she added on a laugh. "I come from a family tree made up of premarital babies."

"Well, I don't," he said. "So, please. Let's just take a few weeks and figure out what we're doing, so we can tell them the whole thing at once."

She nodded, knowing the argument by heart by now, but still hating that she couldn't tell her mother and Savannah and Lovely. And the whole stinking *world*.

"Hey." He tipped her chin up to look into her eyes. "I promise I'll never say the E word again."

She laughed, remembering her reaction when he mentioned "eloping." There'd been tears. Big ones.

"I know I got a little emotional because...you know."

"You want a wedding." He stroked her cheek gently. "And you should have one."

"But not"—she put both hands in front of her belly—"massively pregnant as I waddle down the aisle."

His dark eyes gleamed. "I can't wait to see you massively pregnant."

The way he said it made her heart burst and she reached out for a warm hug. "I'm so excited," she whispered into his strong shoulder.

"Same. It's nuts, isn't it?" He tipped her face up to him. "I can't think about anything else."

She gestured toward his desk. "You were pretty deep into that spreadsheet."

"Well, do or die. This account is huge. My boss is coming in here after lunch and wants..." He shook his head. "Never mind. It's boring."

"It's your work, it's not boring."

He snorted. "An analysis of asset turnover ratio on a consolidation model?"

"Oh. Is that all?"

"And you wonder why I can't make puns about this business? It's un...punny."

Then why was he in it? Well, she knew. He'd told her many times he actually loved being an accountant, that he got excited by numbers, and was very happy back in the business world.

And, the truth was, Val's family had never had much

money. He was the first in the entire clan to go to college, and their pride in his success was palpable. Add that to the fact that they were having a baby, and his ambition made sense.

They were *having a baby*. She still wasn't used to the very idea of it.

"Why are you smiling? You think financial modeling is funny?" he teased.

"No, but being pregnant makes me smile."

"And puke."

"Some days," she agreed. "Today I've been fine."

"I've heard my abeula say that women who get sick have babies with a lot of hair. Oh, and boys."

She smiled at that. "Our li'l nugget doesn't have hair," she said. "But I've heard her Cuban sayings about babies and she's right as often as she's wrong."

"She's going to be..."

"Scandalized?" she suggested.

"No, that'll be my mother. Abeulita will be thrilled."

"Then let's—"

He shook his head. "Please. And not your mother and sister and Lovely either. Can you do that, Peyton? Is it possible?"

"I promise." She crossed her heart and smiled at him.

He let out a low groan and held her close again. "God, I love you."

"I love you, too," she said, "or I would be singing out my news the minute I step foot in Coconut Key."

"How are you going to do this, really? Those women know every thought and feeling you have."

Something about the way he said that made an unexpected sadness ping in her chest.

"They really do," she said softly, missing them with a visceral kick. "But I have a plan for tonight. I'll fake drink a mimosa because if I had sparkling water, Savannah would zoom right in on that. And I'll let Mom talk about the B&B—and her semi-permanent guest."

"The Aussie guy?"

"Yep, that'll take any focus off me."

"Good girl." He dragged his hand from her waist to her belly. "Or boy. I'm thinking boy, aren't you?"

"'Cause Dylan is so cute?"

"I just want a boy…or a gill." He winked at her. "See? That punny guy still lives under this tie."

She took a deep breath, that same sadness pinging some more. She missed that punny guy. And her family. And Coconut Key.

"*Annnnd* she's about to cry."

"Am I?" She stepped back, touching her eyes. "I'm so emotional, Val."

"You're pregnant, Pey. So be good to yourself, eat right, drive carefully, and…" He put both hands on her cheeks. "Be patient. Especially with all this work I have. This is a big account, probably the most important business I've landed since I got here. We get it, and I'll run everything for that client."

She nodded, tamping down the low-grade disappointment she had no right feeling. His job was important to him, and she respected that. "Then I guess I'm right to put that townhouse on the market the instant I own it."

He angled his head and his dark eyes softened. "Pey, I know you love that place, but if you sell it—"

"Then the profit can pay for the wedding," she finished. "The one I've always dreamed of."

"I want you to have that," he said. "Plus, if I reel in this new client? Fat bonus that we can put in a college account for junior."

"Reel in?" She got on her tiptoes and wrapped her arms around his neck for a kiss. "There's my Val."

When she stepped back, she could have sworn she saw some sadness in his dark eyes. Like he missed that Val a little bit, too. The executive and the fisherman were both Val, but he was that all or nothing guy, and couldn't quite find the balance.

True to her promise, Peyton hadn't taken one sip of the drink her sister had made. She'd faked it, and taken the flute with her to get something in the kitchen, dumped it, and then refilled with plain orange juice.

And her plan to keep the conversation on Mom had been easy, since they couldn't seem to get enough gossip about the new man in her life. Beck Foster was downright giddy, which was way too much fun. Savannah had been on a roll joking about "Crocodile Dundee" which kept much of the conversation on Mom.

Although when Jessie had unloaded her struggles about motherhood, keeping her secret had been a challenge for Peyton. *I'm going to face that, too,* she longed to call out into their intimate circle. But she hadn't.

Lovely had been quiet—maybe unusually so. Most Thursday nights, her grandmother's contributions had been words of wisdom. But she let the others do that last night, except for her usual teary speech about how happy she was to have them all. If anything, Lovely was a bit tearier than usual. Mom confided that she thought that was because Oliver was in the picture, but it wasn't like Lovely to be jealous of anyone or anything.

All in all, Peyton had had fun and kept her secret. And this morning, she'd signed the paperwork for the townhouse, then turned around and put it right back on the market before driving back to Miami.

But everyone wanted to tour her brand-new property while it was still officially "hers." No one had seen it completed, because by the time all the construction was done and the punch list finished, Peyton had moved to Miami.

The outing was planned and now, as Peyton pulled into the parking lot, she spotted Mom, Lovely, Savannah and Nick with Dylan, and oh, Oliver was here, too. Normally, this would have been a great idea...if she weren't hiding a secret that was bursting to get out.

The impromptu party also reminded her of all the family, friends, and Coconut Key connections she'd be giving up by living in Miami.

Shaking it off, Peyton parked and climbed out of her car, waving her new key.

"The owner's here," she called on a laugh. "Signed, sealed, and purchased."

Mom came right over with a hug. "You're a property owner, Peyton! I'm proud of you."

"Not for too long," she said with a wistful smile. "Timing is everything, huh?"

"Let's hurry and go see it," Mom whispered, pulling her close. "I think the heat's a little bit much for Lovely."

She looked past her mother to see Lovely fanning herself and leaning a little on Nick as they talked to Savannah, who held the baby, and Oliver.

"Oh, gee. That's no good. It's this unit right here. Remember?"

Mom looked at the two-story row of townhouses. "I do, and I forgot how adorable this little complex is. And a perfect location with an end unit. When you first bought it and called it a condo, I got that image of a high rise in my head."

"No high rises in Coconut Key," she said, thinking of the thirty-story building where Val lived that always made her a little dizzy when she went on the balcony. "This one is bright and comfy, but I don't have any furniture, Mom. What's Lovely going to sit on?"

"Nick has some beach chairs he can bring in."

"And we won't be there long," Peyton added. Because, honestly, she couldn't spend that much time with her mother and not squeeze her hand, yank her aside, and squeal out the truth.

"Don't rush home, Pey," Mom said, sliding an arm around her and pulling her close. "I feel like I get so little time with you. I'm sorry, I don't want to make you feel guilty. It's just...I want your opinion on Oliver, and I know he wants to get to know you more."

She looked at the group gathered outside the door to her new place, her gaze shifting to the tall man with dark burnished gold hair and strong shoulders. "He's a nice-looking man, Mom. Does he have a good heart?"

Her mother smiled. "I think so, but you're a great judge of character. You tell me."

Peyton nodded as they joined the others and she accepted congrats on her new place.

"Remember, I'm selling it," she reminded them. "I bought this pre-construction and pre-Val."

"It's a fine place," Oliver said, stepping back to take in the coastal design of the place. "How big?"

"Not quite two thousand square feet, on two stories. But the view is astounding. Wait until you see the dock in the back."

"It has a dock?" Oliver's eyes widened.

"One for every unit, and there are only four in this section. Come on."

She led them to the entry, taking a moment to nuzzle the baby in Savannah's arms when Nick went back to the car to grab some chairs. "Let me hold him when we get inside," she said, her arms already aching for her nephew. And the practice. "Then you can give yourself the tour."

"You got it, girl. I love this place, by the way. Are you sure—"

"Savannah." She narrowed her eyes. "Mom already guilted me about leaving early. Come on. You know why I'm doing what I'm doing. I love this townhouse, but I love Val more."

"Yeah, yeah, yeah."

Peyton stepped ahead of the group, key in hand. "Here we go." She opened the door and went in first, taking in a soft breath at the gorgeous sunshine pouring in through the sliding glass doors, an extra-wide canal in the back glistening in the sunlight.

"That faces east," she said, pointing toward the dock that would be perfect for a couple of Adirondack chairs and a table. And a man who'd love to fish. Had she been thinking of him when she bought this place? "The morning light is so pink and pretty."

"Stunning!" Oliver exclaimed as he walked in.

"It's the house that saving my publishing salary bought," she joked. "Well, the down payment. But I got a great deal."

"You'll make a profit for sure if you sell," Nick said as he came in carrying a beach chair for Lovely. "It was a brilliant investment."

"That's what Val said. Feel free to look around, everyone. There's the living area and kitchen here, one bedroom downstairs that could be an office, then upstairs is just the master suite and a really small guest room." A room, Peyton had once thought, that would make a fine nursery. When she'd made the decision to buy this place, she'd been seriously considering having a baby on her own. "It's not expansive, but I love it."

"How could you not?" Oliver said as he walked to the wall of sliding glass doors. The patio beyond the doors was small, but the waterway was wide and deep, and the wooden planks of a small L-shaped dock were nothing short of inviting.

Peyton bit her lip, already sad to give up this beautiful little home. But it was just a townhouse with a view. Not a man who loved her and made all her dreams come true.

She shook off the thought and returned to the living room to make sure Lovely was comfortable.

"Are you okay?" she asked, sidling up to her grandmother.

"I'm fine and I don't need to sit, you know." She slid

her arm through Peyton's. "It was hot out there, but I'm good. You made a beautiful choice with this place."

"I know. I'm a little sad being here with all of you now."

Lovely shook her head. "Don't be sad. You're too happy to be sad."

The words were right there, right on the literal tip of her tongue. *You want to know how happy I am, Lovely?* But she managed to swallow them, stepping back to watch Oliver open the sliders and walk out with Mom, deep in conversation.

"Do you like him, Lovely? Mom wants my opinion."

"I like him very much," she said, then let out a soft sigh.

"What?" Peyton asked, frowning at her. "Why the sigh?"

Savannah joined them, shifting Dylan from one arm to the other. "What are you guys talking about? Dundee?"

"Yep." Peyton reached for the baby. "Gimme."

He rewarded her by reaching both hands out with a toothy grin, grabbing at her hair like he always did.

"Well, I don't get an opinion," Savannah said as she relinquished the baby to Peyton. "Since he's my father-in-law, who will also end up as my stepfather, so how weird is that?"

"Step..." Peyton's jaw dropped. "You think Mom's gonna marry that guy?"

"Where have you been, Peyote?" Savannah joked. "Oh, I forgot. Miami."

"Stop it," she snapped back. "I was with Mom all evening and she didn't talk about it being anything *that* serious. Has she even kissed the guy?"

"I don't know," Savannah admitted. "And truth be told? I get a lot more of this from Nick, who gets it from Oliver, who is definitely enamored of our mother. Big time."

"Wow." Patting the baby's back, Peyton looked out on the patio, watching them laugh and talk and look at each other like...well, the way she and Val looked at each other. "Oh," she said on a soft breath.

"What's wrong, sweet child?" Lovely asked.

"FOMO," she replied, and at Lovely's questioning look, she added, "Fear of Missing Out, which I'm experiencing right now. Hard."

"It's going to be fun to watch her fall," Savannah said, biting her lip as she looked out there. "I feel like I have a front row seat."

Peyton shot her a look. "Must you make it harder?"

"I must." She grinned, reaching for Dylan. "Let me have him back so you can go talk to them. Mom really does want your opinion, but, honestly, there's nothing not to like about the guy. I mean, he provided Nick with half his genes. The *good* half."

Reluctantly, she handed Dylan back to Savannah and walked out to the patio, her smile fading as the briny water filled her nose.

"Wow, it's fishy today," she said, waving a hand under her nostrils.

"That guy on the next dock just caught a trout." Mom pointed to a dock about fifty feet away. "And the fish are jumping. Oliver is dying to get a rod and reel."

He turned to her, his dark eyes sparking. "I love this place and I haven't even seen it all."

"Thanks. It really has a great vibe."

"It's perfect," he said in that low Australian accent. "Are you truly selling it?"

She moaned and let her eyes close, not liking the question *or* the salty smell that suddenly wafted from the water.

"I am." She tried to smile at her mother. "Did you put him up to trying to talk me out of it, too?"

"On the contrary," Oliver answered for her. "I might be trying to talk you into it."

"Into moving?"

"Into *selling*," he said. "I can't imagine a place like this comes on the market that frequently in Coconut Key."

She frowned, trying to process what he was saying.

"Oliver thinks he might consider buying it," Mom explained.

"Oh, really?" She blinked in surprise. "Seriously?"

"I'm quite taken with this island," he said, just a hint of a smile sliding toward her mother. "And I can't stay in the best room at the B&B too much longer because Beck's turning away business."

"Wow, that's...yeah." This really *was* serious. "That's awesome," she added, and this time the smile won out, feeling genuinely happy for her mother. He'd move here for her mother...after knowing her a month? Like Nick? All the great guys would, except...Val.

Once again, her stomach rolled.

"I think it makes sense to have a place here," Oliver continued, oblivious to her low-grade sense of sickness. "After all, I have a grandson and..." He looked at Mom. "Friends."

He smiled at Mom in a way that just...was good. Bone deep good. Like it is exactly what it should be kind of good. Wow. What would she give for that front row seat that Savannah had.

"And I can see why you'd stay. I certainly would if I..." Peyton tried to swallow the words, but that just made the smell of the water more intense. "I don't think I ever noticed that it smelled so much like fish out here."

Mom frowned. "I don't smell anything. It's just...the Keys. Salt and sunshine and clean water."

"You don't smell..." She put her hand on her stomach because it felt like the whole thing was turning upside down.

Oh, good God. She was going to throw up. Like...any second. Like...*now*.

Fisting her hands, she took a deep breath, but that only made it worse. "'Scuze me," she said quickly, pivoting before Mom could sense something was wrong.

She made a beeline for the bathroom, but the door was closed.

"Nick's in there," Savannah said. "You okay?"

"Yeah. Yeah." Her throat was thick and time was short. "Need...something. Upstairs." It was the only other bathroom, so she shot up the stairs that no one had yet used.

She whipped into the bedroom, pushed the door to the en suite, slammed it, and barely made it to the toilet in time. It was a bad one, like when she smelled the salmon at the Academy. This was as bad as when she went to Val's house the other night and he made mahi.

It was *fish*, she thought as she wretched. Fish made her puke. How was that for the greatest irony of life? She might have laughed if she didn't have to heave so bad.

After a few minutes on her knees, her stomach calmed down and she stood on shaky legs, glancing in the mirror to see how utterly bone pale she was. She rinsed her mouth, dabbed her lips with her fingers, and took a steadying breath. There. Fine. Done.

She opened the door and came face to face with Savannah, inches from the door.

"How could you not tell me, Pey-pey?"

Peyton stared at her, the little bit of blood left in her face draining.

"How far along are you?"

Still silent, she just looked in her sister's hazel eyes.

"Does anyone know?" Savannah asked.

She finally swallowed. "Just Val and he..."

"Girls? What's wrong?" Mom's voice came from the stairwell seconds before she arrived.

"Am I missing the tour?" Lovely was a few steps behind. "I gave the baby to Nick so I could..." She reached the bedroom door. "Is everything okay?"

No words would form in Peyton's mouth.

"Peyton," Savannah ground out with insistence.

"Peyton?" Mom asked, worry in her voice.

"Peyton," Lovely cooed, coming closer. "You're just having second thoughts about selling, but you shouldn't—"

"I'm pregnant," she whispered, and all three of them stared in a second of stunned silence.

Suddenly, they erupted with questions, squeals, and screams. And so many group hugs, they smashed her.

As tears flowed and kisses rained on her cheeks, all Peyton could think was that she broke her promise to Val.

And that this might be one of the best moments of her life.

CHAPTER SIXTEEN

BECK

"How did I end up with twelve people when I invited three teenagers for Saturday Game Night?" Savannah mused, looking out at the big deck where most of those twelve were gathered listening to Nick give the rules of "React and Act"—an elaborate version of charades that was apparently all the rage in Hollywood. "Thank goodness Jessie brought all that guacamole."

"For one thing," Beck replied, tearing open a bag of chips, "everyone is in a celebratory mood." She bit her lip and squeezed her hands like a kid on her birthday. "Peyton is pregnant!" she whispered. "And don't ask me why I'm whispering because it's not a secret."

"Not on this side of Baby Foster-Sanchez's gene pool," Savannah mused. "Unless they are breaking the news this weekend."

Beck sighed, remembering her last conversation with Peyton. "They are," Beck said. "Peyton told me Val just rolled his eyes and said he should have bet on the fact that the secret could not be kept for a full twenty-four hours. He agreed that they should break the news to his family so no one is hiding anything. Oh, and they're looking at wedding options, not that they'll have that many if she wants to get married within the next month."

"Go to Vegas and call it a day," Savannah said.

"Are you kidding?" Beck scoffed. "That girl has wanted a wedding since she was born."

"She's wanted a husband and two-point-five kids. Does one day of white lace and wedding cake matter that much?"

"Says the woman who got married on national television before an audience of millions."

She shrugged. "Mom, when you love someone and there's a baby in the mix, all that stuff is just...trappings. The real thing is what kind of man he is, and what kind of father he'll be."

Beck smiled at her. "Look at you, getting so wise and mature."

"Also, if he's good in the sack. So, not *that* mature."

When the group on the patio exploded with a burst of laughter, they turned and looked out to see the three teenagers were peppering Nick with questions about the game he was explaining. Lovely bounced little Dylan on her lap. Jessie and Chuck were trying to pay attention, but Beau was zooming all over the patio like an out-of-control race car.

Heather sat on a bench near the railing, where Kenny perched, a beer in his hand, a smile on his face as he took in the group.

Lastly, there was Oliver, incredibly comfortable leaning

back on a chaise, listening intently and wearing that half smile while he gazed at the son he never knew he had. Every once in a while, Oliver glanced at the French doors like he was waiting for Beck to come out, and that just made her feel so good. She felt her smile grow as she looked at him, a warm sense of anticipation pouring over her.

"The gang's all here except for Josh," Savannah said. "Who is, if rumors are to be believed, on a date."

"Hmmm." Beck gave a go-to response because all she could think of was what she was anticipating with Oliver. Was she ready for…more?

"So, let's serve a tray of ground glass and see who notices."

Could she give herself, body and soul, to him and—

"Um…earth to Rebecca Foster." Savannah's voice and snapping fingers broke through her thoughts, and Beck turned.

"Oh, sorry. What did you say about glass?" She blinked as the rest registered.

Savannah leaned over the counter and narrowed her eyes. "You're doubting this one, too, aren't you? You're going into the Doubt Spiral. The 'I don't know what I'm waiting for but I'm waiting' act because Dad wrecked you."

"No." Beck shook her head, clearing it and looking right at Savannah. "I'm not. Dad did wreck me, but that's not what kept me from falling in love with Josh. I wanted something more magical and…"

"And does Oliver have a magic wand?" She wiggled her brows. "Maybe I shouldn't ask that."

"No, you shouldn't, and I don't know." Beck studied

him again, digging deeper for what was working on her heart.

"Look, Mom, I talk to him a lot," Savannah said. "Every morning he joins me with coffee after Dylan's breakfast." She threw a look out toward the deck. "He's a great guy. Real deal. Exactly like his amazing son. And he's *crazy* about you."

And that feeling was mutual. Except... "Does he talk about his wife?"

"His *late* wife? The one gone for more than two years? Rarely. In passing. I think he's trying to move past the pain and really focus on the here and now." She rolled her eyes. "I'm starting to sound like my hippie grandmother. Who hasn't been herself lately, don't you think?"

Beck sighed, shifting her gaze to Lovely who seemed perfectly happy planting great-grandmother kisses on Dylan's head. "I think she's scared of losing me."

Savannah nodded. "You said that and it makes sense. When you were spending time with Josh, it was like you were with someone who is essentially a son to her. Oliver might be more threatening to her. She does have that lovedar, remember. That lady knows what is what."

"She does," Beck said on a smile. "But did you ever hear her say her lovedar was buzzing for Josh and me?"

"Can't recall, but it certainly got noisy when Nick showed up in my life." She leaned in to whisper, "And she made a joke to me about it when Kenny and Heather came in with the kids before. And I have to agree."

"They're good together, wouldn't you say?" Beck asked.

"Good?" Savannah gave her a *get real* look. "I'd say they're...inevitable."

"What are you two whispering about in here?" Jessie came in through the French doors. "It better not be how lumpy my guac is."

Savannah scooped a chip through the dip and popped it into her mouth. "Your guac is a work of art. Relax."

"It's not my guac I'm tense about." Jessie came over to the counter and slid onto a stool. "I'm not hiding in here, okay? That's my story and I'm sticking to it."

"You hate acting games?" Savannah guessed.

"The night air is giving you a hot flash?" Beck asked. "Because every day that we inch toward insane summer humidity, my flashes are faster and furious-er."

"Who can worry about hot flashes when you have a raving four-year-old?" Jessie replied with a humorless laugh. "In fact, who has both at the same time?"

"You do," Beck said, patting Jessie's hand. "And it's challenging, isn't it?"

"So. I need energy. I need patience. I need time. I need..." She grabbed a chip and hovered over the guacamole. "Comfort food."

"Energy, patience, and time are in short supply for any mother of any age," Beck assured. "Am I right, Sav?"

"Thousand percent. You also need babysitters and nights out with your husband."

"And a discipline plan," Beck added with a look. "'Cause Chuck's awesome and wonderful and perfect, but he hasn't exactly set ground rules."

"Right?" Jessie sighed out the word. "And I feel like the bad guy—and I'm essentially that child's stepparent. Oh, by the way, the meeting with the judge regarding the adoption is apparently the same day as the opening performance of *Mary Poppins*. But we'll be there, don't worry."

"If there is a play," Savannah said dryly. "At the rate Nick is directing, it could be twenty kids sitting in a circle talking about how they *feel* about chimneys." At their shocked looks, she added, "Just kidding. Kinda."

"He'll make it happen," Beck said. "Peyton's baby and you officially as Beau's legal mother?" She pointed to Jessie. "We better start planning the after-play party now."

"What party?" Lovely walked in, holding a fussy Dylan.

"The post-*Poppins*, pregnant Peyton, Momma Jessie party," Savannah said, swooping over. "Is his diaper full?"

But Lovely stood stone still and stared at them, the color in her cheeks draining. "Yes, that's...a lot to celebrate."

"And who knows?" Savannah asked, taking the baby without noticing Lovely's reaction. "Maybe by then Oliver will have bought Peyton's townhouse and we'll be planning yet another wedding."

"Savannah!" Beck exclaimed.

"For Heather and Kenny," she stage-whispered.

"Savannah!" That came from all three of them.

"Oh my gosh, this thing is loaded." She patted Dylan's butt. "I'll take him up and change him. Maybe give him a little nightcap and put him down early. You three..." She flicked her hand in their direction. "Plan the future. It's so bright I have to wear shades!"

She sailed out leaving Jessie and Beck both staring at Lovely, who wasn't smiling at all. In fact, she looked downright miserable.

"Are you okay?" they asked in perfect unison.

"Yes. Of course." She waved her hands at her face. "Just a tad warm out there. No real breeze tonight."

"It really is muggy," Jessie agreed. "But you look like something's bothering you, Lovely."

"You do." Beck came around the counter to her. "Don't listen to Savannah's exaggerations and tales. No one is getting married." She gave her mother a squeeze, certain that was at the root of that low-grade air of sadness that seemed to hang over her ever since Oliver arrived.

"Except Peyton, I hope." Lovely smiled and it might have been a little forced, but she was trying.

"Oh, yes, can't forget that. Are you playing React and Act, Lovely?"

"I..." She let out a sigh. "I was wondering if someone might drive me home," she said. "I'm just feeling every one of my seventy-four years tonight."

Beck's heart shifted. Maybe that was it. Maybe her mother was just getting up there, and she had to respect that.

"Oh, of course. And I mean it, Lovey," she whispered the nickname affectionately. "You're never going to lose me." She added a kiss. "You know that, right?"

Lovely patted Beck's cheek. "I love you, Beckie."

She must have really meant it, or have been bone tired, because Beck could have sworn there were tears in her mother's eyes. Beck made a silent vow not to spend all her time with Oliver this weekend, to be sure Lovely didn't feel left out.

"I love you, too," Beck said with one more kiss. "I'd be lost without you."

Lovely blinked, and this time Beck was sure she saw tears.

"ALL RIGHT, this one is for the game-winning point," Nick announced from his perch where he decided to take on the role of game show host. No surprise, he nailed it, keeping the lively game going amid hysterical laughter, some complaints, minor infighting among the teams, and a whole lot of snacking and really bad acting.

Beck honestly couldn't remember when she'd had so much fun. Her only disappointment was that Jessie and Chuck had driven Lovely home, and decided to take Beau to bed, too, because he'd gone over the edge...or would have if he'd run around that veranda much longer.

But the remaining players had divided into two teams, with "couples" acting out the clues for their teammates. Oliver and Beck had racked up a lot of points for their team, and had tied up the match on their last round.

Nick held a basket out to Kenny, only one folded paper left in the bottom. "Last one, dude."

"We got this," he said to Heather who joined him on the "center stage" in the middle of the veranda. She smiled up at him and they shared a look that Beck—and everyone else—could read plain as day. What was the word Savannah had used? *Inevitable.*

"Go team H and K," Heather said, high fiving him as Kenny opened the paper.

And froze. And stared at it. And then gave Nick a look no one could interpret. Except Nick, who was clearly fighting a smile.

"What?" Nick asked. "It's all that was left in the basket."

"What's it say?" Heather asked, leaning close to Kenny to read the paper.

"We can't do this." Kenny started to ball the paper, but Heather snagged it, smoothing it open and taking a slow, deep breath.

"Sure we can," she said, looking up at him. "It's for the game-winning point and it's pretty easy."

"Easy for you," he murmured, softly, just to her, but everyone heard it.

"Then put us out of our misery," Savannah called out. "Act it out and let Marc and me guess. I want to win this thing."

For a long moment, Kenny and Heather looked at each other, their expressions unreadable, as electricity seemed to crackle in the air.

"Go for the obvious?" he asked.

"If you want to win," she replied.

"Or make a fool of myself," he muttered. But Heather reached out to him.

"Don't worry. I'll say—"

"Hey, hey!" Nick interrupted. "Not a word. Gestures only or you forfeit. And Savannah and Marc have to guess in under five seconds. Ready?"

"As I'll ever be," Kenny said.

After taking a deep breath, Kenny signaled Nick to start the timer. Then he very slowly lowered himself to one knee, and mimed opening a small box.

Unlike every other round of the game, the entire patio went silent. Heather pressed her hand to her mouth and gasped, which was probably against the rules, but who could blame her?

"Whoa," Maddie murmured.

"Yeah, whoa," Ava echoed.

But it was Marc who broke the silence by snapping his fingers and pointing. "I know! You cracked a shellfish and it stinks!"

The laughter rang out...and so did the timer.

"And Beck and Oliver win the game!" Nick called out.

Oliver reached over to give her a celebratory hug, but as she returned it, Beck caught a glimpse of Heather offering her hand to Kenny to guide him to his feet, the two of them looking into each other's eyes with a look that was just...inevitable.

"Oh, you're shivering," Oliver said as he caressed her bare arm. "You have chills."

"I'm just...happy to have won," she said quickly.

"Time for dessert!" Savannah called out as the teams broke up and chatter rose in the party.

"You know what I'd like for dessert?" Oliver asked, his low voice and sexy accent in Beck's ear doing nothing to dispel the chill bumps on her arms. "A walk on the beach with my winning teammate."

"I'd love that."

As some people went inside and others just gathered in groups enjoying the night, Beck and Oliver slipped down the stairs toward the sand. At the bottom, Beck kicked off her flip flops and Oliver did the same, taking her hand as if it were the most natural thing in the world.

Almost like it was *inevitable*.

"I'm not quite sure how we won," he said easily as they walked, the sand white under a big moon hanging over them. "Pretty sure Nick didn't get his acting chops from me."

She laughed. "We did have a few easy charades to act out. Plus, Heather and Kenny stunned their guessers into silence with that proposal."

"What exactly is going on there?" he asked.

Beck smiled and shook her head. "Not sure, but it looks pretty good, don't you think?"

"As perfect as everything else around here," he said with a wry laugh.

She eyed him. "Is that a bad thing?"

"Just an observation. Coconut Key is quite the paradise."

"It is," she agreed on a sigh. "Sometimes I have to pinch myself because everything is just so good here. My life is...I don't know. So full of contentment. I'm surrounded by the people I love, living in a tropical dream, running an awesome business. I wake up every day happy to be alive."

She almost added something about him, but a quick read of his expression stopped her. His handsome features looked drawn at the moment, even a little pained in the moonlight that spilled over his face.

"What are you thinking?" she asked with a tug on his hand.

"Oh, nothing."

She tugged a little harder. "Ollie..." She let her voice rise with a tease, knowing the unwelcome nickname always brought him out when she sensed a wall rising around him.

"Really, it's nothing."

"Not nothing," she said, slowing her step. "I think

you're thinking something, and I want you to share it. Even if it's less than wonderful."

"Why should I bring you down on this gorgeous night?"

She thought about the simple question, then decided to answer honestly. "I don't want a surface relationship with you. I've had one...maybe more than one," she added, thinking of how often she and Dan co-existed but didn't really "live" life together.

"Josh?" he guessed.

"Yes, he and I always chose the 'nice' route, the safe route. And I respect that, and I even know why. I was wounded when I got here and he was a good friend. But this"—she lifted their joined hands—"is starting to feel like more than friendship."

He turned to her. "Very much so. In fact, if I don't kiss you tonight..." He got a millimeter closer. "I may consider myself the loser of the night, despite our game victory."

"Then..." She inched away. "Tell me what you're thinking."

"The price of a kiss, huh? You drive a hard bargain, Rebecca Foster." Smiling, he started walking again, in quiet thought. She kept pace with him and waited for what he'd say next.

"When you said your life was perfect," he started, "it reminded me very much of what mine was like...four years ago."

She knew enough about his life—and his wife—to know what probably changed four years ago. "Was that when Margaret was diagnosed?" she guessed.

He just inhaled, silent for several heartbeats.

"Yes," he finally said. "We'd made what, by all

accounts, was a perfect life together. We never had children, which was a deep disappointment, but we had everything else. A successful business, a loving relationship, a beautiful home, another on the beach. We had our favorite times of the week, our inside jokes, our unwavering strength in good times and bad. Although, to be fair, there weren't many bad times. Until...there was *only* a bad time."

Her heart shifted with the weight of genuine sympathy. "I'm so sorry."

"No, I don't want pity. People dream about a life like I had with Margaret. So, when you say everything is perfect, I feel compelled to warn you...that's when things fall apart."

"Oh." She nodded and sighed. "I don't take anything for granted, believe me."

He stopped again. "That's smart, because nothing—and I do mean nothing—is guaranteed."

"I'll remember that."

A hint of a smile returned to his face. "And since nothing is guaranteed, I'd very much like to kiss you now."

"Even when you're..."

"Grieving my life and my wife?" he finished for her. "Yes, Beck. Especially then."

The words touched her, but she hesitated, suddenly realizing this kiss—and everything they'd share—would be compared to what he had before. A much better marriage than she ever had, that was for sure.

"Beck," he said softly, lifting her chin. "Everyone our age has baggage. We just put it under the bed and carry on."

"Or unpack it together."

He made a face. "I'd rather not."

"Ever?"

He spread his hand over her cheek, a strong, warm sensation that Beck didn't think she'd ever felt before. Had any man ever taken possession of her face like that, and held her like...like she was a treasure?

"Let me do this my way," he said. "You might do it differently, but let me show you my way."

"Okay." Before the word was out, he lowered his head and kissed her. At first, it was barely a feather light touch, but then he added pressure, deepened the contact, and angled his head.

She felt her next breath mingle with his as he wrapped an around her waist and slid his fingers into her hair. Her knees went weak. Her toes curled in the sand. And her mind went absolutely blank as she got kissed like...like never before.

Truth was, she had no idea a kiss could feel like this. Dizzying. Electrifying. Even her fingertips were tingling.

After a moment, he broke the contact and looked into her eyes. "How do you like my way?"

She managed a soft laugh. "It's a good way."

Smiling, he hugged her and kissed her on the head. "I don't want to unpack anything," he whispered. "I'd really rather just open a new suitcase and fill it up with Beck."

"Oh." Had anyone ever said anything so sweet? "Well, here's a little something you can slip into the zipper compartment of the suitcase."

"What's that?"

She looked up at him. "That was the best kiss I ever had."

"Wow. Now that's worth packing." He pulled her closer as they walked arm-in-arm back to the house with Beck still humming from the kiss. And the knowledge that you can't shove a suitcase under the bed and never unpack it. That time would come. It had to.

She just hoped he didn't repack and leave, because something about this man felt...inevitable.

CHAPTER SEVENTEEN

NICK

"Good party, babe." Nick snuggled behind Savannah as she stood at the bathroom sink tapping out her toothbrush.

"Wasn't it fun? I was sorry Lovely left early, and Chuck and Jessie, but I think everyone had a great time." She turned in his arms and looked up at him, every bit as beautiful with her face completely natural and unmade-up. Her light came from the inside, and he loved nothing more than basking in it. "Your father and my mother. Who'da thunk it?"

"They were totally making out on the beach," he said. "Did you see the look in his eyes when they came back up?"

"Too busy watching Rebecca Foster pretend to have a hot flash, which she never mentioned before Oliver arrived. All of a sudden, she's all, 'Oh, wow, it's kind of warm in here!'" She fanned herself, raising her voice an octave.

He cracked up, shaking his head. "I really think he's

going to stay here."

"I do, too. I think he's going to buy Peyton's town house." She closed her eyes and let her head drop back. "I could not be happier for her."

"And I could not be happier..." He dipped down and put his mouth on her creamy bare shoulder. "To finally be alone—"

She straightened suddenly. "What's that noise? Is your phone ringing?"

He frowned and turned his head. "At one in the morning?"

"Better get it before it wakes Dylan." She nudged him toward the door.

As he walked, he threw a look over his shoulder. "We *do* have a nursery now, and I thought he was going to sleep in there. He's almost eight months, Sav."

"Tonight's the night," she promised. "I'll slip him into that crib now. Go, get your phone. I don't know who wants you at this hour, but it's never great."

He picked up the cell from the nightstand to see his former agent's name on the screen. "It's Eliza Whitney," he told Savannah as she walked to the cradle to get the baby. "Only ten in L.A. Mind if I talk to her for a minute?"

"Of course not. She's probably having a rough Saturday night. It's only been a month since her husband passed."

He gave her an appreciative nod and tapped the screen to talk to his agent. Well, former agent, but still a dear friend.

"Hey there," he said warmly. "I don't care if it's the best script that ever came across your desk, I'm not interested."

"Well, no worries there," she said. "I got canned."

He closed his eyes, silent while disgust rocked him. Those sons of bitches fired her a month after her husband died?

"And before you blame yourself, Nick, you should know that without Ben's ties to Canyon Studios, I'm not worth the salary they paid me."

"That's ridiculous," he said, rising to her defense. Her late husband may have been one of the original founders of the popular boutique studio, but Eliza had been a strong agent in her own right. "You're the only fair, caring, sane agent in the business, and they should kiss the ground you walk on."

She gave a familiar laugh. "There's no place for fairness, care, or sanity in L.A., as you discovered. And there was no kissing, but decent severance. I'm fine, just a little...humiliated."

He muttered a curse at the sadness in her voice.

"How can I help?" he asked instantly. "Whatever you need, Eliza. Unless you're going out on your own and want a client. Then I can't help."

Her sigh was deep, long, and painful. "On my own? I've never done anything on my own in my life. And Ben, bless his poor departed soul, was an enabler."

His heart turned over at the agony in her voice. "God, I'm sorry, Eliza."

"Me too," she said sadly. "My daughter has invited me to go see her in Seattle. Begged, actually, but...the last thing she needs is her mother breathing down her neck."

"She took Ben's death hard, I bet."

"Yeah, but she has other issues. Anyway, I honestly didn't call to cry on your shoulder."

"You can, you know."

"Thanks. But I have a question about Florida."

"Please tell me you're moving here."

"No, no. But I'm considering a visit, actually to Sanibel Island. I'm looking at a map and I'm wondering what the drive's like from the Keys to Sanibel Island? I might visit you, too."

Savannah came back into the room with no baby in her arms. "Do you know how far it is from here to Sanibel?" he asked her. "Eliza, Savannah's here."

"Hello, Savannah," Eliza said. Though they'd never met, both women had heard a lot about each other, and Savannah had talked to her at length when they'd called together after Ben died.

"Eliza, how are you?"

"Oh, my gosh, it's one in the morning there," Eliza realized with a choke. "I'm an idiot. Did I wake you two?"

"Not at all," Savannah assured her, sitting on the bed and putting a warm hand on Nick's leg. "We had a little family party here tonight and aren't even in bed. And the drive is probably about six hours through the Keys, up to Miami, and across the state to Sanibel. But there's a ferry from Key West, which is only about twenty-five miles from here. I think it takes under four hours and it's a beautiful cruise up the coast."

"Oh, that might work."

"What's on Sanibel Island?" Nick asked.

"My father, who has passed, lived there," she said. "His widow contacted me."

"I didn't know that," Nick said, thinking of the times they'd talked about their childhood and parents. She had very little to say about her father, except that he was gone a lot when she was growing up, and that her parents were divorced.

"Long story," she said, "but I thought I might combine it with a trip to see you. Not for a while, though. I'm still not quite ready to travel."

"I get that," Nick said, aching with sympathy for her. Eliza and Ben had the happiest marriage in Hollywood, and he hoped to emulate their love and strength with Savannah. "I'd love to see you, Eliza. We were so sorry you missed our wedding."

"No one missed it," she said. "I recorded the episode of *Celebrity Wedding* and I've watched it many times. The interview with your father makes me cry every time."

"He's back here, you know."

"No! Is he enjoying himself?"

Savannah and Nick shared a look, both of them grinning.

"I'd say so," Nick told Eliza, "judging from the look on his face every time Savannah's mother is in the room."

"Oh! Isn't that an unexpected twist?" She chuckled softly.

"We really would love for you to visit," Savannah said. "We have a ton of room."

"Well, I'm sure you two are busy with the baby."

"He's pretty easy," Savannah assured her. "The only one who's busy is Nick with a high school play."

"Excuse me?" Eliza's voice rose with disbelief. "You're in a high school play?"

"Not *in* it," he corrected. "Savannah's niece is in it, and the director had to leave town, so...I stepped in to direct, but..." He groaned and closed his eyes. "If my career wasn't already finished, it would be after this production."

She laughed. "I'd pay good money to see something you directed. What play is it?"

"*Mary Poppins.*"

"Oh! 'Anything can happen if you let it!'" She practically sang the line in a dead-on Cockney accent.

"You've seen the movie," Nick guessed.

"Even better. I was in the play on Broadway."

"What?" Nick croaked the word, sitting up.

"Maybe you forgot that before I married Ben and moved to Los Angeles, I was a hoofer on Broadway in the eighties."

His eyes popped as he looked at Savannah, who mouthed with a smirk, "*Hoofer*?"

"I told you." He poked her stomach, then directed the next question to the phone. "I can't believe you were in *Mary Poppins* on Broadway! What part?"

"I was in the chorus, but I understudied for almost every female role they had. Never got to play, but wow it was fun. What a wonderful experience for you."

"Define wonderful," he said dryly.

"Do you know the choreography?" Savannah asked.

"I'd remember bits of it, I bet. When's the performance? That might be just enough incentive to get me out of this house."

"Eliza." Nick picked up the phone as if he could get closer. "I need your help. I need it so bad. The play is in a couple of weeks, and the dancing is a hot mess. No one knows what they're doing. Please help me. Please. You're free now."

"Oh, Nick, I'd love to. But...I'm just not quite ready to

travel yet." She sighed. "I wish I could help you. If I do make that trip to Sanibel, I'll see you, but, not on such short notice."

"I understand." But, oh, how he needed her. "What about over conference call? A video? FaceTime? Anything where you could watch the dances and help me polish them up?"

"I could do that. I could certainly try."

"Can I set up a video call tomorrow afternoon, when the rehearsal starts? If nothing else, you can talk to the kids and tell them about your experience on Broadway."

"I'd love that. Send me a link and I'll be there." Her voice sounded so much lighter than when they started the call. "Thanks for giving me something else to think about, Nick. I do miss having you out here."

"Then come and see us," he said again. "You need to meet Savannah and Dylan."

He heard her sigh. "Let's talk tomorrow. I'll spend the morning brushing up on *Mary Poppins.* Before you know it, I'll be 'practically perfect in every way'!"

They laughed at her English accent and said goodbye, and immediately Savannah scooched up next to him.

"She's going to help you," she said. "And maybe you can help her."

"I hope so. And now, we're going to help each other." He rolled over and wrapped her in his arms, kissing the world's most kissable mouth.

"Is that what the kids are calling it these days?"

Kissable, and sarcastic. "God, I love you, Savannah Foster Frye."

Her response was sweet and genuine, and without Dylan in the room? Kinda noisy.

CHAPTER EIGHTEEN

LOVELY

From the minute she got the call that Dr. Chang wanted to see her, Lovely knew the news wasn't going to be great. So, once again, she got an Uber—same driver as last time, too—to take her to the office. It was getting...easy.

Easy to manage the fear on her own. Easy to make the appointments, use her phone to get a ride, and find her way to the doctor's office on her own. Easy to smile at the receptionist and flutter through a magazine in the waiting room and greet the same young lady who'd brought her back last time.

Only this time, she went to Dr. Chang's office, not an exam room. So this might be where the easy part stopped.

"Lovely." Dr. Chang stood and stepped around her desk, reaching out to take Lovely's hand. Her personal touch was one of the things Lovely adored about this woman, who was gentle and tender and...had a tight smile in place.

"I have cancer," Lovely whispered, letting the three words slip out because she couldn't keep them in any longer.

"We do not know that," Dr. Chang said, taking a guest chair as she eased Lovely into the other one, then reached for a file on her desk.

"Then why am I here?"

"Because the mammogram report shows a lesion." She opened the file and Lovely stole a glance, expecting to see a black and white scan with some huge red circle over a picture of her breast. But there was only a typed report.

"What's a lesion?" Lovely asked.

The doctor angled her head, thinking for a moment. "The best way to describe it is a suspicious spot. There are a number of things it could be, but to determine that, I'm recommending a biopsy which will tell us if what we see is positive or negative."

Her whole body tightened. "You mean benign or malignant."

"Yes, but we usually say positive or negative now," she said. "I know your sister passed of ovarian cancer, but I don't want you going into a spiral. We'll schedule a biopsy at the Keys Breast Center in Marathon, which is the only one south of Miami that does biopsies."

"Oh, that's far."

"We can get into a closer hospital, but I really like the Center, and I strongly recommend Dr. Oulette for this procedure."

"No, no hospital. That would...no. I can't do that."

"Lovely." She put her hand over Lovely's, her palm warm and reassuring. "The law requires me to honor confidentiality and tell no one about this. As your doctor, I'd never dream of intruding on your privacy. But as your friend, I'm begging you to share this burden with your family."

But how could she? Everyone was so happy right now. How could she throw a bucket of cancer on her darling Beck and sweet Jessie or her deliriously happy granddaughters? All of them were on a cloud these days and Lovely would be the one...

"I'll think about it," she said as the doctor pierced her with a gaze. "I really will."

"I doubt you can get scheduled until early next week, so you have some time to think about it." She added pressure on her hand. "We have not—I repeat *not*—detected cancer. This isn't a death sentence, Lovely."

She closed her eyes and whispered, "But what if it is?"

Dr. Chang shook her head and returned the file to her desk. "You can't go there yet. It's important that you stay positive and strong and optimistic. It will help you get through whatever lies ahead."

Like chemo. Radiation. Long goodbyes and...

She absently stroked the braid that nearly reached her waist. What would happen to her beautiful hair? She'd had it long her whole life, and now it was gray... except for those few months when Ava had dyed it pink.

Oh, Ava. She had to see that child grow up. All of them. She couldn't—

"Lovely."

Dr. Chang's voice broke through the mist in her mind.

"Yes, yes, I'm sorry. I'm just thinking."

"Please share this with your family. They will have love and advice and support. They will understand that a biopsy is quite often the last step because a negative result means you're free and clear."

"But a positive result?" She pointed at the doctor. "Do not sugar coat, please."

She exhaled and nodded. "We'll get you with a good oncologist, who will run tests for proteins and genes. The entire tumor would be removed, and additional tests would tell us if anything has spread, especially to the more vulnerable areas like lungs or lymph nodes. With that information, we'd make an educated and considered decision regarding treatment options, which could include a mastectomy, chemotherapy and radiation."

The words all ran together, like a jumble of oncologist and tumor and lymph nodes and tests and decisions and, oh God... "Mastectomy. Chemotherapy. And—"

"Lovely." Dr. Chang gave her a look of gentle warning. "You're getting ahead of the process. One step at a time, so let me have you stop and talk to my front desk staff. Danielle will handle the referral for you. Then, I want you to go to the person, or people, you are closest to, sit down and calmly tell them what's going on. If you want to have them call me, I will happily have this conversation with anyone you like. Anyone. Who might that be?"

"Beck."

"Your daughter," she said, "who will lovingly hold your hand through every minute."

Lovely nodded, hating the pressure clamping down on her chest. "Okay."

"Good girl." She stood, taking Lovely's hand to help her up. "We will meet after the biopsy results are in. I hope you don't come here alone."

"Okay," she repeated, knowing she sounded dazed.

Well, she was dazed. Sucker-punched and gobsmacked and scared to death. Scared...*of* death.

But somehow she managed to get herself home and before she did anything, Lovely cuddled up with Sugar, Basil, and Pepper and let her precious dogs soothe her into the sweet escape of a nap.

It was late afternoon when Lovely woke, a sense of déjà vu pressing down on her.

Yes, she'd felt this way before. After the accident. After she'd died and gone to heaven and seen her sister, Olivia, who had given Lovely permission to break a promise and tell Beck who her real mother was.

Blinking into the late afternoon sun that streamed into her bedroom, Lovely pushed up, absently rubbing Sugar's head as the little dog panted with a never-ending need for affection.

"Why did she do that?" Lovely whispered to Sugar. "Why did Olivia let me tell Beck the truth?"

She closed her eyes. Up there, in the field of yellow flowers and endless peace, maybe Olivia could see things that Lovely couldn't see down here. Like...the future. Maybe Olivia knew that this dark chapter of Lovely's life lay ahead and that she would need a daughter to get her through whatever happened.

Maybe not telling Beck was selfish, not self*less*, and made a mockery of the mother-daughter bond they'd formed.

Beck would be shattered to not know, and Lovely was wrong to keep the secret.

After all, hadn't they promised each other they would never have another secret between them? Yes, life changed since then. It got better and brighter and bigger. But Lovely couldn't break that promise.

With a clarity she hadn't felt for a long time—certainly not since before that mammogram—Lovely pushed off the bed. She showered, dressed, rebraided her hair, and gathered up the dogs, ready to walk the short distance between her cottage and Coquina House.

Just as she closed the sliding glass doors to the patio, she heard a familiar laugh from down on the beach. Stepping outside, she saw the hammock that hung between two palm trees swaying under the weight of not one, but two bodies.

The sounds of Beck and Oliver's conversation floated up, and from this vantage point, all Lovely could see were two sets of bare feet propped up at the end of the mesh hammock.

Another trill of Beck's lighthearted laughter was carried up to the balcony where Lovely stood, the sound like a sharp warning in her head.

Don't steal her joy. Don't wreck her time with him. Don't—

She swiped the air, like she was knocking the devil away from her. "I have to do this," she murmured, turning to go down the outside steps and walk straight to the beach. "If I wait for a better time, I'll talk myself out of it."

She kicked off her shoes at the bottom and walked barefoot, her maxi dress tickling her ankles, the sand cool on her toes.

"Do I have intruders on the hammock?" she called out as a light warning.

She wanted to tell Beck now, but she didn't want to interrupt an intimate moment.

"Lovely?" Beck's foot slipped out of the side, rolling the mesh netting as she somehow managed to gracefully push up. "I peeked in on you a while ago and you were napping."

Beck brushed her blond hair back, as if a little self-conscious at how messy it was, but her smile was bright and genuine. Behind her, Oliver extricated himself from the hammock, too.

"You've been missing all day," Beck said, taking a step closer. "Are you okay?"

No, my darling, I am not.

But Lovely swallowed the words, just smiling and nodding hello to Oliver.

"I thought you were coming over for lunch," Beck said as Oliver moved next to her, suddenly seeming very tall and protective. "Remember?"

"I..." Oh, God. She *had* to do this. "I need to talk to you, sweet girl."

"Lovely, what's wrong?" Beck reached for her.

"We better talk alone."

Beck looked confused, but Oliver immediately held up both hands. "Please, ladies. I'll head back to the B&B. Do you need anything, Lovely?" he asked, looking at her with the same concern. "Can I get you something while I'm there? Scones and tea? We've left them out for the guests."

She smiled at him, struck, as always, at how much like Nick he was. Or, the other way around, she guessed.

"I'm fine." Well, that was a lie. "But Beckie and I need

to…" She glanced up at her cottage. "Sit with me for a bit, please?"

"Of course, of course." She turned and put a hand on Oliver's arm. "We'll talk later."

"I'll handle the guests and afternoon tea," he assured her. "You stay with Lovely."

Lovely watched him walk away, taking in how strong and masculine he was. Beck would need that kind of man to lean on in the coming months, so Lovely was deeply grateful he'd come to Coconut Key.

"What's wrong?" Beck put both arms around Lovely and pulled her in. "You do not look happy."

She turned and put a hand on Beck's face. "But you do."

"I am," she whispered, the simple, sweet confession just making this so much harder.

"Beckie. I'm afraid I have some news that could put a damper on that happiness, and you cannot imagine how much I don't want to do that."

Color drained from Beck's cheeks. "What?"

She took a deep breath, closed her eyes, and the words all came tumbling out.

CHAPTER NINETEEN

BECK

With each passing hour, the news hurt a little less. At first, Beck had stared at Lovely and processed the words and hadn't really been able to breathe. She said all the right things, managed to hold back tears, and fought the feeling of déjà vu when she relived Olivia's battle with ovarian cancer. Those years had been brutal, and she wasn't nearly that close to the woman she'd thought was her mother.

With Lovely? The woman she now knew was her mother, best friend, business partner, and soul sister?

She almost couldn't bear to think about the possibility of cancer.

But then they got Jessie over there, and Savannah, who brought Dylan and called Ava. Heather received Jessie's text and before long, they all gathered in a literal circle, and even had Peyton and Callie on a FaceTime call for a while.

Through all the pep talks, and positive anecdotes, and constant reassurances that this could still be a negative result, the group of women proved that family was blood and bond. And not one of them would let Lovely Ames go through another challenge in life without their undying support and love.

As the daylight slipped away, Ava helped Savannah clean up from the sandwiches Heather brought for all of them. Dylan slept in Beck's arms while she sat next to Lovely, quiet for a bit, enjoying the first breezy notes of what promised to be a cooler evening.

"Beckie!" Lovely said suddenly as if she'd just realized something. "You left Coquina House in Oliver's hands?"

"The Adamsons checked out this morning, and we only have two couples currently. There were snacks and drinks ready, and the rooms were clean. I'm sure he's handled any questions they have."

"Did you tell him?" Lovely asked, biting her lower lip. "You know his wife..." She couldn't even finish the sentence, which would end with...*died of breast cancer.*

"I did, I texted him," Beck said. "Josh and Nick know, too, but we all just thought for today, it should just be us girls propping you up."

"I shouldn't need propping." Lovely let her eye lids drift closed. "But, oh my stars, am I glad I have it."

"I can't believe you ever considered going through this alone. That you went for a mammogram without me!" Beck shook her head and let out a sigh. "I should have known down in my soul that something was wrong with you."

"I should have told you," Lovely admitted.

Jessie came out on the patio and put her hands on Lovely's shoulders.

"We're all kind of mad at you for that, you know." But

her voice didn't sound mad, only as tender as the kiss she planted on her head. "However, all is forgiven, and I hope you expect to take your entourage to the next appointment in Marathon. We'll have to bring extra chairs to the waiting room."

Lovely gave a soft laugh, then leaned her head back to look up at Jessie. "You've been through hell with me already, sweet girl."

Jessie patted her shoulder and came around to take a seat at the table, the waning light behind her. "Nothing is hell with you, but this little bump in our road is going to be much, much easier. For one thing, it still could be nothing."

"Or it could be...something." Lovely looked from one to the other, her eyes filling. "I'm not ready to go."

"Lovely," they said in unison.

"I want to see him grow up." She reached over and touched Dylan's smooth head. "And Ava go to college."

"You will." Ava stepped out to the patio, dish towel in hand. "I was hoping you'd help me write a killer essay when I put my applications in next fall."

"And Peyton's going to want you to see every minute of her baby's life," Beck added.

"Don't forget Beau," Jessie added. "You'll want to be here for the day he finally discovers there is such a thing as an inside voice."

"And Marc will play varsity baseball for sure." Heather joined them, along with Savannah, who pointed at Lovely and came closer.

"You, Miss Lovely Ames," Savannah said, "are not going anywhere at any time. Period. End of discussion, end of list of wonderful things, end of this nonsense.

There's nothing wrong with you." Her voice wavered but she kept her chin up and her eyes focused on her grandmother.

With her heart cracking in her chest, Beck reached over and took her daughter's hand. "Savannah has spoken," she said, trying to lighten the mood. "So shall it be."

"Damn straight, Mom," Savannah added.

Lovely smiled, her green eyes filled for what had to be the twentieth time since they'd all arrived. "Well, then, I guess I have to hold you all to this. And more. How about another baby, Savannah?"

"Absolutely," she said without a second's hesitation. "We're already talking about it."

"Whoa." Lovely leaned back and laughed, looking at Beck, who shrugged as if to say that was news to her, but, of course, it wasn't.

"And you," Lovely continued, reaching out to touch Jessie's hand. "Teach the child what an inside voice is and if he doesn't use it, teach him what time out is. And get him off sugar!"

Jessie's jaw dropped a little, then she sighed. "You're so right, Lovely. I needed to hear that. I've got to be a little more assertive with him, and remember he's my son now, too."

"Amen. And you." She turned to Ava.

"Me?"

"You will write your own college essay, thank you very much. You can use my life as your subject though."

"But not your death," Ava shot back. "Because I'm with Savannah. You aren't going *anywhere.*"

Lovely conceded that with a tip of her head. "Who

have I missed?" she asked with a sly smile, shifting her gaze to Heather, who'd been quiet as they'd discussed cancer, and then shared some painful insider's knowledge about her late husband's experience.

"Uh oh," Heather joked, her smile firmly back in place. "I already moved here, Lovely, what more can I do?"

"Don't be a fool, child."

Heather—all of them, actually—blinked at her.

"You can mourn for too long, you know. You can wear blinders of grief and miss true happiness when it's standing right in front of you."

"Holding a tool belt and a Bible," Savannah muttered under her breath, cracking them all up except Heather, who just stared at her.

"Lovely," she whispered, "I'm not..." She glanced at Ava, who held up both hands as if to say she wasn't going to help her out.

"I'm with Lovely on this one, Heather," Ava said. "The man's a goner, sorry."

They all kind of laughed and looked at each other, not sure what to make of that, or the new Lovely who seemed to emerge from a usually docile cocoon. And she wasn't done, not based on the way her attention zeroed in on Beck.

"Oh, dear," Beck whispered. "What am I supposed to do?"

"You're supposed to love again, plain and simple." Lovely leaned forward. "Do you believe me now that it wasn't you and Oliver that had me down these past weeks?"

Beck nodded.

"Then, what are you doing here, sweet girl? He's waiting for you. Get on back to Coquina House, have a drink and a long talk. Maybe break your endless spell of abstinence and have some fun with that gorgeous man!"

The outburst at that was loud enough to be heard on the beach, with Beck choking, Savannah hooting, and the others laughing—except for Ava who put her hands over her ears and exclaimed, "I did not hear that!"

But when it died down, Beck leaned closer to her mother. "I may or I may not, but I will say this. I love you so much, Lovely Ames. The day I found out you are my mother was the best day of my life." She fought tears and managed not to say the rest of what she was thinking.

I have not had enough time with you, dear sweet mother of mine.

So they all hugged again and laughed and teased the heck out of Beck when she did slip away, but only after Jessie said she wanted to stay with Lovely tonight. They all agreed that until that biopsy result was in, Lovely wouldn't spend a single night alone.

But tonight, her mother was right. Beck needed to go home…to Oliver. Because she was more than ready to love again, in every possible way.

BECK HADN'T EXPECTED both couples who were her guests to be out on the veranda, laughing and talking as if they were on a double date.

"We spotted each other in Mallory Square watching the sunset in Key West," one of the women, Jennifer, told her. "I said, 'Aren't you staying in the same B&B we are?'

and wham, we had dinner and have been hanging out ever since."

"Wonderful!" Beck said. "And did Oliver get you drinks and dessert?"

Her guests shared a look.

"We haven't seen anyone else," one said.

"Oh, I'm so sorry. You got coffee, though? And wine?" She gestured toward their drinks, which were obviously from her kitchen.

"We're good, Beck," Jennifer said. "Half the fun of staying in a B&B is making yourself at home, which we did. Relax, we're all set for tonight."

"Thank you, but I'll be here if you need anything." She tamped down a little disappointment that Oliver hadn't helped, since he knew that she wanted to run the kind of B&B that offered much more than "self-service" in the kitchen. But maybe he never even heard the guests come in. Everyone who stayed here had their own entry code for the front door lock, so that was possible.

Still, it didn't seem likely.

She'd texted him hours ago about Lovely and he'd answered with one simple line that she didn't even remember. As she walked through the dimly lit kitchen, she checked her phone and tapped his texts. Yes, very simple.

So sorry to hear. Hugs to her.

She'd texted again, letting him know she'd be back later. Did he think that was weird? That she was "checking in" with him? He said he'd take care of guests, so...

She headed up to the Coconut Room where he was staying, tapping lightly on the closed door.

"Oliver?" she called. "Are you in there?"

At first, she heard nothing, then some movement. Shuffling. Silence. Her whole body tensed as she knocked again.

After a moment, she heard his footsteps coming to the door and watched the knob turn. When he opened it, she sucked in a breath to see his ravaged expression and red-rimmed eyes.

"What's wrong?" she asked, instantly reaching for him.

He inched back, avoiding her hug. "Beck," he rasped. "I'm struggling."

"I see that." She came into the room and closed the door behind her, searching his face and seeing nothing of the easy-going Australian man who'd stolen her heart. This looked like a man...grieving.

"Is it...Lovely?" she guessed.

He gave her a pained look and sighed, gesturing for her to come all the way into the room, which was when she saw the open suitcase on his bed.

"You're leaving?" she practically croaked the words as she stared at the bag.

"No. Yes. I don't know." He stabbed his fingers through his hair and pulled it back, the gesture so familiar now that it did something to Beck's heart. With a soft groan, he walked toward the open sliding doors and stepped out to the small balcony that overlooked the water.

It was too dark to see much now, but there was enough moonlight for her to see a glass on the table, next to the bottle of sherry she supplied in every room.

"Why are you drinking alone?" she asked softly, following him out there.

"I haven't had much." He leaned against the railing, looking out at the darkness. "I don't think I can be here for you...for this," he finally said.

"For my mother? We don't have a diagnosis yet, Oliver. She has to have a biopsy, then—"

He held up his hand to stop her. "I know every step, from the first spot on a scan to the last...day. I know what to expect, how to deal with it, what to take for the chemo vomiting, how badly the radiation burns..." He finally turned to face her, his eyes full. "I've been reliving it since I got your text and..." He tried to swallow and failed. "And I don't think I'm strong enough to go through it with you."

"Oliver." She closed the space between them, getting her arms around him, relieved that he let her hug him this time. "We're not there yet, and if we are..." She leaned back to look into his eyes.

"If you get there, you'll need someone strong, Beck."

She squeezed his muscular back, feeling the sturdiness of him. "You're strong."

"I'm not sure," he murmured, pressing his lips against her hair as he pulled her against his chest, which felt way past strong, even with his heart beating as hard as it was. "I want to be. I want to be that man you need, that solid rock, that soft place, that unflappable source of peace and hope that, trust me, you *will* need."

She sighed into him, not wanting to need any of that, but if she did, she'd want it to be him.

"Just thinking about it has wrecked me," he admitted. "I've fallen back a few years, dropped headlong into mourning, and now I feel like I'm somehow not honoring my wife by being here."

She eased back and looked up into his eyes. "Are you sure you've fully grieved her death?"

"I thought I had, but tonight? I feel like it happened yesterday and I'm raw and desperate and so not what I want to be for you." He stroked her cheek with one hand. "You make me want to be a man, Beck."

She felt a frown pull. "You are a man, Oliver."

"*The* man. The only man. The right man." He lifted her chin toward him. "Not some simpering, sad sack of…widower."

She gave him a soft smile. "You're not simpering or sad, my darling. But I have felt for a while that you still have some…issues. Some grieving. Some broken bits to put back together."

"I guess I do," he confessed, "or I wouldn't have bawled like a baby and downed a glass of your good sherry to numb the pain."

"Did it work?"

"No. But I didn't want to face your guests afterwards. Am I fired as your stand-in?"

She smiled. "On probation. Get rid of that suitcase and I'll give you another chance."

He closed his eyes and lowered his face, kissing her with so much tenderness, her heart folded in half. She returned the kiss, lost for a moment, then dragged her hands over his nicely carved arms to wrap around his neck.

His heart was still pounding, and he let out a moan from deep in his chest, a mix of desire and pain and…sorrow.

Very slowly, she eased back.

She might be more than ready for the next step...but not when there was sorrow in the air. When she finally dove into the deep end of that ocean, all she wanted to feel was joy.

They looked at each other for a long, long time, and she could easily see that he was thinking the same thing.

"I'd love it," he whispered. "But..."

"We might regret it," she finished.

"It would feel great, Beck, but it's not fair to ask you to put me back together."

"I can talk," she said. "I can stay with you all night and talk. You can tell me everything. About the loss. About her. About your grief." She squeezed him a little tighter. "I'm here for you."

His eyes lit, but then shuttered. "No. Not...yet."

"You're not ready for that?"

"You're not ready for it," he countered. "Your mother has a potentially life-threatening situation. You don't need to hold me in your arms and hear all about one with a sad ending, even though it is just about the nicest offer anyone has ever made."

"Then we'll talk tomorrow."

He inched back, slowly shaking his head. "I'm going to use that suitcase, Beck."

She felt some blood drain from her head. "You're leaving?"

"I might spend a night or two at The Haven. Maybe. Or drive around and see some of Florida. Or the whole country. I can't..."

"You can't stay here if Lovely's sick," she said. "It's too hard for you."

"That's not it."

Wasn't it? She believed it was and she wanted to understand that. It had to hurt just to hear the words *breast cancer* again.

"I just need some breathing space," he said. "Please, I want you to know that—"

She put her fingertips on his lips, not sure she wanted to hear the rest. "I get it," she said. "You need space. I've suspected this from the very beginning."

He didn't say anything, but held her gaze as she eased out of his arms.

"It's fine," she said. "I am going to be consumed with Lovely and..." A sob formed in her throat but she managed to fight it off. "This is better."

He looked a little confused by that, but let go of her so she could step back. "Do your work," she whispered. "You can't love anyone until you do."

He nodded slowly, and she turned, stepping out into the hall and closing the door behind her.

On fairly unsteady legs, she made it down the stairs, and checked on her guests who'd all apparently gone to their rooms. In silence and without turning on any lights, Beck washed their glasses, cleaned the kitchen, and straightened the furniture on the veranda.

While she was out there, she heard footsteps outside, then saw the lights of Oliver's rental car as he turned the ignition on and drove off, the shells of Coquina Court crunching under his tires, breaking, just like her heart.

CHAPTER TWENTY

PEYTON

"Hey." Val stood in the doorway of Peyton's apartment, his dark eyes full of concern and sympathy. "I'm sorry it took me so long to get here. I had…a call."

She caught the little hesitation at the explanation; probably because he truly felt bad that work took over at a time like this.

"It's fine," she said, reaching to take the hug he offered, wishing it took away the ache in her heart. But nothing short of getting in her car and driving to Coconut Key could do that.

"How are you?" He added a squeeze and inched back to look at her. "How is Lovely?"

"Remarkably fine, surrounded by the women who love her." Her heart hitched at the thought of not being in that circle of support, but Peyton wanted to stay in Miami until Val came over so she could talk to him in person. And then…well, she had no choice.

She was going to Coconut Key. Tonight.

"Callie and I talked to her for a while," she added as she drew him into the living room, where Callie sat surrounded by books that might be open but hadn't been studied.

"Hey, Val." She lifted a hand.

"Hey, Cal," he lobbed back, exchanging their standard greeting since Peyton had moved here and Val became their most frequent visitor. "You doin' okay, kid?" he asked.

She shrugged. "I've spent the last few hours doing research on this."

"Shocker, huh?" Peyton joked as she went to the kitchen to get Val's favorite beer and her iced tea. "Callie did the academic stuff."

"Someone has to," Callie said defensively. "And the odds are pretty good for Lovely. The vast majority of these biopsies are negative."

"But some aren't," Val said softly, speaking with the heavy tone of a man who knew more about cancer than Callie could get from searches on the internet.

"Lovely's very strong," Peyton said, coming back with the drinks. "She's already cheated death once and cannot stop talking about all she has to live for. Attitude is everything, right?"

Val just looked at his beer bottle, quiet.

"I couldn't find a lot of studies on, you know, attitude," Callie said, leaning forward and closing two textbooks, then putting them in her backpack. "But Lovely's is good."

"You don't have to move your work, Cal," Peyton said. "We can go in my room and talk if you need to study."

"I'm going to the library," she said. "I want to power

through a paper so I can get down to Coconut Key, too, as soon as possible."

Val looked up. "Too? Are you leaving?"

"I have to," Peyton said, knowing she wouldn't have to defend that decision to Val, but that didn't stop him from looking disappointed and worried.

"For how long?" he asked.

"Hold that discussion, you two." Callie stood and scooped up her backpack. "And I'll hit the library." She added a sad smile to Peyton, leaning over to give her a kiss. "I'll be there this weekend and stay as long as I can."

Peyton patted Callie's hand on her shoulder and added a squeeze. "Love you, baby sis."

"Love you, too. Drive safe. It's dark out there." She blew a kiss to Val. "Stay good, Val."

As she walked out the door and latched it behind her, Val turned, looking a little...stricken.

"You're leaving tonight?"

She nodded.

"Why not wait until tomorrow? Let me stay with you." He took her hand and threaded their fingers. "I'm worried about her, too, you know. Not like you are, but..."

"I know, honey." She lifted their joined hands and kissed his knuckles. "But I have to see my mom. I have to be there for her. I just got a text from her and she sounded...wrecked."

"Yeah, I get it." He heaved a sigh. "Damn, I wish I could go with you."

"Can you come down this weekend? You can stay in The Haven guest house with me."

He didn't answer for a long time, and for the first time

since he got there, Peyton started to get the sense that something wasn't quite right.

"I can't do that, Pey," he said, tugging at the collar of the dress shirt, even though he'd loosened the tie sometime on the way over here. "I have to...work."

Why did that not sound quite right? "But you got the Onaway account," she said, "and they love you. They told your boss you were the reason the firm nailed the business."

He nodded, but still had a somewhat ravaged look in his eyes.

"Val." She took his other hand. "What's wrong? Is it Lovely? Is it—"

"I have to tell you something," he said, his voice rough. "It's...not easy."

Oh, God. Could she take more bad news today? "What is it?"

He dropped back and closed his eyes. "Onaway."

"Yes?"

"They more than like me, Pey. They want to hire me. That was the call I've been on. They want me to fly up to Boston tomorrow and meet a ton of people and spend a few weeks learning the business, and looking around at real estate and—"

"Real estate?" She could barely form the word in her mouth. "To *move* there?"

He swallowed. "Maybe."

She really tried to react but for a moment, all she could do was catch her breath and press her hands to her chest. "You would move to Boston?"

"Well, we would. I'm not going without you. Would

you come up, too, and look around? We could maybe see what the housing market is like and—"

"In *Massachusetts*?" Was he serious? "I don't want to go as far north as Miami, Val. And you want me to move to Boston?"

"Hang on, hang on," he said, taking her hands again. "This is a huge opportunity, Pey. It wouldn't be forever, but a couple of years and—"

"The years when the baby is born and learns to walk and becomes a toddler and..." She bit her lip, determined not to cry. "I thought you had to be in Miami, near your family. I thought that's why you won't consider living in the Keys. And I was ready and willing to do that, but..."

"I love living near my family, but I'm in Miami for the job. A job you know I couldn't get in the Keys, or I would have. But this job? Look, I know it's in Massachusetts, but..." His voice trailed off as he searched her face. "Never mind. I'll turn it down."

"And resent me for the rest of your life?"

"I could never resent you," he said. "But this opportunity isn't just about money, although it's huge. I'd be in management, reporting directly to the CFO. It's an amazing next step in my career."

"But I thought you loved Miami, and your firm." Because, compared to Boston, Miami was a dream.

"I do love Miami, and I loved the Keys. I might love Boston, too. I know I'd love this job, which I swear, I'd only do for a few years."

A few years. Could she live in Boston for a few years? On a long exhale, she let her eyes close. "I have to think about it. More importantly, I have to think about Lovely. I can't quite handle this right now."

"I understand. I'll be gone for a week or so, unless you come up with me."

"I can't leave now," she said, standing up slowly and rubbing her arms as the magnitude of it all hit her. "I won't leave my mother or Lovely, not until that biopsy is done and we know what's happening next."

He stood and reached for her. "Peyton, I'm a man who has to do what's right for all the people I love. I studied for a long time and, before I went to the Keys, I worked hard for this opportunity. It's not one that comes along frequently and…" He sighed. "It certainly isn't a job I'd find in the Keys."

She nodded, trying to understand. Trying like hell. But if he went to Massachusetts, then she had to go, right? They had a baby on the way, and she loved him. "I just need to think it through. Is it a done deal?"

"Not by a long shot. I have to accept their terms and they have to accept mine."

But who was accepting Peyton's terms? And their baby's? She stepped back and tamped down the argument. It wasn't her style to fight, and she didn't want to start now.

"Pey, I'm so worried about you," he said, genuine concern in his voice. "And about Lovely."

"I just have to be there for them," she said. "This week and next. And, I'm not going to lie, if this is bad news? If Lovely is facing months of treatments and appointments, I can't…"

"Go to Boston?" he guessed.

"Or stay in Miami."

He flinched at the words. "Peyton, we can't live apart. I love you, and we're having a baby."

"I know, I know," she said. "But we're not married yet, and the baby is still the size of a cashew, and I'm needed more there than I am here. So, brace yourself. If the news is bad..."

"You're taking your townhouse off the market and moving in."

"That's a little extreme," she replied. "I could leave it up for sale and live with Savannah in the guest house. And then we'll figure it out from there."

"I don't want to lose you," he whispered.

"Then maybe you ought to reconsider Boston."

He sucked in a soft breath. "Is that an ultimatum?"

Oh, God. Was it? And look how that turned out last time. "Val, I don't know. I don't know anything now. I just can't—"

He interrupted her by pulling her close, stopping her with a kiss that took her breath away.

When it ended, she could barely open her eyes. But as she did, she got dizzy for a completely different reason.

He had tears in his eyes.

"I can't stand this," he said on a ragged whisper. "I'm not giving you the life you want."

But if he did, he wouldn't get the life he wanted. So what was fair?

All she could do was sigh. "Can you help me get my bags in the car?" she asked. "I'm not supposed to lift anything heavy."

"Of course."

He did and they kissed again before she drove off.

But as she pulled onto the highway and saw the lights of Miami in her rear-view mirror, she knew that something major and monumental had just changed in her life.

IT WAS DARN near three in the morning when Peyton's car rolled past the sign that welcomed visitors to Coconut Key. Her eyes were burning, her heart was heavy, and all she wanted to do was curl up and sleep. It was tempting to slip into the guest house at The Haven, wake no one, and crash. But something in her gut told her to go to Coquina House. Something sent her to the one person she knew needed her.

Peyton would have let Oliver do the honors of comforting Mom, but that last text had really thrown her. She couldn't reply while driving, but she could read the message, which she'd missed when it first came in.

Oliver's gone. Can't wait to see you.

Gone? Gone where? Now? Why? Since it was well past one by the time she saw that text, Peyton didn't call. But she hit that accelerator and zoomed from mile marker to mile marker until she reached Coquina Court.

It looked dark and quiet, but when Peyton parked, she slipped around the side and peered up to her mom's bedroom window on the first floor of the raised beach house. Was that a light? Maybe.

Did it matter? She was going in.

Using the code set for her, she unlocked the front door and slipped in without making a sound. Coquina House smelled like scones and salt air and family love.

Yes, Peyton had had a wonderful childhood in Alpharetta. Her mother had made a beautiful home for three daughters and a husband, and it had always been a pleasure just to walk in the door and be comforted by the warmth of it.

But something was so much better in this home. Maybe it was because a wholly different Beck Foster had created it—a woman determined to put a broken life back together again. She infused everything with that special something that made Mom extraordinary. The only other person Peyton had ever met who was anything like that was Lovely.

God, she hoped to be like them. To make a home and family that just oozed with joy and comfort.

Holding that thought, she slipped around the staircase to the tiny vestibule opening that led to Beck's owner's suite. She tapped lightly and waited.

"Momma?" she whispered, her mouth near the door jamb. "I'm here for you."

"Peyton? Oh, honey, come in."

She inched the door open to see Mom in the middle of the bed, the only light from her phone. But that was enough to see she'd been crying. Hard.

On a moan that came from her soul, Peyton practically flew across the room to her. "It's going to be okay, Mom. Lovely's going to be okay."

She put the phone down, reaching out her arms to take Peyton's hug. "I know. I mean, I have to believe that, no matter what the diagnosis."

"What did you mean when you said Oliver's gone?" She smoothed her mother's hair back, so not used to seeing this always-together woman look quite this messy.

"I mean he's gone. He...left. I don't know where he went."

She settled on the side of the bed, frowning, feeling a little like she was having déjà vu. Another man taking off?

"Like...forever? Or a trip? Or staying with Nick and Savannah?"

"I don't know," she repeated. "But the possibility of facing everything involved with breast cancer again was too much for him. He was very upset about it after I came back from Lovely's. He said he needed time and space and...I don't know." Her face crumpled with a sob. "But I feel incredibly abandoned."

"Oh, Mom!" Peyton folded her into another hug, her own tears threatening. "You're not abandoned. I'm here to stay. In fact, tonight I'm sleeping right here with you. And I'm not leaving again. Not until we're through this, whatever this may be."

"You can't do that to Val."

Couldn't she?

She popped off the bed and went to get her overnight bag in the hall. "I can and I did," she announced as she brought it in and placed it on a chair, eyeing her mother and making a very quick decision not to deliver any more bad news to her tonight. Boston could wait until the light of day. "This bag is small, but the other two in the car means I can stay as long as I have to. Or," she added with a look, "*want* to. And I want to."

"Don't pick up heavy things," her mother said, sitting up.

"This is light. And Val carried the other two for me." She unzipped and pulled out clean pajamas and underwear, plus her cosmetic bag, carrying it past the bed into the en suite bathroom.

"How does he feel about you coming here?" her mother asked.

At the bathroom door, Peyton paused, tempted to unload but sensing this was not the time. "He understands," she said, but the words didn't feel genuine.

"Any news on the Culinary Academy? I thought you said you'd know by today."

"Holy cow," she whispered. "I forgot to tell him."

"Forgot what?"

"I got in." And with Lovely, and then Boston, she'd totally forgotten that.

"What?" Mom popped all the way up. "Way to bury the big news."

Peyton shrugged, realizing that maybe it wasn't big at all. "All focus is on Lovely," she said. "That's all that matters right now. And I'm not leaving until she or you are through this. And classes don't start until the fall, anyway. So I have nothing to do for the next few months but help with Lovely."

Except, you know, to buy a house and move to Boston. She cringed and stepped into the bathroom.

"And *grow a baby,"* Mom said with a dry laugh.

"Which has been pretty easy so far, as long as I don't meet up with a wayward fish."

She came out in her jammies, wiping off mascara with a cosmetic pad, to find Mom sitting straight up, staring at the bathroom door, two rivers of tears pouring down her cheeks.

"You're crying again."

"I'm just...emotional. This is all so much. Too much. And I love you."

Definitely a good call not to mention Boston until

tomorrow. "I love you, too." She hugged her, then slipped back into the bathroom for some extra tissues she suspected they might need, bringing them back to the bed. "Move over, snuggle bun."

"Oh, I used to say that to you girls when you were little and needed me to sleep with you." Mom's voice cracked. "I loved being a mother."

Peyton smiled and scooted down, finding her mother's hand and holding it tight. "You were—and are—the best mother in the world. I want to be just like you."

"You'll be better."

For a few moments, they lay in the dark, side by side.

"You remember the first night we got here, Pey?" Mom whispered.

"Yeah. We had dinner with Jessie and Josh and wandered all over this house, which was in fairly sorry shape back then."

"It was just you and me," she said. "Running away from our way-less-than-perfect lives."

"We weren't running...yeah. We were." She laughed. "Dad and Greg sure let us down."

"But we never let each other down." Mom squeezed her hand. "If it weren't for you, I'd have never come here. I'd have never known Lovely was my mother. I'd have never experienced life on Coconut Key, which is..."

"The best life," Peyton finished, hating that sadness pressed on her chest when she said the words. She wanted to live here so much. So, so much.

She felt her mother turn as the sheets rustled. "I can't believe he just left," she whispered. "I honestly was ready to..." Her voice drifted off. "Anyway, I'm sure glad I didn't."

"Maybe he'll be back, Mom."

"Maybe. But I can't help feeling a little like I did the night Dad told me he wanted a divorce. I know it's not the same in the scheme of things, but I still feel...abandoned."

"You're not," Peyton assured her. "You have your family."

"But what if Lovely..." Her voice cracked with a sob.

"Shhh. Don't." Peyton put her arm around her mother and patted her back, drifting back to her childhood when the roles were reversed. She rubbed her back, like Mom used to do for her, and stayed very still. "Everything will look better in the morning," she said, echoing a lesson she'd learned as a kid.

It must have worked because after a little bit, Mom fell asleep.

And Peyton placed her other hand on her stomach, imagining her nugget, suddenly confident that she did have the skills to be a good mother. They'd been modeled for her from day one. And that gave her all the peace she needed to sleep.

CHAPTER TWENTY-ONE

KENNY

"I'm not gonna lie, Dad. There are parts of that play that are just this side of a dumpster fire."

Kenny looked up from his plate, pulling his brain back to the present instead of the fog it had been in since baseball practice. Before...well, he'd been in the fog all day. Ever since he heard about Lovely's biopsy, so, a few days.

"I thought Nick's agent, Eliza, was on the job." He got up and carried his not-quite-empty plate to the sink.

"She's on the computer screen, for whatever that's worth." Ava sighed. "She's awesome, too. Has great ideas, is funny, and knows the play inside and out, but it's really hard to choreograph over Zoom, you know? And our first performance is in, like, ten days!"

"I'm sure it'll be fine." He stared at the dirty pan in front of him but could barely find the brain power to clean it, he was so distracted.

"Can you believe that, Dad?"

He frowned and tried to replay what she'd said, but he hadn't heard a word. "Believe what, A?"

"What is wrong with you?" She came over from the table, crossing her arms and scrutinizing his face. "You've been a million miles away since you got back from baseball practice. Is Marc messing up? The coach being a jerk again?"

He didn't answer right away, sensing that she had no idea what was bothering him, and that was probably a good thing. Still, he needed to talk to her, needed to prepare her. "I'm worried about Lovely," he admitted.

"Oh." Her narrow shoulders sank with a sigh. "I know. But this isn't for sure cancer. Or is it? Are you adults not telling me everything?"

"You know everything," he assured her. "But she's an older woman, and she's been through a lot, and..." He shook his head and gave a sad smile. "I'm not entirely sure how this happened, but she's family. And I'm worried."

"Dad." She closed the space between them and wrapped her arms around him, the gesture almost putting him over the edge it was so sweet and natural. "Don't worry."

"Do you remember when you got here, you wouldn't hug anyone. 'I'm not a hugger' you used to say."

"Well, I'm a hugger now," she replied flippantly, sounding, as she so often did, like Savannah. "And you need hugging. Don't worry."

"That's easy for you to say, honey, because you don't know how many people *do* die of cancer."

She inched back. "Mom used to say something about

worry. It was—shocking no one— from the Bible. Do you remember it?"

He thought for a moment, trying to catch Elise's voice in his head, as she'd quote one of the hundreds of verses she'd memorized in her far-too-short life. "I'll go with 'Cast your anxiety on Him because He cares'?"

"No, it was the one about birds and flowers. How birds always have food and flowers have clothes, and they never worry about either of those things. And then something about how worrying doesn't make life longer but if you look out for His kingdom, God handles it all." She lifted her brows. "I know, not exact, but does that ring any Bible bells?"

"Some."

"What's the real quote?" she asked, looking genuinely interested.

"Umm...seek first the kingdom of God, I think." He frowned, digging into ancient memory banks that were, for the most part, locked. "And... 'Do not worry about tomorrow, for tomorrow will worry about itself.'"

"Yes!" She snapped her fingers and pointed at him. "'Each day has enough trouble of its own.' Can't you just hear Mom saying that?"

Sadly, he couldn't. There were days when, without the help of an old video, he had trouble conjuring up the sound of Elise's voice.

"Dad, you know what you should do? What Mom would do in this situation?"

"She'd pray," he said without giving it any thought.

"For Lovely? She'd go straight to church because she'd say, 'Jesus will know how serious I am if I go to His house.'" She smiled and gave a little whimper. "Mom was something, wasn't she? That faith was..."

"Strong." He swallowed the emotions that welled up. Not grief, but something else. Maybe a swell of pride in his daughter, at how wise she was, and how right. "And you know what, A? I *am* going to take a drive to clear my head. You okay here for a while?"

"I got mountains of homework," she said, giving him another one of her no-longer-rare hugs. "You go do what you need to do."

Before he left, Kenny stopped in his room, opened the top drawer of his dresser, and grabbed Elise's Bible from the place he'd put it after Hurricane Dylan. He'd even opened it once or twice since then, but he hadn't really read it.

Maybe it would help for him to go to God's house and read it. That was exactly what Elise would have done.

Our Redeemer wasn't that far, and he pulled into the lot a few minutes later, noticing a surprising number of cars there. Then he remembered it was the night of some Bible studies, including one that he and Heather had gone to together for a while.

Heather.

Well, at least the news about Lovely had taken his mind off the *other* thing that distracted him for hours every day.

He went into the church, which was open for the groups, and headed to the sanctuary. In the far corner, a small group of about five people were gathered with their heads down, so deep in prayer that they didn't notice him as he slipped into the second-to-the-last row.

It was where he and Heather had first sat when they'd come here, and where he'd continued to sit after she went back to Charleston. It felt comfortable and homey; easy to open the Bible and flip the pages to the Gospel of Matthew, where he believed he'd find the verses Ava was suggesting.

The words—those printed on the page and the many written by hand in the margins by his sweet, late wife—swam in front of his eyes for a moment, but then he focused and found what he recognized as the Sermon on the Mount.

Good place to start, anyway. But it wasn't his own worry that he wanted to pray about. It was Lovely. And how much their family and this world needed that strong, kind, amazing woman who was such a powerful role model to Ava. Could his little girl endure losing another woman in her life, after Elise and then her grandmother?

Lovely was her great-grandmother by blood.

And how great she was.

He flipped a few pages, skimming until he reached a healing scene. A centurion with a sick servant, who proclaimed that Jesus didn't need to show up in person to heal anyone, but say the word. That sounded...hopeful. He focused on one line.

But just say the word, and my servant will be healed.

He read the words over and over and over again, burning them in his brain, and looking up to the cross, whispering them so they crossed his lips. *Please heal her, dear Lord. Please—*

A hand on his shoulder pulled him from the prayer, making him jerk his head up in surprise.

"What are you doing here?"

He blinked at the angel, thinking, as he so often did when he saw Heather, that she had been sent by God. "Praying for Lovely," he said, too lost in the moment to even attempt anything but the truth.

"Oh, my group just prayed for her." She tipped her head in the direction of the half dozen or so people currently hugging each other goodbye. "I rejoined our old Bible study, but it's over now. Can I sit with you?"

"Of course. I was just..."

"Praying, I know." She smiled and slipped into the pew next to him, glancing down at the open Bible. "Whoa. Someone's spent a lot of time in the Word."

"This was Elise's," he said, fluttering the pages. "She liked to write in her Bible."

"She certainly did. May I?" She eased it out of his hands and started slowly turning the pages, studying the scripts and notes in the margins. "Wow. I feel like I'm looking at her photo albums or diary."

"Honestly? Those notes *were* her diary. And that book is a better reflection of Elise than any pictures."

She grazed a page reverently. "What a blessing to live a life like that."

"A short life," he said.

"A good life." She looked up at him. "Don't ever forget that."

He looked into her eyes and forgot...everything.

"You keep praying," she said. "I'm going to find a scripture for Lovely. Someone mentioned it in our study tonight, and I want to read it. Not sure where it was, though. I could search it on my phone."

"What is it? Maybe I'll know it. I realized tonight I remember more than I thought."

"The one about 'whatever is good, pure, and lovely.' I forget the book."

"Philippians," he said without thinking, then smiled. "Go me."

"Go you," she echoed with a laugh. "Now pray. I'll find it."

He exhaled and tried to get back to what he'd been begging for, but couldn't concentrate because God had answered a different prayer. The one he secretly prayed when his feelings consumed him.

Give me a chance with her, God. Just a chance.

Well, here they were, practically alone in church, close and praying and both needing the comfort of a friend.

"Here it is," she whispered, putting a light hand over his. "Listen." She leaned into him, her familiar floral scent filling his head. "'Whatever is true, whatever is noble, whatever is right, whatever is pure, whatever is *lovely*,'" she grinned up at him when she said the word, "'whatever is admirable—if anything is excellent or praiseworthy—think about such things.'" She let out a long sigh. "What do you think about when you hear all that?"

"True, noble, right, pure? Lovely and admirable? Excellent or praiseworthy?" He just looked at her, the gaze drawn out for several long heartbeats. "I'm in church, so I can't lie."

"You can't lie anywhere, but...why would you?"

"Because that?" He tapped the verses on the page. "Is God's permission to think about you."

"Oh." The word slipped out from between her lips, and her eyes lit. "That's so sweet, Kenny."

"It's the truth," he said softly. "And don't look at me that way because you're just going to say I'm...I don't know. Drowning out the memory of your husband, which I know I am, but I can't—"

She touched his lips with her fingertips. "Shhh. You're not drowning anything. Except me. In...feelings."

"Really? What kind?" Because if they were anything like his? Yeah, prayers had been answered.

"A feeling of peace."

"Oh." He heard the disappointment in his voice. Peace wasn't...love.

"Like when I'm with you, I'm where God wants me to be," she finished on the softest whisper.

He looked at her, hoping he'd heard that right.

"After you mentioned the class on God's will that I dragged you to, I went back and read the notes," she said.

"You didn't drag me, Heather. I'd have crawled through broken glass to spend two hours on a Thursday night with you."

She smiled at that. "Well, one of the things we learned was about when you hear God's voice, whether it's in your head or from a friend or you read something, whatever. When the

message you get gives you a sense of peace? Then it's right. If it gets you all churned up with anxiety and worry, then it's not from God."

"And you feel...peace." He couldn't hide the hope in his voice.

"Nothing but," she said. "Like, with you, I can handle anything. I can raise those kids and face this world and figure out all the problems." Her eyes filled and he was pretty sure his were doing the same thing. "I know you have feelings for me, Kenny. And I know you've been fighting them and hiding them."

"Not that well," he admitted.

"But the fact that you do fight them is just a demonstration of what a good, good man you are." Her fingers clasped his hand, tight and warm and real. "I think He's telling me to let you into my heart. I think God has blessed this..." She squeezed his hand. "I really do."

His heart felt like it was bursting as he pressed their joined hands to his chest. "Heather. You know what I think?"

She shook her head.

"I think I'm going to kiss you so maybe we better go outside so Jesus doesn't see."

She chuckled. "He's out there, too."

"Oh, yeah." He laughed and leaned closer. "Then...can I?"

"Please."

He closed the space between them and placed the lightest, most delicate kiss on her angel lips.

"Well, that's one answered prayer," he said, his eyes still closed.

"Then let's pray for Lovely."

He nodded and put his arm around her shoulder, holding her lightly.

"Heavenly Father..." As the words came from his heart, Kenny felt nothing but peace. He was where God wanted him to be, too.

CHAPTER TWENTY-TWO

NICK

She wasn't answering? What the hell?

Nick tapped the laptop keyboard, glancing up at the still-empty stage, knowing he had just minutes before the teenagers descended. Just minutes until he had to start the run-through of the Cherry Tree Lane Reprise, which was just unthinkable, since they barely knew the steps for the first Cherry Tree Lane number in Act I. How could they reprise anything?

So where was Eliza? And Ava? She always came early, with Maddie—who'd been invaluable to him as a second set of eyes and ears. Eliza had promised she'd had a plan for Act II when they'd closed up last night, but refused to tell him what it was.

"Hey, Uncle Nick." Ava strolled in through the backstage, weaving around the chimney and chair sets. "How's it going?"

"Pretty bad," he said. "I can't reach Eliza by phone or video call."

"Ava!" Maddie came blasting in from the back.

Ava leaped off the stage and landed like a gazelle, arms outstretched to hug the other girl.

"Didn't you two just see each other at lunch?" Nick asked.

"And again in sixth period," Ava confirmed. "But we're always happy to see each other."

"Well, I'm glad someone is happy around here, but it isn't the director," he said.

"You'll feel better when Miss Eliza shows up on the computer," Maddie said. "Every time she's helped you this week, you've been more relaxed."

"Because she knows what she's doing."

"You know what you're doing," Ava told him and at his look, she laughed. "Mostly. But I promise, everyone is going to work so hard on Act II this week, we'll be ready. In nine days."

He bit his lip to keep from swearing, trying the laptop and cell phone again, but he still hadn't reached Eliza when the stage starting filling up with familiar faces.

Joelle, of course, who breezed in with the confidence of the lead; then came the goofball who played Bert, and did it quite well. The younger kids from the middle school showed up on time, as always, along with a few members of the ensemble chorus.

It wasn't long before they were looking at him, waiting for direction.

After greeting them all, getting high fives, and a few updates, he cleared his throat and stood in front of them.

"I think what we should do first is—"

"Dance."

Every one of them, including Nick, turned to the voice coming from the very back of the auditorium.

"And that's what I'm here to teach you to do."

"Eliza!" Nick practically flew off the stage at the sight of Eliza Whitney, her auburn hair skimming squared shoulders as she made her way down the center aisle, a wide, wonderful smile softening her face.

"What are you doing here?" He ran to meet her, arms outstretched.

"Saving your"—she wrapped him in a hug—"dance-challenged ass."

The entire cast gave a noisy hoot and cheer, but no one could have been happier than Nick.

"I can't believe it," he said, pulling back to look into the warm gaze of a woman who'd done so many, many favors for him as his agent; who negotiated his contracts and frequently went to battle for him. And of all of those show business skirmishes, this one meant the most. "I can't believe you flew here from L.A."

She smiled at him, searching his face as if trying to memorize it. "I needed a kick in my behind, too," she said. "Plus, I can't let your reputation go down in flames on a high school play."

"My reputation went down in flames long before this, but..." His voice faded as he scanned her face, taking in a few new lines and some shadows under her eyes. Grief had made its mark on a remarkably attractive face. She had a timeless beauty with great bones and an elegant way of carrying herself, always in understated and classy clothes. She hadn't bothered with all the injections and face tucks that most fifty-something women in Hollywood depended on, either.

Because Ben, she always said, loved her just the way she was.

"I don't deserve you," he said, because expressing his sympathy seemed awkward right then, and this sentiment was the truth, too.

"It's fine," she whispered, as if she knew the real reason for the hug. "I needed the distraction more than you know. I'm unemployed now, remember."

He stepped beside her and kept an arm around her back. "Well, distractions I can offer. Here's about two dozen of them, plus two acts, twenty-five musical numbers, a forty-two-page script, and more costume changes than I can count."

Her whole face lit up as she took it all in. "Hello, actors!" she called.

They responded with an enthusiastic cheer and a shower of comments and calls.

Taking a deep breath, she started walking toward the stage.

"I've come to choreograph, practice, dance, and perform." She held out her hands. "Let's make this play a hit, what do you say?"

As she started to greet them all—individually—Ava and Maddie came shooting over to him, flanking him on each side.

"My mom would say this is a miracle," Ava said.

"So would mine," Maddie agreed. "She came home from church last night and told me something amazing was going to happen."

"So did my dad!" Ava said.

Nick looked from one to the other. "Something amazing just did, ladies."

"THIS IS the first time you've finished a rehearsal and come home looking like you had fun." Savannah put her hand on Nick's cheek and added a kiss. "Thank God for you, Eliza."

Eliza lifted her wine glass and tipped her head from the counter where she had been sitting since they'd come back to The Haven after the rehearsal. "Happy to help. It was the best distraction I've had in weeks. Months, really."

Nick studied her as he twisted off the top of a beer. Eliza had never been a Hollywood agent powerhouse, never been one of the deal-making sharks who terrified producers. Not only had her underlying gentleness been a secret weapon, it had always made Nick more comfortable than, say, his manager, who bared his teeth during every negotiation. Of course, that was who his mother preferred way back in the day when Nick was a young actor and Diana called the shots as the ultimate stage mother.

But at twenty-four, when his career absolutely skyrocketed, he met Eliza through her husband, a studio head. And he was instantly calmed by her demeanor. Her inner, quiet strength impressed the hell out of him.

As it had today, when she managed to get those kids to listen and dance without ever raising her voice or getting frustrated. It couldn't have been easy for her to roll up her sleeves and help with a high school play, especially on the heels of losing her husband and her job.

"I don't know if you're the best director in the land," Eliza mused, pulling him from his thoughts. "But, dang, Nick, you are an excellent acting coach. I loved what you brought out in those kids."

He considered that before taking a drink, nodding slowly. "I like doing that," he said. "It feels natural."

"People would pay good money for someone with your credentials to teach them the craft," she continued. "And I won't even ask for ten percent, even though it was my idea."

He smiled at her, as he had a thousand times that day. "You're the best."

"I think she's right," Savannah said as she set up the sushi tray they were going to share for a late dinner. "You should start a little acting school."

"In the Keys? Who'd want acting classes here?"

"Wannabe actors," Eliza answered. "And, trust me, those are lurking everywhere. And with your name? You could also teach online and maybe connect with a local acting troupe and offer your services." She leaned forward and narrowed her eyes at him. "So, it's for sure and certain. You are never going back?"

"I told you I'm staying." He put his arm around Savannah. "This is home for us. And Dylan. And any other little rug rats we are lucky enough to have. This is it, Eliza. This is the stuff."

"Aww." Savannah dropped her head against his chest with a satisfied sigh.

Eliza leaned forward and dropped her chin on her knuckles, looking at the two of them.

"Well, you did it, Nick," she said, lifting her glass in another toast. "You escaped the bonds of Hollywood and found the true contentment that all those fake and desperate people are looking for."

"Amen, sister." He tapped her wine glass with his bottle. "Neither one of us ever fit in that place, you know."

"Oh, I know. Ben was the only reason I could take it. He saw through them all and was such a rock. Yes, I loved working with you and a few other actors. But I'm done, so..."

"Maybe it's time for a new chapter," Savannah said. "You should talk to my mom. She totally reinvented herself at fifty-five and has never been happier."

"She did," Nick agreed, snapping his fingers and pointing to Eliza. "You should move here and open that acting school with me. Teach people the ropes of the business."

For a moment, Eliza looked like she loved the idea, too, but then she shook her head. "Please don't take this personally, but I've had enough of actors, scripts, contracts, royalties, producers, and..." She rolled her eyes. "Elevator pitches."

"Then what will you do?" Savannah asked.

She looked down at her wine. "You know, I have some unfinished business to take care of before I do anything," she said. "Family business."

"With your late father?" Nick guessed.

Eliza looked up, some pain in those gray-sky eyes. "Yes," she said simply. "And I truly did come here with the intention of heading up to Sanibel Island to pay my last respects to his widow, but..." She blew out a breath. "My father and I were...not close. I hadn't seen him in many years. He died while I was in the throes of hospice with Ben, and I didn't make his memorial service. But now that I'm here, I feel like I should go up there, but..."

Nick and Savannah waited for her to finish, but she just looked out the window toward the water, her eyes misting.

"I'm not sure I want to," she finally said. "I've lost my husband and my job in the space of a month. Facing the fact that I lost my father, no matter how I felt about him..." Her voice grew thick and she tried to laugh it off. "I think I'd rather teach teenagers how to dance."

Nick smiled but Savannah came around the island and put her arm around Eliza. "Please stay here as long as you like," she insisted. "The guest house is yours. If you want to get on the ferry and go up to Sanibel, you can. If you want to veg on the beach, take Dylan for long walks, or hang out with the world's most wonderful family, you can do that, too. Heal. That's what people do in Coconut Key."

Eliza's eyes filled as she placed her hand over the one Savannah had on her shoulder. "Thank you." Then her gaze shifted to Nick. "Well, I understand why you married her."

"She's a gem." He smiled at his wife, affection rolling through him.

Just then, Dylan squawked, the familiar cry coming through the baby monitor.

"And there's the other reason he married me," Savannah cracked, breaking the heavy emotion of the moment.

Nick put the bottle down. "I haven't seen my son in hours. Let me get him and bring him down." He blew Savannah a quick kiss and jogged toward the stairs.

As he turned the corner, he heard Eliza say, "Thank you for the offer, Savannah. I think I'll take you up on it and stay at least until the play, maybe longer. And, thank you for helping Nick figure out what some people take their whole lives to learn, if they ever do."

"What's that?" Savannah asked.

"That love is all you need."

Savannah laughed. "I think that song is on my grandmother's playlist from way back in the day."

"'All you need is love,'" Eliza sang, her voice as clear from the kitchen as it had been when she'd broken into "A Spoonful of Sugar" on the stage.

Humming the tune, he took the stairs two at a time, a free man who had, indeed, cracked the code.

CHAPTER TWENTY-THREE

BECK

"You're sure I'm not going under?" Lovely asked the question for maybe the tenth time that morning, including twice since they'd gotten in the car with Peyton and Beck to drive to Marathon.

"I promise you're not," Beck said, shooting a smile from the driver's seat. "And so did Dr. Chang, so you don't have to worry. It's just a little twilight sleep, not full blown anesthesia."

"I wasn't worried"—Lovely put a hand over her breast and rubbed lightly—"until I woke up this morning."

From the back seat, Peyton put a gentle hand on Lovely's shoulder. "We're here for you, Lovely."

"And based on the number of calls and texts you've gotten," Beck said, "so is the rest of Coconut Key."

Lovely let out a sigh. "I don't want to be a bother."

"A bother?" Beck asked. "How about everyone's favorite person?"

"You're well-loved," Peyton told her. "Val must have texted me six times this morning."

"How are things in Massachusetts?" Beck asked, trying to keep her tone neutral. Ever since Peyton had told them, they sort of managed to dance around the subject of…just how far away he wanted to take her. Any conversations brought her daughter to tears, and there were enough of those as they all prepared for the biopsy and what lay ahead for the family.

Beck knew in her heart that if Lovely had cancer, Peyton wouldn't go. She just wouldn't. But no one quite knew how that could work out, and Beck hadn't pressed.

"Things are fine in Boston," she said. "Cold. Even in May."

Lovely turned. "Maybe he'll hate the weather," she said brightly.

"Maybe."

Beck glanced into the rear-view mirror to gauge Peyton's expression, but she couldn't read it.

"What about Oliver?" Lovely asked, softly enough that Beck knew her mother didn't want to intrude, but couldn't help herself.

"I haven't heard much from Oliver," she said, trying so very hard to keep all the emotion out of that statement.

"That's sad," Lovely said.

This time, when she glanced in the rear-view mirror she caught Peyton's gaze, and they shared a silent look of solidarity. The two of them were hurting, but it wasn't the right time to share or focus on the men who'd let them down.

"He texted me a picture of a seashell from Captiva Island, and then Savannah said he shot a text to Nick that said he was in…Destin? Santa Rosa Beach?" Beck shrugged. "Somewhere way up in the Panhandle. He did say he wanted to go driving and exploring, so I guess he's making his way up the west coast of Florida."

And every day he stayed away, Beck missed him a little more. Much more, in fact, than she'd expected to.

She felt Lovely's gaze on her, too, aware that both of these women knew her heart and soul and just how much this had rocked her. So, she dug for something—anything—to change the subject.

"Did you see Dylan's got another tooth?" she asked.

That did the trick, or at least they played along, and they chatted about the baby, and Ava and the play. They dished more on the woman Josh was apparently dating, although it still stung when Beck thought about how Lovely had met her while getting a mammogram alone. They stayed on more fun, distracting topics, like Kenny and Heather, who were doing a terrible job of hiding the fact that they were obviously falling hard for each other.

Anything and everything but the different weights that were currently on their hearts.

But Beck's mind kept slipping back to them. A week or ten days ago, everything had been perfect. Now she missed Oliver more than she wanted to. Peyton was struggling with living a thousand miles away. And Lovely... well, Lovely was stroking her long gray braid as if she were holding one of her dogs and getting comfort from the action.

Lovely's problems were all that mattered right then.

Beck reached over the console and took her mother's hand. "Don't worry," she whispered, "this will be over in a jiffy and we'll get good news."

She responded with a sad smile, the one Beck had gotten used to seeing these past few weeks.

She kept that smile in place until they arrived at the Keys Breast Center, housed in a three-story building in Marathon that looked like an absolute skyscraper to a person who lived on these islands. But when they opened the door to the office on the second floor, Lovely's smile grew genuine.

"Oh, goodness," she said, stopping as she looked around the waiting room at the familiar faces. Many familiar faces.

Savannah and Nick, holding Dylan, sat next to Kenny and across from Jessie and Heather, both in their Coquina Café uniforms. Josh was there, too, and Callie. Wait. Callie?

"Callie!" Beck blinked at her daughter in surprise. "When did you get here?"

"Ten minutes ago," she said, getting up to come closer and give both Lovely and Beck a hug. "It didn't make any sense to go all the way to Coconut Key, so I thought I'd come and surprise you." She kissed Lovely's cheek. "Skipped a class for you, which is my way of showing how much I love you."

Lovely pressed her hands to Callie's cheeks, looking into her dark eyes. "Sweet, sweet angel. Thank you." She eased Callie to her side and looked around. "Thank you all for coming. I don't know why I thought for one second I could go through this alone."

"Ms. Ames?" a woman from behind the desk called. "Can I get you to check in?"

"But I'm having a little party here," she said, sounding light and happy and so much like Lovely again.

Beck put her arm around her and nudged her toward

the desk. "We'll all be here when it's over and then we will have a real party."

"No, Beckie," she said as they walked. "No party until I get told it's negative."

Beck's heart dropped a little, trying not to think about what it would feel like if the report wasn't negative.

One challenge at a time, she told herself, staying next to Lovely as she filled out a form at the desk.

"Thank you," Lovely whispered under her breath as she leaned into Beck.

"Please," she replied. "You're my mother."

Lovely looked up, her eyes filling with unshed tears. "No matter what happens, you are the greatest thing I ever did in my life. Even giving you up for Olivia to raise."

"And you are..." Beck smoothed that braid over Lovely's shoulder, which was obviously a source of comfort for everyone. "Mom," she whispered. "My real and most beloved Mom."

Lovely folded into Beck's arms and they squeezed each other for several seconds before the door to the back opened.

"Lovely?" a nurse holding a clipboard called. "We can go back now."

"Do you want me to come?" Beck asked.

"I'm sorry," the nurse said, "Dr. Oulette doesn't allow anyone but medical staff in the procedure, but we will come out the minute he's finished and get you. Then you can sit with your mother."

"I'm fine," Lovely assured her. "And you just called me Mom."

"You like that?"

Biting her lip, Lovely nodded. "You have no idea."

"Then good luck, Mom. I love you."

She got a blinding smile in return and when Lovely walked through the door with the nurse, Beck could have sworn there was an actual bounce in her step.

Peyton was next to Beck when she turned back to the waiting room.

"I guess the gang's all here," Peyton said.

"Almost all of them," Beck mused, giving Peyton a look. "Some are missing."

Peyton lifted a brow. "Then you better look at who I just saw getting off the elevator in the hall."

For a moment, Beck thought she meant Val, but when the glass door opened and Oliver walked in, Beck sucked in a breath.

"Oh," she let out the tiniest whimper that only Peyton heard.

She watched his dark eyes scan the crowd gathered, acknowledging their greetings, but his gaze didn't stop until it landed on Beck, and then his smile was so real and right it actually made her dizzy.

"Beck." He mouthed her name as his whole body seemed to exhale with relief.

As he came right over to her, he held out his arms with some hesitation, as if he wasn't sure if she would hug him.

"Ollie," she whispered, a half-smile pulling at her lips.

"If that's what you want to call me..." He wrapped his arms around her. "I'm fine with it." He squeezed her lightly and pressed his lips to her ear. "You were right." His voice sent a thousand chills up her spine. "I needed to do some thinking..." He inched back and looked her right in the eyes. "And now I know exactly what I want."

She stared at him. "What is it?"

"Let's get through today and Lovely's procedure, and I'll tell you tonight."

She just let out a breath it felt like she'd been holding for days. "I can't wait."

THAT WAIT DIDN'T END until very late that evening, when Beck stepped out of Lovely's bedroom, confident that her mother was asleep. She'd planned to spend the night in Lovely's cottage, sleeping on the sofa, but when she turned the corner in the living room, Peyton was in pajamas, making up the sofa as a bed.

"I don't think we'll both fit there," Beck said.

"Just me, Mom. Let me stay here tonight."

"I promised—"

Peyton cut her off by pointing toward the beach. "Oliver's down on the hammock waiting for you," she said. "I told him I'd send you down."

She sighed and smiled. "Okay. I'll go spend some time with him, but don't get comfy. I promised my mother I'd stay."

"You promised her someone would, and she's my grandmother, and I'm happy to stay." Peyton tugged at the sheet and smoothed it out. "I think he's very anxious to talk to you, Mom."

"You think?" She walked toward the sliding glass doors that looked out over the beach, the moonlight bright enough to see the hammock that hung between two palm trees, the mesh swaying slightly with the weight of a man.

Her heart tumbled around a bit, the way it had been since he'd arrived so unexpectedly. Yes, she'd been consumed with thoughts of Lovely, even though her mother had sailed through the procedure and been surprisingly alert when Beck had joined her afterwards. She'd been aware of Oliver all day as he hovered on the outskirts of her consciousness, but she kept her attention on Lovely—or Mom, as she suddenly wanted to be called —from the drive home to an afternoon of caretaking.

While she'd made Lovely dinner and managed the flow of visitors to her cottage, Beck had been deeply aware that Oliver was at the B&B. And he wasn't just waiting for her, but greeting a family who'd just called the night before wanting two rooms. He'd checked them in, arranged for drinks and snacks, and basically stepped in as the proprietor in her absence.

Peyton had gone to help, but he seemed to have everything well under control, leaving Beck to tend to Lovely and think about Oliver.

Finally, it was time to stop thinking and start talking.

"All I know," Peyton said as she snapped a case over a pillow, "is that he has been asking me about my town house—square footage, fees, price, availability, and when, uh, someone who bought it, could move in."

Beck turned and blinked at her. "You really think he'd buy it?"

She shrugged. "The real estate agent said someone was calling with a ton of questions and sounded like they might make an offer."

Beck inhaled slowly, letting this news wash over her.

"Mom." She pointed outside again. "Go talk to him."

"I will. I—"

Peyton came closer, putting both hands on Beck's shoulders. "Listen to me."

She laughed. "The daughter becomes mother?"

"I'm speaking as your friend," she said. "Your best friend who picked up your broken bits more than a year ago and dragged you to Coconut Key to meet an 'aunt' you didn't like."

"You did, Pey."

"Then listen to me. That man down there? He *cares* about you. He had to work through some grief, and I think he has. He wants to make a life with you in it, and, my God, woman, if you don't at least give him a chance..." Her voice cracked. "You deserve to be happy, Mom."

"Oh, Peyton." She wrapped her daughter in a hug, fighting her own tears. "So do you." She stopped when she felt Peyton shudder. "Honey, are you crying?"

"What am I going to do?" Peyton asked on a sob. "I just want to raise my baby with you right down the street, not a thousand miles away. And, honestly, I just want to come first, you know? Like Savannah. Like you. I just want to be the one who doesn't sacrifice." Tears spilled. "But that seems so small and selfish. I have a man I love. I have the baby I always wanted. I don't want to be...greedy."

She stroked Peyton's hair, not sure what to say. Sometimes it was better not to say anything. Peyton was a grown woman and she'd make her decisions; all Beck could do was love her.

"It's okay," Peyton said, working so hard to pull herself together that Beck could feel it. "We'll get back here eventually. In the meantime, please, Mom. Go talk to Oliver."

She gave Peyton one more hug, then separated. "I'm going now. What should I say?"

"Yes," Peyton whispered. "Take your walls down, Rebecca Foster, and say yes."

"Good advice."

"Do you have permission to be on this hammock?" Beck called into the dark night, smiling when one hand emerged from the cocoon of the mesh netting to reach the sand and stop the swaying.

"I know the original owner," he called, still lying down. "She told me she used to play here as a child. Invented games and sang songs with her best friend."

Touched by how well he'd listened to her on their many long walks along this beach, she continued closer, the sand chilly on her bare feet, the salty air so clean and fresh it almost made her lightheaded.

No, Beck. Not the air. The man.

"And she said anyone could just show up and swing," he added.

"Not just anyone," she said softly, coming closer. "Only special people."

He held his hand up, fingers splayed. "Am I?"

So, so special. "That remains to be seen," she said lightly. As she reached the hammock, she took that hand.

He threaded his fingers through hers. "Please join me and let me show you how special I am. Or, better yet, how special we could be together."

As always, her heart tilted when she looked at this

man who only needed to smile to send butterflies dive-bombing her stomach.

"How's Lovely?" he asked, sitting up as much as anyone could in a hammock.

"Resting and comfortable and calm." She brought their joined hands to her lips. "How are you?"'

"Same. Resting, comfortable, and calm. Please." He scooted a bit and drew her closer, giving her a chance to ease into the hammock and lie down next to him.

"There we go," he said, tucking her into his strong body and using his arm to give her a pillow. "That's where you should be."

Was it? In the hammock, yes. In Coconut Key, definitely. But with him? She looked up at him, snuggling closer. It sure felt right.

"First of all, Beck, I'm sorry I left so...abruptly."

"It's fine—"

"Nope. Not fine, not by a long shot. But you were right. I had thinking and...grieving to do." He grunted under his breath. "So much, it seems."

She studied his profile, her hand on his chest so she could feel just how hard his heart was beating. "Did it help?"

He exhaled softly. "It gave me closure, and I needed that," he said. "I've been grieving for a while, but I had... the fog. The last bits of fog that just hadn't lifted. And when I met you, it was like a beacon of light shone on that fog and revealed just how thick and...kind of blinding it was. You were the light I needed." He turned his head to look down at her. "It's warm around you," he whispered. "Bright and welcoming and fresh and clean and new. I just want to...inhale you."

She laughed softly at the words, but he didn't smile. If anything, his gaze grew more intent.

"I don't want to leave this island, or...this woman. Can I stay?"

The simplicity of the question took her by surprise. "You can do whatever you want, Oliver."

"Not without your permission."

"You don't need my permission to stay here."

He let out a soft moan as if he didn't agree with that. "I drove all over this state," he said. "Hours in the car. Walked all over beaches and piers and boat docks and little islands and you know what I thought about the whole time?"

She had no idea. "I'm going to guess it was...your late wife? Maybe the island life?"

"I did think about my marriage, and living here. But mostly, I thought about sharing a new life with you. About years—not weeks or months—but years together. Not a fling, not a fun relationship, not a visit that ends when I go back to Sydney. But years. Life. Forever."

Her heart absolutely stopped. "Forever?"

"Nothing is forever," he said softly. "But if you go into it thinking it will be, then..." He stroked her face with a gentle fingertip. "Then we have a chance, don't you think?"

She blinked at him, lightheaded from the emotions rising up. Joy and hope and astonishment and anticipation and...love.

"I know that marriage let you down, Beck. I know you were treated unfairly and the word *husband* might not mean...are you crying?"

Was she? "I don't know. Are you...*proposing*?"

He smiled. "The fog lifted when I realized that I wanted everything, long-term, for good and for real. So, that's my endgame. That's why I'm staying. For the chance to show you there is such a thing as a happy ending. What I'm proposing is that we try and get there."

For the longest time, she couldn't speak. She just stayed completely still, drinking in the moment. The tender, touching words spoken with the soft Australian accent. The white beams of moonlight slipping through the palm fronds. The soft splash of the Atlantic Ocean and the heady smell of honeysuckle in the air. The warmth of his body, the peace in her heart, the utter completeness of the world around her.

She forgot about everything except this man and this moment.

"What do you say, Beck?"

Take down your walls, Rebecca Foster.

"I say..." She closed her eyes and leaned in to whisper the word into his mouth. "Yes."

CHAPTER TWENTY-FOUR

LOVELY

Friday was interminable. It had been more than a week since the biopsy, and each day had ticked by at a snail's pace for Lovely. No matter how much she painted, walked the beach, chatted with Beck, babysat Dylan, rehearsed lines with Ava, or stopped by Coquina Café to have breakfast with Jessie and Heather, nothing distracted her from...

Cancer.

She'd gotten used to saying the word in her head, especially because no one else would say it at all. They skirted around it, using euphemisms like "if you are sick" or "should the news be bad" but no one would say...*you could have cancer, Lovely.*

She knew that was out of love and respect and even a little fear, but she longed for someone to be blunt with her.

So when Beck came up to the cottage late Friday afternoon to pick her up to take her to the opening night performance of *Mary Poppins*, Lovely had already decided she was going to be straight with her daughter.

Beck didn't knock, of course, but stepped inside, looking lovely in a blue sundress, her face glowing with that inner excitement that a new man—*the* man, Lovely was certain—had brought.

"Hey...Mom." She searched Lovely's face, wearing a smile as she did every time she called Lovely that wonderful word, as if they both knew what a gift it was. "Dr. Chang didn't call."

It wasn't a question. "No, Beckie. And now I have to wait until Monday."

"Oh." Beck moaned the word. "Well, she said it could be ten days. And at least you have three performances of *Mary Poppins* to keep your mind off things. You look very pretty, by the way." Beck gave her a hug and fluttered the lavender and white maxi dress with flowing sleeves she'd chosen for tonight's performance. "And you smell like a rose," she added.

"Beckie." Lovely inched back, forcing herself not to throw her arms around this amazing woman who'd been the Rock of Gibraltar for her.

"What's wrong?"

"Say it," she whispered. "We have to both say it."

Beck frowned, then shook her head. "I don't know what you mean."

"Cancer," she hissed. "We have to acknowledge this."

"Not yet we don't." Beck took her hand. "We've been given until Monday—"

"To fret."

"To forget," Beck corrected, squeezing her hand. "This isn't like you, Lovely. You're not a worrier."

"But it's cancer," she said softly, hating the word but having to put it out there. "We can't keep dancing around it."

"We can," Beck said. "Tonight we're going to dance to Supercalifragilistic...stuff. Or Ava is. And Chim-chiminee, and spoonfuls of sugar, and...and... 'anything can happen if you let it.'" She smiled. "Isn't that what Ava keeps telling us?"

"Cancer can happen."

"Lovely Ames!" Beck blinked. "You need to stop. No news isn't bad news, it's just no news."

Lovely tipped her head. "I'm sure it's bad news," she said. "That's why it's taking so long. They're probably re-running all the tests, just to make sure, and Dr. Chang decided that she would wait until Monday so the weekend isn't ruined. She might know my granddaughter is in the high school play. Everyone knows Nick is directing it and she likely decided to—"

"Stop," Beck ordered. "That's not how it works. Not with the testing, and no doctor would ever sit on bad news over the weekend because your family was involved with a play."

"You don't think? Then you haven't lived in Coconut Key long enough."

"I have, and I can assure you that Dr. Chang doesn't have the results yet." Beck gave an apologetic look. "I called her office this afternoon."

"Oh." Lovely covered her lips. "Really? What did they say?"

"That seven to ten days meant seven to ten days, which will be Monday, so in the meantime, you should—"

"If you say relax or forget or have fun, Rebecca..."

"You should stay close to me," Beck finished, giving Lovely's knuckles a kiss. "I'm just as worried as you are, but I'm doing my level best to keep your mind off it."

Lovely let out a long sigh, so deeply grateful for this daughter of hers. "All right. Let's go watch Ava sing and dance and say...what was that phrase again?"

"'Anything can happen if you let it.'"

But cancer wasn't something she could "let" happen or not. Still, Lovely picked up her white wrap and handbag, gave the dogs extra treats, and walked out into the evening air with Beck, where Oliver waited in the car.

"You don't mind if he goes with us, do you?" Beck asked.

"I love watching you two together, sweet girl. He's so smitten, it makes me smile."

"As am I."

Lovely tucked her arm into Beck's, silently saying a prayer of gratitude that her darling girl wouldn't miss her so much when she was gone, because she'd found Oliver.

BECK WAS RIGHT ABOUT one thing—Lovely temporarily forgot about the biopsy as she sank into her seat in the very front row of the auditorium like a VIP. A low-grade hum of excitement seemed to vibrate in the air as the seats filled up with family and friends, many of them hugging hello, and several stopping by to say hello to Lovely and her group, which filled much of the first two rows.

Seated on the aisle next to Beck, Lovely glanced over her shoulder to catch Savannah's eyes.

"Nice seats," Lovely said.

"Sleeping with the director has its privileges," Savannah teased on a whisper. She seemed as bubbly as everyone else, even though she'd left Dylan home with a trusted babysitter. When Jessie and Chuck came in with Beau between them, the whole group let out a soft cheer, knowing that the legalities were over and Jessie was officially Beau's mother.

Normally, they'd have had a huge party this weekend, but Beck said they'd wait because of the play. But Lovely had asked Beck to wait until they knew the results, so there'd be a party next weekend...or not.

"You're on your best behavior, young man," Lovely said to Beau, reaching forward to brush one of his dark curls.

"I promised I would be," he said, his big brown eyes earnest. "Papa and Mama said there will be ice cream if I don't make a peep."

Lovely blinked, not sure if she was more surprised that he'd called Jessie "Mama" or that someone had introduced discipline. Next to him, Jessie put a gentle hand on his tiny shoulder and whispered something in his ear, getting a great big grin in reply.

Kenny and Heather sat with their heads close, talking with Callie who was holding a seat for Peyton, but didn't seem to know why she wasn't here yet. Marc was near Heather, looking around to greet some kids from school. Everyone was here except—

"Hello, Lovely." She looked up to meet a familiar

smile, taking a moment to place the big eyes and thick black bangs of a woman about Beck's age.

"Julie!" she exclaimed, then glanced to her left to see Josh next to her, a light hand on the woman's back. Lovely couldn't help a smug smile at her successful matchmaking efforts. "How nice to see you again."

"And you." She leaned over and whispered, "Any news yet?"

She shook her head, then inched back, realizing that as a medical professional, she might know something. "Is that bad?" Lovely asked.

"Absolutely not," she replied immediately. "The tests take time. And I'm praying for you."

"Thank you, dear."

Josh stepped closer and nodded to Beck and Oliver. "I don't think you two have met Julie Ellis," he said, and as they stood, he finished the introductions.

Lovely held her breath for a moment, certain everyone else did, too, as Josh introduced his date to Beck...the woman he'd dated for the better part of the past year. But there was no need to worry. Beck was warm and kind, and if Julie knew she was meeting an "ex," she was also far too classy to do anything but exchange friendly greetings.

The lights dimmed once, and Beck turned, looking toward the back of the auditorium. "Where's Peyton?" she asked Savannah.

Savannah turned, too, then pointed to her sister, rushing in. "There she is."

"Oh, thank goodness." Beck stood to wave at her as Peyton hustled toward them, stopping in front of Beck, Lovely, and Oliver with a funny look on her face.

"I know you made an offer," she said breathlessly to Oliver. "But we haven't signed papers and, honestly, I'm not sure I want to sell."

Lovely and Beck exchanged a quick look, but Oliver shook his head. "I was outbid. Just got a text a little while ago." He gave an apologetic look to Beck. "I was going to tell you after the show, but not to worry. I have my eye on another place already."

"It's not you?" Peyton asked, crouching down and frowning. "Oh, no. I was hoping it would be easy to get out of the sale."

"The agent told me it went to a young couple with a baby," Oliver said.

Peyton flinched like that news hurt.

"You don't want to sell your townhouse?" Lovely asked, surprised as anyone by the news.

"I don't...think so."

"You're not going to Massachusetts with Val?" Beck sounded shocked.

"I don't...well, of course I'll have to, but I want a place here. I decided I'll live here part-time. I don't want to move to Massachusetts."

The lights dimmed twice, warning the audience the show was about to start.

"Honey, are you sure?" Beck asked.

"I'm not sure of anything," Peyton admitted, "except that I don't love the idea of living in Boston. And I have a great townhouse and I'm keeping it." She pushed up and gave Beck a challenging look, as if she expected her mother to disagree with this.

But then she slipped over to the empty seat next to Callie.

"Whoa," Beck whispered to Lovely. "Didn't see that coming."

Before Lovely could answer, the lights went out completely, bathing the auditorium in darkness. Everyone hushed but for a smattering of clapping and cheers, which broke into full applause as the sound system suddenly opened up with the familiar refrain of "Chim Chim Cher-ee."

From this vantage point, the high school stage seemed as big as Broadway to Lovely. And when the curtains opened and the young man who played Bert began to narrate in a hilarious and quite authentic British accent, she wasn't just distracted, she was transported.

Her eyes burned with tears when Ava came on stage looking glorious and beautiful, shining with a light from the inside that they all knew had been dimmed by grief when she arrived a little over a year ago.

Lovely and Beck exchanged a look of indescribable pride while Savannah let out a hoot as she clapped for her "grasshopper." Lovely stole a quick glance at Kenny, who looked like someone had plugged him in, beaming at the stage, his eyes openly full of fatherly love and his hand openly wrapped around Heather's, who was clearly sharing the moment with him.

So much, Lovely thought, blinking back a tear. So *much* to live for. So many people and relationships and love in this world. Her life had never been better or fuller or more satisfying. Would God take that away from her now? Would the universe challenge her with a daunting and impossible mountain to climb? Would her body fail her after it cheated death once?

She shook off the emotions and forced herself to go

back to the turn-of-the-century London. Ava strode across the stage like she was born for it, her long hair up in a period-specific hairdo, a bright blue dress with a bustle swishing around, a tiny dog—a toy, although she'd practiced for hours with Sugar—in her arms.

She delivered her opening line, lecturing her dog about barking, and getting a noisy laugh from a warm and receptive audience. As one scene flowed into the next, the laughs were frequent, the acting surprisingly good, and the dancing? Well, there were a few missteps, but for the most part, those kids glided over the stage like they'd been practicing all year, not just like crazy since Eliza—the dancing queen, Savannah had dubbed her—had arrived.

The intermission was far too brief, with so many people to chat with, including Nick and Eliza, who came out from the back for a quick hello.

Nick was surrounded in seconds, but he handled it like the pro he was, shaking off any attention with comments about how proud he was of these kids. He introduced Eliza as the head choreographer, and showered her with accolades for saving the play, and then they were gone.

The lights dimmed again, and the second half started with a palpable confidence on the stage. The nerves had disappeared as the performers belted out their songs, danced with pure joy, and put on a show that truly was *practically perfect* in every way, as they said over and over.

Just as Mr. Banks gave his heart and soul into a number about dreams, Lovely felt her handbag vibrate with a text on her phone. Who would be texting her? Anyone she knew or loved was in this room, so...

She ignored it.

But as the scene changed and Ava made another appearance as Miss Lark, Lovely felt the vibration again and couldn't resist reaching down to the aisle to the pocket of her handbag and sliding the phone out to squint at the screen without Beck seeing her.

Dr. Amy Chang.

Her breath caught in her throat as she saw the words, unable to stop herself from pulling the phone a little closer and tapping the screen with her finger so she could read the message, still hiding the phone, her heart already hammering.

Lovely, please call me.

Oh, God. Oh, *God.*

She trembled as the phone slid from her fingers back into the bag. Call her. Now?

She tried to focus on the stage, but the colors of the clothes were swimming and she couldn't hear the music because of the pulse pounding in her head.

Anything can happen! The stage was full of youthful, exuberant faces, their feet and arms moving in unison as they sang the theme of the whole play.

Anything...*anything.*

She had to know. She couldn't sit here and watch this play or stand and clap or do the honors of giving Ava the bouquet that was under Beck's chair without knowing what would happen.

"I'll be right back," she whispered to Beck, who looked startled that Lovely would leave so close to the end.

"Are you okay?"

Lovely nodded and snagged her bag, slipping into the

aisle and hustling away without taking even a minute to see if anyone was looking askance at her. Let them assume the old lady couldn't hold it for one more minute. Because she *couldn't*.

Her legs were quivering when she stepped into the empty lobby, the music and singing suddenly quiet when the doors closed behind her. She looked around for a private corner and walked to the table where a few programs were scattered, using it to brace herself as she took out the phone.

Anything can happen. The words echoed in her head as she stared at the screen and the request to call the doctor who held Lovely's fate in her hands.

Wait. Did she really want to know? Did she want to go back into that auditorium and somehow hold it together when her heart was breaking with bad news? Could she even do that? It would hurt everyone. It would ruin the night.

But she *had* to know.

She tapped the screen with a shaky finger, not sure who would answer at a doctor's office this late on a Friday night.

"Hello? This is Dr. Chang."

That's who. The doctor herself. This must be very, very serious. "This is Lovely Ames," she croaked, then cleared her throat. "Hello, Doctor."

"Lovely. I had to call you. I had to tell you myself and not let you wait until Monday."

"You did?"

Just then, the door from the auditorium popped open and Beck stepped out, her whole expression crumbling when she saw Lovely. Only then did Lovely realize there were tears pouring down her own face.

Dr. Chang spoke, but so did Beck, running toward her. "Mom. Mom!"

And that made her cry...almost as much as the words Dr. Chang said in her ear.

"Excuse me?" she said, not sure she heard right. Could she have? Was that—

"It's okay," Beck said, taking Lovely's shoulders and pulling her in. "We can do this. We can beat this. I am here for you, every single step of the way. You won't—"

"It's negative," Lovely whispered.

Beck froze. Lovely smiled. And in her ear, she heard Dr. Chang laugh softly. "Yes, Lovely, that's exactly what I'm saying. There is no cancer in your body. It was a completely benign cyst."

"Negative?" Beck managed to mouth the word.

"Negative," Lovely confirmed again. "It's negative, Beckie! Negative!"

Somehow she said a clumsy goodbye and a thousand thank yous to Dr. Chang as she and Beck hugged and danced with just about the same enthusiasm as those kids on the stage.

"Did I miss the end?" Lovely asked as the explosive applause and cheers seeped out through the door.

"Still time for the curtain call. Come on!"

Hand in hand, they practically ran back into the auditorium and this time, no one noticed them in the aisle because every person was standing to cheer and clap and whistle. Lovely and Beck made it to the front row just before the announcer called Miss Lark, who came bounding out with her dog, to curtsy, bow, and blow a kiss at her extremely noisy family.

Lovely might have been the loudest of them all. She let cheers pour from her body as she bellowed with gratitude for this moment, this family, and this precious life that proved every day that anything really could happen.

CHAPTER TWENTY-FIVE

PEYTON

"Are you sure you don't want me to go with you?" Savannah asked. "I can be scary. I'll tell those people to back off and tear up that contract."

Peyton smiled over her coffee cup. "You can be scary, Sav, but it's not going to be a big deal. Nothing is official. The agent had instructions to accept the highest offer, and theirs was, but I haven't signed the papers. It might cost me a fee, but I don't care. I'm not selling."

Her sister leaned forward. "Are you one hundred percent certain, Pey? Have you even talked to Val about this?"

"I kept getting his voice mail last night, and didn't want to be *el desperado* and call him forty times."

Savannah rolled her eyes. "You're not desperate. You're his pregnant fiancée. And you're making a rather major decision for your lifestyle and bank account."

"I'll call him on the way over there." Peyton looked past Savannah to the deck where Nick came bounding up the stairs from a run, with a backpack that held one happy little baby. "Did they just run together?"

Savannah followed her gaze and laughed. "His new thing. Exercise with Daddy."

Peyton swallowed as a black ball of envy threatened to choke her. "I've always been a little jealous of you, Sav," she confessed on a whisper, "but never more than now."

"Don't be jealous." She put her hand on Peyton's arm. "I kind of hate it when you are."

"How can I not be? Look what Nick did for you. The ultimate sacrifice and you two hardly knew each other."

"Maybe that's why," Savannah joked. "If he'd really known me..."

"He'd have done the same thing," Peyton finished. "The man loves you so hard." And, of course, her stupid body betrayed her with tears.

"Val loves you." Savannah squeezed her hand. "He's not independently wealthy, like Nick. Val has a fantastic opportunity with this company and it isn't going to be forever."

"No," Peyton said. "I'm not spending the better part of the next few years up there, away from everyone and everything I love. I'm keeping the townhouse, spending the winters here, and maybe every holiday. And maybe every...weekend."

Savannah looked away, clearly not enamored with that plan.

"What?" Peyton demanded, needing her opinion.

"That's not a good way to start a marriage, Pey," she said. "We'll always be here and you can come anytime. But if you do this...this part-time living arrangement?

You're starting off with a great big crack in the foundation. I'm not sure we're worth it."

She let out a groan and looked at her phone, ostensibly to check the time but...why hadn't he returned her text?

"Sometimes I don't think he cares," she muttered.

"I don't agree." Savannah put down her coffee cup. "I think you don't fully believe a man like Val can love you, and you sabotage it."

"Hey, you were the one who told me to give him an ultimatum last year," Peyton said. "Thanks for that."

"You spurred him on, and didn't lose him. And you have a ring on your finger and a baby in your belly. You're welcome."

Peyton looked skyward and exhaled noisily. "Am I sabotaging this, Savannah? Or am I demanding that I be put first? Isn't that what we want from our husbands?"

"I wish I knew the answer." Savannah put her hand over Peyton's. "All I can tell you is that whatever happens, I am here for you, sister. Now and forever."

Peyton smiled, then slowly stood. "I'm going to dress and head over to the townhouse. I'll be early, but I don't care. I want to walk around and think about furniture and decorating."

"All right," Savannah said. "Don't be surprised if that couple and their baby change your mind, though."

"How could they do that?"

Savannah gave her a *get real* look. "You're going to take one look at Mr. and Mrs. and child, and know how *you* should be living your life. With your husband, not away from him. Not trying to be in two places at once."

Maybe she was right. Truth was, she hadn't made a

final decision yet. Something would point her to the right thing to do. Some sign, some...thing. She just wanted clarity.

Savannah's words echoed in her head while she dressed and drove over to the townhouse. Her heart was heavy with doubt and disappointment, two emotions she never dreamed she'd feel when she had...what had Savannah said?

A ring on your finger and a baby in your belly.

Yes, she had them, but did she have Val? Did she have the man who'd put her first, like he'd promised? He *had* promised.

I want to be by your side...forever.

She remembered the words he'd spoken when he'd proposed. That was a promise. But what he really meant was he wanted her to be by *his* side forever, which was a subtle but major difference.

A difference that, she thought as she slipped the key into the front door, wasn't right.

And neither was that.

She frowned into the morning sunshine that bathed the dock in a pinky gold light that she loved. But it wasn't the beautiful colors of the water that made her stop and stare. It was the sight of a small skiff tied up to the dock, and a stranger in a baseball cap sitting on the wood planks...fishing.

A rise of resentment rolled through her at the intrusion, but as she took three steps closer, she froze.

That was no stranger. That was no intruder. That was...Val.

Her whole body felt weak and light and stunned by the sight.

He turned just then, squinting into the house, then standing as he saw her. Very slowly, she walked to the sliders and unlocked the latch to push it open, her whole being suddenly feeling weak and joyous and hopeful and so crazy in love.

"What...are you..." Words just weren't coming.

He lifted the fishing pole. "They're biting, Pey. This spot is magic."

It was *magic...with him standing on it.*

She took a few more steps, crossing the small patio to the dock. "You should have called."

"And ruin the surprise?" He reached out an arm, beckoning her. "C'mere, gorgeous. I've missed you."

Her heart—and every other part of her body —melted.

"Missed you, too," she said, sliding next to him and wrapping her arms around his waist. "Did you come for the *Mary Poppins* performance?"

He laughed. "Oh, sure. That's why I came."

She didn't quite know what to make of that answer, but she had too many other questions to ask first. "Why are you on this dock...with a boat?"

"Well, I figured the place would be locked, and I wanted to fish, so I borrowed the skiff from my friend and came that way. Oh!" The end of the fishing pole bounced with a catch that he reeled in like a pro, producing a tiny trout.

Really? He came here on a Saturday morning without telling her...to fish?

"Hello, little one." He put the pole down, freed the fish, and looked right into its eyes. "Don't worry. You can see yourself trout." He grinned and tossed him back in, turning to her. "I have missed fishing more than anything except you. I swear I will never go another week without this pole in my hand. And this dock? What an amazing place to fish." He frowned. "Although...maybe it needs a railing or something to make it a little safer or child-proofed if there's going to be a kid living here."

He knew who'd made the offer on the townhouse?

"Val." She breathed his name because it was all she could manage. "I don't know why you're here, but I need to tell you something." She glanced over her shoulder. "And fast."

"You expecting someone?" he asked.

"As a matter of fact, yes."

"The new owner?"

How did he know that? Had she told him today was the day she'd meet them to finalize the sale? Maybe. She didn't remember.

"They'll be here soon," she said, "and I..." How did she tell him? How could she tell him that she wasn't selling and she wasn't going to live full time in Boston and she wasn't—

"They're already here," he said.

She drew back, then glanced around. "They are? Did I miss them?"

"No, they're here."

She frowned. "A couple with a baby?"

"Here." He pointed to the dock where they were standing. "Dad." He tapped his chest. "Mom." He tapped hers. "And bambino." He slid his hand down and flickered his fingers over her stomach. "How's our little one doing, by the way?"

All she could do was shake her head. "I'm confused."

He grinned and opened his arms, pulling her in, filling her senses with the strength and scent and body that she loved. "I don't know what you're confused about, Pey. We're the couple who bought the townhouse...well, technically, I made the winning offer. And I'm willing to pay it, unless you want to back out of the sale. I just had to be sure you didn't sell this place to anyone else." He inched back and narrowed his eyes. "Not even your mom's new boyfriend and, dang, he drove the asking price up."

Now her head buzzed. "Val, what are you talking about?"

"C'mere." He took her hand and led her to the edge, pulling her down to sit next to him. "Turn this way and look at that."

She looked out to the water. "I love that view," she said. "It's one of the reasons I bought the place."

"I love it, too." He turned back to her. "But not nearly as much as I love you. So, I'm here to tell you, this is where we're going to live. Right here, in this townhouse. The three of us. The Sanchez family."

"Val!" She blinked at him, gripping the dock under her hand, not trusting herself that this was real. "Did you turn down the job?"

"Nope. I got the job."

She stared at him and he gave a slow, easy smile that transported her back to the day when he walked into the kitchen at Jessie's restaurant and rendered her speechless with one bad joke about crabs. Here she was, more than a year later, still speechless.

"Actually, to be perfectly honest, I did turn the job down."

"What?" She grabbed his arm. "Will you just be straight with me?"

He dropped his head back, laughing. "But I'm having so much fun. I definitely loosen up when I'm down here, have you noticed? It'll make me a better, more balanced dad."

She glared at him. "Straight. Now. I'm kind of dying here."

"All right, all right. I turned them down because..." He shrugged both shoulders, making a face. "It's a great town, Boston, but...not for us. Not for you. And I had to think about you."

Her heart slipped around a little.

"First and foremost, I had to think about what you wanted. About what makes you happy, because when you're happy, I'm happy."

Tears—some of joy, some of a little guilt for how she'd imagined he didn't feel that way—sprung to her eyes. "Thanks, Val."

"And I started thinking about Coconut Key." He huffed out a soft breath and looked around. "The first time I came here, I was running away. Away from my pain and grief and memories. And then I met you, Pey. And I realized that I'd run away and..."

"You went back to Miami."

"And I like it there, but I like it better here. Because you're here."

"And the fish," she murmured.

He smiled. "I like to fish," he acknowledged. "But this time I'm not running away, Peyton. I'm running *to* something. To you." He cupped her cheek. "Because I love you."

She sighed into his hand, still a little confused. "So you're moving here? What about your job in Boston?"

"Well, I walked out of that one. Literally, out the door, down an elevator, and through the lobby. Just as I was walking out, Tom Gerritt—he's my boss, the CFO—was coming in from lunch. Rushing in, trying to act like it was a chance meeting in the parking lot, but he'd just gotten the call that I turned down the offer. And he came out with guns blazing."

"Wow. Dramatic."

He grinned. "It kind of was. He's a cool dude, actually, with three kids. Very smart. We talked and I was straight with him. Told him you didn't want to live here, and I wasn't about to do anything to rock the boat of a brand-new marriage and family, and just as I was about to leave, he said five simple words."

"Please reconsider our offer..." That was four. "Val?"

"Why don't you work remote?"

She blinked at him. "Remote...like from home?"

"Bingo." He touched her nose. "The job can be done anywhere, Peyton. I'll have to go up to Boston a few times a year for quarterly meetings, but with video calls and a home office? Honey, you are looking at the next senior financial analyst for Onaway Shipping. Who will work in shorts, and catch your dinner during his lunch hour. And who"—he leaned in—"will be living right here as your husband, I hope to God."

Good thing he was holding her or she might have just fainted right into the water.

She tried to breathe but he stole that with the lightest, sweetest, softest kiss.

"We're staying here," she murmured against his lips, still not able to believe how happy that made her.

"We're staying right here in Coconut Key." He kissed her one more time and put his hand on her stomach. "Right where all three of us belong."

EPILOGUE

BECK

Beck had plenty to do as the Mother of the Bride and "attendant of honor"—they all agreed *maid* or *matron* was wrong—for Peyton's wedding. But the official wedding toast was the one thing Beck *didn't* want to do. She hated public speaking and, try as she might, she didn't know exactly what to say. What was the magic formula to success? How would she, a woman who'd been summarily dumped after thirty-four years, have any credibility on the subject?

"Well, she did it." Savannah sidled up to Beck as they gazed out over the hundred or so guests milling around the massive waterfront deck of the Ocean Key Resort & Spa in Key West.

"And she did it in fine style," Beck agreed. "Although twenty folding chairs on a beach would have been easier these past four weeks."

"No kidding," Savannah agreed. "But this is Peyton Foster. The girl who used to come down the stairs at our house with an entire roll of toilet paper as her train, and your best silk flower centerpiece as her bouquet. I love that my sister got her big white wedding."

"A June wedding, too." It hadn't been easy, especially since the unexpected cancellation at this resort fell just a few days after Callie graduated—with the highest honors, of course—from the University of Miami. On top of that, Peyton started culinary classes in Key West, but that had been the blessing. She'd met a wedding planner in her class who told her about a last-minute availability of a highly desirable wedding venue.

Savannah gave her mother a long sideways look, adding a sly smile. "And can I just say that you are a gorgeous woman of honor?"

"Thank you, honey. Standing next to Peyton certainly was an honor, but..." She wrinkled her nose. "You'd give a better toast."

"Oh, don't worry. Just be your lovable, nurturing, honest self, Mom. And don't cry."

"As if that's possible," Beck said. "I get teary every time I look at her. I mean..." She gestured toward Peyton, currently chatting with her father-in-law and laughing at something the charming Cuban man said. "She's everything a bride should be."

"Including pregnant, which is apparently how we Foster women roll," Savannah cracked just as Lovely and Jessie joined them. "Good thing I found that spectacular dress that hides her little baby bump, right?"

"She's not hiding her joy, though." Lovely put an arm around Beck. "I don't think I've ever seen a happier bride."

"Savannah was mighty happy," Beck recalled.

"And you will be, too." Jessie gave a teasing grin and pointed at Beck. "Just sayin'."

Beck didn't bother to deny it—they all knew where she and Oliver were headed. Maybe not to anything as lavish as this, though.

"We have a long way to go until then," she said, her gaze skimming the crowd for Oliver. She spotted him instantly, talking to Nick and another couple.

Oliver laughed at something Nick said, then, as if pulled by a force, he looked to his right and caught Beck's eye. Like he could feel her looking at him, they were that connected. And, as always, Beck felt herself fall a little harder for the man who somehow managed to surprise, delight, and adore her every day.

"But we're having quite the time getting there," she added, always happy to share her contentment with these women she loved.

"So are those two." Jessie gestured toward the railing where many of the guests had gathered in preparation of a spectacular sunset. There, Heather and Kenny stood side-by-side, not-so-secretly holding hands, smiling at each other. "My little sister has the most indescribable air of peace around her, doesn't she?"

They all agreed that was true for Heather, and Kenny, too.

"Oh, and Jessie, kudos on Beau's performance as the ring bearer," Savannah said, giving a playful elbow jab. "As much as I would have loved to somehow insert Dylan into the festivities, he'll have to wait for Callie's wedding, but your son did a magnificent job."

"Didn't he?" She let out a little chortle of pride. "He's getting better every day, I have to say. And with Heather taking over so much of the work at Coquina Café, I'm really looking forward to an easy summer so I can spend lots of time with him. Time is kind of what we both needed more than anything. More time and less work."

"Exactly," Beck said. "And with Callie helping out at the B&B this summer, I am hoping to have some of that myself."

"Did someone mention me?" Callie came over to the group, her dark eyes gleaming.

"We're just discussing what an amazing addition you're going to be for Coquina House these next few months," Beck told her.

"Oh, Mom, I'm so happy to not be in an office over the summer for once in my life," Callie said. "I've already completely reorganized the linens and dishes, and have a spreadsheet for all of the jobs, and a minute-by-minute daily planner."

Savannah snorted. "Why am I not surprised?"

"How did Dad take the news that you weren't working for him—or any firm—between college and law school?" Beck asked Callie.

"How you would expect. 'Big mistake, Callie,'" she imitated him in a low voice. "'Only slackers step aside from their careers for a summer.'"

"Did you talk to his date?" Lovely asked. "She seems very..."

"Young," Savannah finished, making them laugh. "Proving that Dad's affair with his law partner was only the start of his mid-life crisis."

"What's her name again? Amy? Angie?" Beck asked.

"Andi," Savannah said. "Blandy Andi." When they laughed, she shrugged. "Just keepin' it real, y'all. She has the personality of a doorknob and the knockers to go with it."

Beck eyed the voluptuous woman who was definitely twenty years younger than Dan, waiting for a twinge of jealousy that never came. "Whoever she is, she is *not* the woman who wrecked my marriage, that's all I know."

"Wrecked your marriage," Lovely said, "*and* changed your life."

"Speaking of changed lives..." Savannah notched her chin toward another couple not too far away. Josh and Julie had their heads close in conversation, punctuated by laughs and long, warm looks.

"Lovely, you skillful matchmaker." Beck nudged her mother. "Finally putting that lovedar to great use."

They all cracked up at that, just as Ava joined them, sauntering over in a pale pink dress that made her look a little bit older than her sixteen years.

"Grandma Beck," she said, "the planning lady asked me to find you. You're supposed to make that toast the very moment the sun touches the water. It's some kind of Keys tradition for good luck."

Beck groaned. "I'm going to need all the luck I can get."

"You'll be wonderful," Lovely said. "Just speak from your heart, sweet girl."

Ava reached for her. "Come on. They're serving everyone champagne now. Can I drink some?"

"No," all five women answered at once.

Ava gave an easy laugh. "And here I thought I lost my mother, only to get so many, many more of them."

Savannah pointed at her. "Count your blessings, grasshopper."

"I do, Aunt Savannah," Ava assured her. "I have to because now Dad makes me say grace even before breakfast."

Beck couldn't help smiling at that, knowing that Kenny's return to faith, lost after his wife died, had been anotherwonderful change for her son.

As they started to walk, Eliza Whitney joined the group, reaching out to them. "Before all the festivities are underway and I don't get a chance to say this..." She took Beck's hand, and put a hand on Savannah's arm, bringing all of the women closer. "I want to say thank you for how you've welcomed me this past month."

"We've loved getting to know you, Eliza," Beck told her.

"Plus so much good dirt on celebrities." Savannah winked.

Eliza pointed at her. "Savannah, you are one of a kind and I love you for the gift you've given Nick. He couldn't be in better hands. But, I do want you all to know that I've made a decision—I'm taking that ferry up to Sanibel Island tomorrow."

All of the women looked at her, surprised. They'd included her on more than one Thursday girls' night this past month, and she'd shared enough for Beck to know the decision hadn't been made lightly. Eliza carried around some deep resentment, and no small amount of guilt, where her father was concerned. And she had no idea what his widow would be like, or why she wanted to see Eliza.

"I think that's the right thing to do," Beck said. "I hope that a good, honest conversation with your stepmother answers your questions and eases your pain."

"Thank you." Eliza smiled at her. "All I know is I'm going to a place called Shellseeker Beach. I don't know what I'll find."

"Sounds like you'll find shells," Ava said.

"And bring some back for us." Lovely gave Eliza's arm an encouraging squeeze. "We'd love to see you again."

Eliza looked from one to the other. "What an amazing group of women you are," she said. "I'm so happy I met you. Each of you are just inspiring to me. What is your secret?"

Beck thought about that for a moment, glancing at her mother, her daughters, and her granddaughter, wondering how to explain the magic that they'd found. "I guess...it's leaning into the strength of family and friends."

"Lots of laughter," Savannah said.

"And never losing hope," Lovely added.

"Mom?" Peyton glided up to the group, arms out. "It's time for the toast."

Beck dropped her head back. "Now I'm the one who needs some words of wisdom for how to make a marriage work."

"I think you just got them," Eliza said. "All you need is family, friends, laughter, and hope."

"Let's go before the sun hits the water," Peyton said, putting her arm around Beck and ushering her through the crowd toward the stage.

Beck beamed at her daughter as they walked together. "So, best day of your life, Pey?"

"One of many," she said. "Past, present, and future." She leaned over and lightly kissed Beck's cheek. "Thanks for bringing us all to Coconut Key."

"You brought me here, remember?"

"Something brought us here," Peyton said. "Fate. God. Timing. Hey, even Dad had something to do with it. I don't know, but I'm sure happy we're here."

"Me too, honey."

They reached the small stage and stopped, but before Beck took one of the flutes, Oliver stepped to her side and placed a light kiss on her cheek. "For luck, luv."

She smiled up at him, emotions already threatening to get the best of her. "That makeup artist better have used waterproof mascara."

"Mom." Peyton pointed toward the sunset. "Now."

Beck stepped up and blinked into the golden light pouring over the faces she knew and loved. Her three daughters. Her granddaughter. Her son, and sons-in-law, dearest friends, new acquaintances, and there, in the middle of it all, her mother, the most aptly named person on earth.

She took a deep breath, stepped to the microphone, and let the sun warm her face as she shared the secret to happiness and toasted not just this marriage, but all the ones they had and those to come.

All you need is friends, family, laughter, and hope. And love. So much love.

Beck's remarkable journey in Coconut Key may have ended, but the stories of friends, family, laughter and hope will continue! You are welcome to join Eliza Whitney as she journeys up the coast to gorgeous Sanibel Island nestled in the Gulf of Mexico for a life changing experience. Want to know more? Sign up for Hope's newsletter...and read on for a sneak peek from the first book in the Shellseeker Beach series, *Sanibel Dreams.*

The Shellseeker Beach Series

When Eliza Whitney loses both her beloved husband and her high-powered job in the same month, she's uncertain what the next chapter of her life will look like. At fifty-three, she's too young to retire and too old to start over. Then her estranged father's widow contacts her and asks her to come to Sanibel Island to help settle his affairs. Eliza sees the trip to a place called Shellseeker Beach as a distraction from her loss, and maybe a way to get some closure on the difficult relationship she'd had with her father.

For more than seventy years, Theodora Blessing's sole purpose on this earth has been to heal the hurting, and to run Shellseeker Cottages, a cozy beachfront resort that has been in her family for decades. But Teddy no longer owns the gorgeous property, and Eliza is her only hope to get it back. Will Eliza help Teddy and save the family business...or claim it as her own and sell it to developers?

Before long, the two women begin to unravel the mystery of Eliza's father, the late, great "Dutch" Vanderveen, an enigmatic pilot who led multiple, secretive lives. And they forge a friendship that changes both their lives. With the help of Teddy's healing heart, Eliza discovers a family she never knew she had, a purpose she never knew she needed, and a life she never dreamed was possible.

Come to Shellseeker Beach and fall in love with a cast of unforgettable characters who face life's challenges with humor, heart, and hope. For lovers of riveting and inspirational sagas about sisters, secrets, romance, mothers and daughters...and the moments that make life worth living.

The Shellseeker Beach Series

Sanibel Dreams
Sanibel Treasures
Sanibel Mornings
Sanibel Sisters
Sanibel Tides
Sanibel Sunsets
Sanibel Midnight

ABOUT THE AUTHOR

Hope Holloway is the author of charming, heartwarming women's fiction featuring unforgettable families and friends and the emotional challenges they conquer. After a long career in marketing, she gave up writing ad copy to launch a writing career with her first series, Coconut Key, set on the sun-washed beaches of the Florida Keys. A mother of two adult children, Hope and her husband of thirty years live in Florida. When not writing, she can be found walking the beach with her two rescue dogs, who beg her to include animals in every book. Visit her site at www.hopeholloway.com.

Made in United States
Orlando, FL
17 March 2022